Murder by the Book

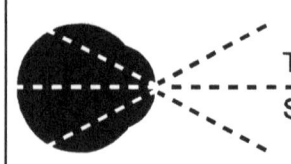
This Large Print Book carries the
Seal of Approval of N.A.V.H.

A BEYOND THE PAGE BOOKSTORE MYSTERY

MURDER BY THE BOOK

LAUREN ELLIOTT

WHEELER PUBLISHING
A part of Gale, a Cengage Company

Farmington Hills, Mich • San Francisco • New York • Waterville, Maine
Meriden, Conn • Mason, Ohio • Chicago

Copyright © 2018 by Lauren Elliott.
A Beyond the Page Bookstore Mystery.
Wheeler Publishing, a part of Gale, a Cengage Company.

ALL RIGHTS RESERVED
Wheeler Publishing Large Print Cozy Mystery.
The text of this Large Print edition is unabridged.
Other aspects of the book may vary from the original edition.
Set in 16 pt. Plantin.

**LIBRARY OF CONGRESS CIP DATA ON FILE.
CATALOGUING IN PUBLICATION FOR THIS BOOK
IS AVAILABLE FROM THE LIBRARY OF CONGRESS**

ISBN-13: 978-1-4328-6519-1 (softcover alk. paper)

Published in 2019 by arrangement with Kensington Books, an imprint of Kensington Publishing Corp.

Printed in the United States of America
2 3 4 5 6   26 25 24 23 22

Murder by the Book

Chapter One

Addison Greyborne breathed in the intoxicating scents of tangy sea air and New England autumn leaves infused with the comforting aroma of fresh-baked bread. Of course, standing on the sidewalk admiring her newly installed red awning with its overhead sign, "Beyond the Page — Books & Curios," contributed to her giddy state of mind, and she pinched herself to make sure it was all real.

Her eyes rested on the bay windows on either side of the glazed entrance. The one to her left displayed knickknacks, gemstones, and candles, and the one on the right was her beloved used bookshop. Both windows were decked out in the fall harvest displays that she'd created herself. She inched backward on the sidewalk, marveling at how eye-catching they would be to passersby. Images of all the other seasonal showcases she'd be able to create flashed through her mind, but then her shoe heel slipped over the curbing.

She teetered backward. Feet spread-eagle, arms pin-wheeling in the air, she glanced over her shoulder. A car was coming directly toward her. To her horror, it sped up instead of slowing down. She scrambled and regained her footing. The rush of air across her back rocked her as the black sedan swooshed by. "Slow down!" Addison shouted, but the Honda sped to the next corner, squealed around the sharp left turn, and disappeared down the back side of Town Square Road.

"I guess there are idiots everywhere," she mumbled, taking a deep breath. Addison straightened her navy boyfriend jacket, brushed dust from her dark gray, skinny ankle jeans and rummaged through her purse for the key. Her hand trembled as she tried to fit it into the lock. She gritted her teeth, counted to ten, calmed herself, and tried again. The door swung open. Bells rang overhead, and she let out a comforted sigh. The door chime was a sound she knew she'd never tire of hearing. Excitement bubbled through her as she stepped across the threshold into Beyond the Page.

I'm proud of you, pumpkin, she envisioned her father saying, imagining him standing next to her smiling. A chill quivered across her shoulders. "Thanks, Dad." She smiled, disarmed the alarm, and flipped on the lights.

She scanned the large room, pleased with the past months of hard work. It was done. Perfect. Her best-loved books were prominently displayed along the wall shelves, while standing bookshelves, varying in height and with books arranged by genre, stood in orderly rows in the center of the room. She'd even managed to tuck soft leather armchairs into every nook and cranny, arranging them on small, richly woven area carpets to create cozy reading spaces.

Addison eyed the large glass curio cabinet by the window filled with her beloved collectibles. It fit perfectly at the end of the restored, ornately carved Victorian bar she used as a cash and coffee counter. She wrapped her arms around her chest, hugged tight, grabbed the *"Now Open"* sandwich board, and dashed outside to erect it on the sidewalk beside the front door. She stood back, and grinned.

"Is this your new shop, then?" called a plump, white-haired woman from the bakery entrance next door.

"Yes. Yes, it is," Addison said, sweeping

long strands of hair from her eyes. "Hi. I'm Addison. My friends call me Addie." She walked toward the woman, her hand outstretched.

"Hum." The woman nodded, but didn't reach for her hand. "Thought I heard someone yelling out here a few minutes ago." She cocked her eyebrow.

"Oh. Sorry, yes, that was me. A car almo—"

The woman sneered and walked back into the bakery, smoothing wrinkles from her stained apron.

"Um, I didn't catch your name," Addie called cheerfully, but the woman had disappeared inside.

"Don't worry about her," said an amiable voice behind her.

Addie spun around and came face-to-face with a rather attractive, petite, fiery-haired young woman sporting a poncho as brightly-colored as her hair.

"Martha's just getting crotchety in her old age. She can be pleasant enough, sometimes." The woman laughed.

"Good to know. I was afraid I'd offended her."

"Naw, she's just being Martha. I'm Serena, by the way."

"Hi, I'm Addison," she said, extending her

hand. "Call me Addie."

"Will do." Serena shook her hand and gestured with her head. "I'm just on the other side of you."

Addie turned. "SerenaTEA — how perfect for a tea shop name."

"Kind of clever, isn't it?" Serena chuckled. "I like yours, too."

"I had a hard time thinking of one — you know, something that said I sold more than books — so Beyond the Page it was."

"I like it . . . especially the graphic of the steaming coffee cup on the glass door."

"Thanks. I designed it myself."

Serena cast her eyes downward. "So you sell books, curios, coffee, and . . . what?" She shuffled her feet; her toe kicked at a pebble. "Food, too?"

"No, just coffee, and I don't sell it. It's free and just for customers who want to sit and read or browse. Come in, I'll show you around."

"I'd love to." Serena's face lit up. "I've been curious this past month, but there wasn't a sign up, and the windows were covered with newspaper." She laughed. "No one could figure out what was going on in there during all hours of the day and night."

"You should have knocked. I'd have loved the company."

"I did, a few times, but there wasn't any answer."

"Sorry, I must not have heard you." Addie smiled and held the door open. "I was pretty focused."

"Wow, this is fantastic." Serena looked around. "It's so comfortable and homey. The carved wood beams and pillar post finishes are amazing. Are they original?"

"Yes, I had a restoration specialist come up from Boston to —"

"And look." Serena pointed. "You have a huge section on murder and mystery. That's my favorite reading. I *love* Agatha Christie." Her visual review of the shop took in the gleaming, wide-planked wooden flooring, which Addie recently had restored and came to rest on the Victorian counter.

Addie, who had been following Serena's inspection of the room, blurted out, "that piece isn't original to the store. I found it and had it restored. It made such a perfect cash and coffee bar, I couldn't resist."

Serena smiled and then her eyes focused on the coffee maker on the far end of it.

"And see, that's only one of those one-cup pod dispensers. You know, just to make readers and customers feel at home. We could work out something between us. I don't want to take away any of your business."

"Naw, I'm not worried." A smile crept across Serena's lips as she continued to scan the storefront. "There's a big difference between tea and coffee drinkers. I was just a bit afraid when I saw your sign that it was an actual coffeehouse, too. I do sell some pastries."

"No, don't worry. Books and collectibles are all I can manage."

"Good. With the new restaurant down the street, I already have enough competition." Her smile broadened. "So we should get along just fine. Welcome to the neighborhood."

"Thanks. I don't know anyone in town, so . . . hopefully we'll become friends, too?"

"Well, we've gotten off to a good start." Serena's dark brown eyes flashed with amusement. "We have an enemy in common with Martha." She chuckled, tossing back her long, crimped red mane. "I've been on this street for almost five years, and she'll still hardly speak to me. She actually called me a 'wannabe hippie' one day. Can you believe that?"

"Oh dear, that bad, hey — ?"

"Shh." Serena's gaze shot to the back of the shop. "Do you hear that?"

Addie's skin prickled at the scraping sounds, then a voice yelling and a loud thud. "What the — ?" She dashed toward the back room, Serena at her heels. After a quick glance around the empty storage area, Addie flung the metal door open, burst into the alley and skidded to a stop. Serena thudded into her, sending Addie staggering forward into a strewn bag of garbage.

"Oh God, sorry," Serena said as she offered a helping hand.

"Not your fault." Addie hauled herself to her feet. "I really should have brake lights installed." She grimaced, wiping trash off her jacket and slacks. "And it looks like I'll need to know the name of a dry cleaner in town, too."

"I'll pay for it, but it really was an accident." Serena's face crumbled as she helped remove bits of bread and other unidentifiable matter off Addie's clothing.

"No, you won't. It's just been one of those mornings, and it started long before this."

"Hum," huffed Martha, who stood in the back door of her bakery. "If you girls are finished gabbing about clothes, and you're interested," she said, crossing her plump arms, "an intruder had a crowbar wedged in your door when I came out with the trash. I chased him off when I threw that bag at his head."

Addie eyed the scratches by the latch. Her eyes trailed up to the garbage drizzling down the door. "Yes, good thing you came out here in time to throw the bag and stop him. Thank you."

Martha took a deep breath. "He ran that way, down the alley toward Birch Road." Her ample chest puffed in and out as she turned back toward her shop. "Oh, you should probably call the police." She called over her shoulder, "I've never seen him around here before. Too many strangers comin' and goin' these days." Martha looked back at the two women and shook her white head. "And I expect you gals will clean that up." The bakery door slammed shut behind her.

Wide-eyed, Addie nodded and looked at Serena, then back at her door and the mess on the ground. "Does this kind of thing happen often around here?"

"No, this is a quiet town . . . usually. I'm guessing maybe it was Old Bill? He hangs out back here looking for scraps from Martha's, but he's harmless and he's never been known to try to break in anywhere. Martha would've recognized him, though."

Addie scanned the lane and shook her head. "I'll go get some garbage bags and a broom, but you don't have to help. It's my shop."

"Nonsense, we're in this together. It's the least I can do."

"Thanks."

"See if you've got any rubber gloves while you're at it." Serena cringed and gingerly picked through the garbage.

"Sure thing." Addie popped into her shop. "Oh no!" she shrieked. "Come look at this."

"What, what, what?" Serena sprinted to her side, stopped short, and gasped.

The sight of the disheveled bookcases brought a lump to the back of Addie's throat as she eyed their contents, which had been pitched across the floor. She glanced at the venetian glass display in the showcase by the window and breathed a sigh of relief that it was still intact. Now, hopefully, she'd find that her beloved books weren't damaged either.

Chapter Two

"I really appreciate you helping me clean up all the mess this morning, but what about your shop? Won't your customers wonder why you haven't opened yet?"

"No worries." Serena laughed. "My customers know I don't keep regular hours. They'll come back later, and this is the least I can do for a new friend on her not-so-welcoming first day." She placed the last three books on the bottom shelf. "There, we're done." Serena stood up and stretched her back. "Besides, you needed a witness aside from Martha for the police statement."

"Yes, and it helped having a friend who is related to the investigating officer." Addie winked.

"And he's taunted me my whole life, as you saw. Brothers." Serena shuddered. "Well, I'd best be off."

"You know, before you go, think about this

and tell me if I'm crazy or not — but I'm thinking now . . . and wondering . . . if there were perhaps, um . . . two people involved, not just the fellow Martha chased off."

"What makes you say that?" Serena's hand paused on the door latch.

" 'Cause she said he ran off, not drove toward Birch Road, and we weren't outside long enough for him to run around the two blocks and come back in the front door."

"What are you saying? That it was planned?"

"Yes, and the guy in the lane was just a diversion to get us outside. That there was someone else on the street waiting till we were distracted."

"Hum, but why? It was only the books that were messed up, and the only one that you said appears to be missing is a copy of Alice in Wonderland, and none of your collectibles were stolen, so I don't get it."

"Neither do I." Addie frowned. "The 1961 edition that seems to be gone wasn't worth much. So I don't know why they would break in to steal that."

Serena's brows knit.

Addie shook her head. "I don't even know if it is missing." She shrugged. "It might still be in one of the crates I haven't brought in yet, although . . ." She bit her lip and frowned. "Oh, never mind, it's not worth much anyway."

"If you think of anything else, give me a shout, and we'll call my brother. Maybe he's aware of a crime ring operating in these parts I don't know about. But, personally, I think it was just a crime of opportunity or kids messing around. Don't worry." Serena's brow rose. "I'm sure it's fine. Cheers, see you later."

"Yes, thanks again. See you later."

Addie leaned against the counter waiting for her cup of coffee to finish brewing. She gnawed on her lower lip as the events of the morning ran through her mind like a slow-motion movie reel.

Why didn't the bells chime?

She strode toward the front door and opened it inch by inch. When it was ajar by about a foot, the bells rang out. "That's it," she said aloud. Addie grabbed her purse and keys, locked the door behind her, and dashed next door into SerenaTEA.

Breathless, she bolted into the small, empty tea shop. "Serena," she called, "are you here?"

"I'm back here." Serena's red head appeared around the doorjamb leading to the storeroom. "You okay? You're flushed."

"I'm fine, but I think I just figured something out."

Serena stepped out and tossed the kitchen towel she'd been holding into the room behind her before walking over to a kettle steaming on a side table. "Really? What? Take a seat." She motioned to a counter stool. "I was just going to make a pot of Heavenly Delight tea. Want some?"

"Please, sounds perfect," Addie, said glancing at the variety of large, wooden storage bins behind the counter. She noted the sidewall shelves held silver bags in varying sizes, all bearing the red SerenaTEA label. "Do you make all your own tea blends?" Addie inhaled the heady scents of spices and herbs that enveloped her. "It smells wonderful in here," she said as she settled onto a high counter stool.

"Yes, as you can see, the prepackaged ones of my most popular blends come in small, medium, or large bags, but custom blends are my trademark. It's what makes me different from other tea shops around here." Serena smiled as she poured hot water into a stoneware teapot. "So what's up? Have you figured out what he was after?"

"No, not yet. But I'm certain now someone must have been watching me, or us, enter the shop this morning to know about the door chimes. Unless you heard them jingling when we ran into the alley?"

"No, I don't remember hearing anything."

"I don't either, and I know I didn't hear them when I went back in to get the garbage bags, which must have been when he slipped out the front door." Addie took the teacup from Serena's outstretched hand. "Which means whoever was out front must have been tall."

"What? Why?"

"Because I'm nearly five nine, and I can't reach the chimes well enough to silence them. But when he came in he knew he'd have to reach up and grasp them while he slipped in and out. The ceiling height is at least fourteen feet, and the chimes hang down over the top of the seven-and-a-half-foot door. It only makes sense that whoever ransacked the place was tall enough to reach them. Like I said before, I don't think it was one person, but we'll need a full description of the fellow Martha ran off to see if my hunch is right."

Serena laughed. "Whoa, slow down, take a breath." She reached for the phone on the counter.

"Are you calling Martha?"

"No, I'm calling Marc. I'd rather he question her than us. She's in a real mood today."

"I don't think involving your brother at this point's a great idea. We need proof, not just theories. I know because I've been down this road before. Trust me. The police won't act on hunches." Addie swirled the tea in her cup and knocked back a gulp.

Serena cringed. "It's hot."

"Yeah, I see that." Addie grimaced. "I wasn't thinking."

"You look like you need a stiff drink, not a cup of tea."

Addie shook her head. "A bit too early for that, but I might have one later. Until then, hit me with another one, tea-tender." She held up her empty cup.

Serena went to the side table and poured a refill. "I'm guessing you've been through something like this before?"

"Um, sort of, a few times." Addie sighed.

"Wanna talk about it?" Serena handed her the cup.

"Not much to say other than I've had my share of botched police investigations and dead ends this past year."

"That doesn't sound good. No wonder you don't want to involve Marc right now." Serena frowned but kept her eyes fixed on Addie's.

Addie squirmed in her seat, but Serena's eyes didn't waver. Her sweet face and big, round, innocent eyes tugged at the painful recess of Addie's heart, and she felt a sense of trust. "Okay. I'll talk." She laughed nervously and shifted on her stool. "But you're in the wrong profession, Serena. That look would break down the most notorious mobster in any interrogation."

Serena sat down on a stool behind the sales counter and propped her chin in her hands, but remained silent.

Addie swirled her teacup, set it down, drummed her fingers on the counter, and took a deep breath. "The first incident was almost a year ago. My fiancé, David, was murdered in our apartment in Boston."

Serena gasped and placed her hand over Addie's and gently clasped it.

Addie bit her lip. "It was ruled a crime of opportunity, and the police never found out who did it. The case is still open, I guess, but they're not investigating anymore. Even though I had a few theories of my own, they wouldn't look into them. They just walked away, writing him off as another victim of the current crime wave sweeping the neighborhood."

"Oh my God. What a horrible thing to have gone through." Serena's slight frame shuddered.

"Oh, it gets better." Addie sighed. "About

six months ago, my father was killed in a car crash, not far from here, actually. Pen Hollow, just down the coast."

"Yes, I know that drive. There's a switchback curve at the top of the cliff — pretty scary at times."

Addie nodded.

"You don't mean . . . ? Oh jeez. I'm so sorry." Serena squeezed her hand.

Addie's eyes moistened. "There were too many unanswered questions about his accident, and the state police just brushed me off and closed the case, ruling it an accident. They said he was driving too fast for the heavy fog conditions at the time. I thought there had to be more to it — maybe a brake malfunction or a heart attack or something. I knew my dad. He was always a cautious driver. But they just wouldn't listen to me."

"That must have been horrible. Did you ever get any answers?"

Addie shook her head. "And then —"

"There's more?" Serena leaned closer, gripping Addie's hand even tighter.

"Yes. Three months ago, I got a call from a lawyer, informing me my great-aunt had passed away. They'd done an extensive family search and discovered I was the only surviving relative, so I was to inherit her entire estate."

Serena's eye widened.

"My old supervisor from the Boston Public Library, who is an extremely logical person, and who became my rock through a very dark time in my life" — she cleared her throat — "advised me to put the whole estate up for auction, take the money, and retire."

"Obviously by opening up your own store, you didn't retire."

"No, I'm not one who enjoys being idle. I get bored easily," she said, tapping her fingers on the counter.

"Judging from all the books you have, I'm guessing you were a librarian?" Serena's brow rose. "Isn't that kind of boring anyway?"

Addie laughed. "No, lots of people love that work, but I was the assistant to the curator of acquisitions."

"Oooh, sounds fancy and important."

"Not really." Addie shook her head. "I researched and cataloged old and rare books. Well, that is, until I did a six-month work exchange at the British Museum."

Serena leaned closer. "London? Wow, what did you do there?"

"Same thing, but with some museum artifacts, too, not just books — although really it was anything crated up in storage that hadn't been appraised yet. Now that I think about it, it was kind of grunt work."

"But living in London must have been fantastic. I'd love to travel . . . anywhere . . ." Her voice trailed off.

"I loved being there even though David couldn't go with me because of his work and I missed him so much. When my term was over, I couldn't wait to get home to him. But he was murdered right after I came back, and that's when my world fell apart." Addie sighed.

Serena bit her lip.

"After the whole David thing and then my dad passing, I knew there was nothing left for me in Boston. I needed to get out of that city, and with my aunt's inheritance, it became possible. And that's how I ended up here. To move on and start a new life." She gulped down a mouthful of tea. "But taking in this morning, trouble seems to be never far behind me lately."

Serena shook her head. "So much tragedy for such a young woman." She clasped both of Addie's hands in hers and gently squeezed them.

"Young?" She winced. "I'm thirty . . . *something*."

"Okay, but you haven't turned gray yet, and that's a good sign. I know I would be after all that, and I'm only twenty-seven."

Addie turned up her chin, smiled demurely and fluttered her eyelashes. "Don't tell anyone," she whispered. "But it's the honey-brown color with salon-enhanced golden streaks. It hides the gray."

"You really are something else," Serena said, and she poured them more tea. "After all you've been through, you've still managed to keep a sense of humor."

Addie sighed and stared down into her cup. "Funny thing is, if there is anything funny about all this, I didn't even know I had a great-aunt, and here I am living in her house."

Serena's brows shot up. "Which house is it? I grew up here, and I know everyone. I probably knew your aunt, too."

"It's the big one on the hilltop overlooking the harbor at the end of the road."

Serena grasped the counter edge and stood up. "You mean Greyborne Manor?" she whispered.

"Yes, that's it. Why? Do you know it?"

"Who doesn't around here? You're a Greyborne?" Serena's eyes widened. "Why didn't anyone know someone had moved in?"

Addie chuckled at the stunned expression on Serena's face. "I kept mainly to myself because I had so much to do with the move and sorting out the house, and then when I decided to open a shop, there were renovations and . . . well, the list goes on."

"I understand that." Serena's face reddened. Addie noted that when she flushed, freckles burst out across her cheeks. "But another Greyborne back in Greyborne Harbor? That's big news. We all thought the family line had ended with your aunt."

"It's not that big of a deal, is it? You know, that I'm a Greyborne?"

"This town was named after the Greybornes, who founded it back in the early seventeen hundreds."

"I know. I read that, but it can't mean that much today, can it?" Addie sipped her tea, looking over the rim of her cup at Serena. "After all, it's grown into so much more than its pilgrim beginnings over the years, hasn't it? The tourist sites say it's a booming, to quote, 'quaint little seaside town.' From what I can tell by the tour buses I've seen, I can understand why. It looks interesting. It's picturesque, and I've seen lots of posters up advertising art and entertainment events. The name didn't seem like that big of a deal these days." She set her cup down.

Serena choked on her mouthful, sputtering tea down her chin. "You really have no idea of the legacy that's been left, do you?"

Chapter Three

Addie plopped onto her aunt's old sofa. She could feel the prickle of the horsehair stuffing where the fabric had been worn thin in places as she ran her palm across the ancient surface. Exhausted, she put her feet on the eighteenth-century marquetry coffee table, not caring whether her aunt would have approved or not. This was her house now, and she was going to be comfortable living in it. Her eyes closed for a moment, and she breathed in deeply, exhaling slowly, her limbs finally relaxing. Each time she closed her eyes, she could see the constant stream of curious locals who had filled her shop this afternoon. She'd made a few small sales, but for the most part, it was nosy tire-kickers who had come in to assess *her*. Word seemed to have spread quickly about her links to the place and her ancestry. Serena would be the one she'd have to thank for that. In spite of her good intentions, the chaos her spreading the word had caused only added to what already had started out as a most bizarre day. Right now, Addie was nothing more than a bowl of jelly.

Perhaps a drink would rejuvenate her. She eyed the walnut bar trolley across the room, guessing it to be of American 1920s vintage. It reminded her that there was still work to be done around the house, sorting and appraising, but the thought was too daunting right now.

She sniffed her jacket lapel — and cringed. A bath was definitely needed after the fiasco with the garbage this morning. She decided a glass of something, anything, with a long hot soak in the tub, would be perfect, if she could only will her body to move.

Her heavy eyelids fluttered. She rested her head on the overstuffed sofa back, peering through her long, thick lashes and surveyed the somewhat updated living room. She smiled and recalled the feeling she'd had when she first arrived at the three-story Queen Anne Victorian called Greyborne Manor. She'd pulled down the driveway, and her mouth had dropped open. The sheer size of it, with the wide wraparound porch, gabled roofline, two tall brick chimneys and a second-floor, glassed-in sleeping porch, took her breath away, sending her mind reeling.

She had arranged for the lawyer, Raymond James, to meet her at the house, and when she arrived, he was sitting in one of the white wicker chairs on the porch. He rose when she dashed up the wide porch staircase. She was surprised to see his tall stature, as it didn't seem to match his meek telephone voice. She had guessed him to be middle to late sixties, and she saw that she'd been right. He introduced himself, bowed slightly, and with a wave of his hand directed her through the front door.

She remembered vividly how she had felt as she walked into the entry hall. It was as though she'd stepped back into the eighteen hundreds. He proceeded to conduct her tour, guiding her from one room to another. He had seemed pleasant enough, although he remained aloof and lawyer-like as he answered the million questions she had about the antique furniture, the ornately carved doorframes and staircase banister, the custom tile work around the four fireplaces, and the beautifully restored Walter Crane wallpaper. She knew her head was spinning and suspected that, with her nonstop babbling, his was, too.

Little did she know then that the real treasures were yet to be found. A few days later, she climbed the narrow back staircase to the top of the house, an area Raymond hadn't included in the initial tour. When her foot hit the top step, she knew she'd stumbled onto a significant find. She'd plopped down on an old crate completely lost for words.

Perched on the dusty mahogany shelves were her aunt's journals, first-edition books, and relics from her years spent traveling the world. When she caught her breath and began to explore, she discovered that every shelf and box contained one fantastic prize after another. Her training and work experience made her very aware of the importance and value of such a collection.

But some of the books she discovered were just old and well loved, so she began to separate them all into three piles. One for the books she recognized as being of library or museum quality — she would call the head curator at the British Museum for those. The second pile was for books she knew were valuable but had no idea of their worth in today's market. Those she'd send to her former supervisor, Jeremy, in Boston for value appraisal, as soon as she could find the time. The third was for the leftovers. When she looked at that pile, her heart had sunk. There were so many; what a shame.

She bit her bottom lip, staring at them. Then she jumped to her feet and twirled around, clapping her hands.

"I'll open my own used and rare book shop." She danced around the mountain of books and stopped short. She shuddered at the thought of still having to sort through the rest of the stacks piled floor to ceiling. Even so, it was too late. The seed had been planted, and her mind raced with ideas.

Here she was, three months later. Her store had opened, and she wasn't half done with the sorting. She shook her head. "All that work still to do, and now a day job, too." *What was I thinking?* Heavy-eyed, her gaze wandered back to the liquor cart. She urged her shoulders forward but instead fell back and snuggled deeper into the sofa, eyes closed.

A noise echoed through the house and Addie jerked. Dazed, she rubbed her stiff neck. She must have drifted off. The sound had probably only been in a dream, because the living room was dark now. She got up to turn on the Tiffany lamp by the window, but stopped short when there was another thud. She peered outside just in time to see the taillights of a dark-colored car speeding up her driveway to the main road. Her mouth was arid and her heart raced. It looked like the same car that had tried to run her over in the street this morning.

She grabbed a silver candlestick from the side table. Armed now, she entered the foyer. She checked the front door, but it was secure, and nothing appeared out of place. She made her way toward the back kitchen, glancing in the study, library, and dining room as she passed.

When she neared the kitchen entrance at the end of the long, wide corridor, a cool breeze drifted across her hot cheeks. She took a deep breath, reached her hand around the doorjamb, and flipped on the light. Her heart hammered against her ribs. Pearls of perspiration trickled down her brow, stinging her eyes. She squeezed them tight, counted — seven . . . eight . . . nine . . . ten — and peeked into the large room. The back door was ajar. Addie slid her hand into her jacket's side pocket. With trembling fingers, she took out her cell phone and dialed 911.

Her eyes remained fixed on the door. Her breaths came short and fast. The only sound she heard was the clock on the wall ticking off the minutes. Five minutes. Eight minutes. Then she heard a creaking on the back step. A gun barrel appeared through the door crack. She sucked in and pressed her back hard against the wall. Her hand gripped the candlestick. She raised it.

A police cap appeared around the doorframe. "Marc?" Her arm dropped to her side. "Thank God it's you."

"Addie. You okay?" he whispered.

She nodded.

"Have you checked upstairs?"

She shook her head.

He signaled behind him, and two more officers carrying guns slipped through the doorway. "Don't worry. I've got more men at the front door. Is it locked?"

She nodded.

He whispered to the men behind him. "We'll make our way to the front door and unlock it. Go." He motioned. "Stay here and don't move," he murmured as he slid past her into the hallway.

She took another deep breath and clenched her jaw to keep her tears in check.

"Clear. . . . Clear. . . . Clear." Their voices rang out one by one as they scanned each room along the corridor to the front entrance.

Addie heard shuffling on the stairway, and then the hardwood floors above her creaked.

A few minutes later, Marc returned. "All clear on the second and third floors."

"Thank you. Oh God, when you came in

you scared the life out of me. I hadn't heard any sirens."

"Nope, didn't use them. Hoped to catch the perpetrator in the act, but looks like we're too late."

"Yeah, I spotted the car racing off. I guess that's what woke me."

"So you were upstairs in bed?"

"No. I fell asleep on the living room sofa."

She glanced over at the splintered doorjamb, biting her lip.

"Don't worry, I'll secure that before I go."

She nodded with relief.

He cleared his throat. "Twice in one day to the same person. That's not something that usually happens around these parts." His eyes narrowed as he studied her face. "Were you involved in anything criminal in Boston?"

"No. Of course not," she snapped. Her eyes flashed. "I worked at the library."

He rubbed the day-old growth on his chin, a wave of chestnut-brown hair dangling over his forehead, holding his dark eyes steadfast on hers.

She tucked a wisp of hair behind her ear, huffed, and planted her feet. "Why? Do you think I brought this with me from some sordid past I have?"

"No, no, just trying to figure out why

you're a target in this sleepy little town."

"All clear, sir," said an officer from the doorway. "I've checked the cellar, too, and nothing, but thought I'd bring these two-by-fours up to fix the door with."

"Thanks, Steve but I'll take care of that. You can just leave them there for now. You guys can head back to the station. I'm going to stay with Miss Greyborne while she does an initial check of her property to see if anything's missing."

"Very good, sir." He nodded and tipped his cap at Addie as he left.

"Look. I know you're tired, but we need to do a quick inspection tonight to see if your intruder made off with anything." He nodded toward the door and stepped back as she passed.

She paused and looked at him. "You don't like me much, do you?"

"Don't know you well enough to form an opinion, ma'am." He cleared his throat. His lips arched into a half smile.

She huffed and strode down the hall to the dining room.

They explored the rooms on the main floor, and although drawers and cupboards were opened and appeared to have been searched, nothing seemed to be missing. Nothing on the top two floors even looked like it had been touched.

"I suspect since you were dozing right here" — he motioned to the living room — "the intruder didn't have time to check upstairs. Afraid you'd wake up and all. Probably just looking for quick grabs that would sell easily."

"But it doesn't look like anything's missing, so it doesn't make sense."

"Tells me it was probably a kid, not a professional. Didn't know the value of some of this stuff, I guess."

"Or someone who is looking for something very specific, like whoever ransacked my shop?"

"I doubt they're related." He jotted something down in his notebook. "These types of break and enters are usually just a quick in and out before the homeowner wakes up. So in future, if you are a heavy sleeper and someone can break in, and you wouldn't hear —"

"I'm not normally," she snapped, "but I was exhausted. It was a trying day. You know how it started off, and besides, the kitchen door, and any noise he might have made, is a long way from the living room. There's a lot of house between them." She tapped her foot. "I feel like you're back to suspecting me of doing something wrong, so are we almost done here?"

"Yup." He nodded, still writing. "But . . . as I was going to say, if you are a heavy sleeper, and since this house is the size that it is, then I'd suggest you make sure your security system is turned on even when you're in the house."

"Oh, sorry." Her cheeks grew warm, and she glanced down at the floor. "I don't think there is one."

He shook his head and jotted another note into his book.

They went to the kitchen. Addie felt the awkward tension she had created with her sometimes-too-quick-to-respond tongue. While he proceeded to secure the damaged door with the two-by-fours, she busied herself cleaning nonexistent smudges off the large center island, grateful that the kitchen had been updated with all the modern conveniences.

When Marc finished securing the original mahogany door, they returned to the entry foyer. He advised her in a very matter-of-fact tone to call the local handyman and locksmith first thing in the morning, and then he handed her his official police business card. "I wrote his name and number on the back. The number on the bottom is my cell."

"Chief Marc Chandler? I didn't know you were the chief of police. Your name tag says 'Lieutenant.'"

"Yeah, need to get that changed." He glanced down at it. "I was promoted by the mayor last month when Chief Ryan retired."

"Well then, belated congratulations." She smiled, noting his square jaw and sharp cheekbones.

He nodded. "If you think of anything else, just call the dispatcher, or . . . maybe my cell number." A flush swept across his cheeks.

She flipped the card over and smiled up at him. "Thank you. I'll remember that."

His eyes held hers. The corners of his mouth twitched with a slight suggestion of a smile, but then he tipped his cap, turned sharply on his boot heel, and left.

She stood alone in the foyer and began shaking. She wished there was someone she could call to come and sit with her while she processed the day's and evening's events. She looked down at the scrawled phone number on the back of the card and turned it over a few times before stuffing it in her pocket.

With a deep breath, she marched into the living room, picked up a crystal decanter from the cart, took a whiff of the contents, poured a tall glass of the scotch and took a gulp. Out of past experience, she winced and waited for the burning in her throat to start, but to her amazement, it didn't. The drink went down as smooth as silk. A warm glow coursed through her veins. She flopped onto the sofa, swirled the amber liquid in the glass and took another gulp. Her cell phone vibrated in her pocket.

She tapped the speaker button. "Hello?"

"Addie? It's Serena. Marc just called me and told me what happened. I can't believe it. I'm on my way over now."

"You have no idea how much I need the company."

"Yes, Marc said you looked a little shaken up when he left. How about if we have a sleepover? You shouldn't be there alone tonight."

"You don't even know me that well. Why would you want to put yourself out like that?"

"Don't argue with me. I insist. Besides, I feel like I do know you well enough, and if my brother calls me and tells me anything about a case, then I know I should listen."

"He's worried?" Addie's brow rose.

"Not worried, but concerned. Twice in a day is enough to rattle anyone. So I'll see you soon."

Addie took another sip of her drink and laid her head against the back of the sofa. The events of the day replayed through her mind. She hadn't been robbed either time, so it made no sense. She bolted straight up. Was someone trying to scare her out of town? But why?

Chapter Four

Addie's head pounded as morning light streamed through her shop's windows. Her stomach pitched. Even the faint pungent odor wafting off the recently varnished countertop seemed sharper today. A spasm of pain shot through her temple. She cringed and downed a couple of painkillers in hopes that this would all subside before any customers wandered in.

Serena informed her last night that the scotch she had consumed like water was a very rare old blend. Although smooth, it had a real kick to it. So today, she had no one to blame but herself and her own stupidity.

Despite her foolishness, it had been a good night. They had chatted until late, starting to develop a real friendship. Addie smiled. It had been a long time since she had a close female friend, and she missed that camaraderie. In the working world, she found many of her woman colleagues to be so professionally driven that they ignored any overtures of friendship. Even Sheila, whom Addie vaguely remembered this morning having told Serena about last night and who was the junior curator she had worked with side by side five days a week at the British Museum, had shown little interest in developing a friendship until it was too late and was time for Addie to return to Boston.

The door chimes rang. Addie squeezed her eyes shut and pasted a smile on her face.

"Hi." A mound of tousled red hair appeared around the corner of a bookshelf.

Addie let out a deep breath. "Thank God, it's only you."

"Only me?" Serena stepped forward, a sardonic twinkle in her eye. "Thanks. That makes me feel *great.*"

"I didn't mean it like that."

"I know. I figured you could use a cup of this, and I see I wasn't wrong." She grinned and waved a steaming paper cup under Addie's nose. "An old family remedy for what ails you."

"Mmm, smells like . . . I'm not sure. What is it?"

"Family secret," she whispered. "If I told you, I'd have to — never mind. I wasn't thinking."

"It's okay, Serena." She smiled over her cup and took a sip. "Mmm, this is good, and exactly what I needed."

"I thought so. Just remember the next time that I have the cure so you won't have to suffer. I'd better run. I see a woman pacing the sidewalk in front of my store." Serena called over her shoulder, "Cheers, till later."

"Cheers."

The morning flew by, and come lunchtime, when her stomach growled, she knew she needed something to eat, so she went off in search of food and to distribute her advertising flyers to some of the area merchants.

Addie hadn't been back in the shop for two minutes when Serena bounced through the door. She took one look at Addie's sandwich sitting on the counter, and her face dropped. "Oh, I see you have lunch already. I just picked these up from Martha's. I thought we could eat together."

"We still can," smiled Addie, eyeing Serena's sandwich wrapper. "I'm surprised you bought something from her now that you know she's selling lunches. Doesn't that conflict with your shop?"

"No, I only sell a few organic-made and gluten-free rolls and pastries. She doesn't . . . at least not yet. Her food is typical bakery stuff, but I'm sure the new restaurant and coffee shop won't be too happy with her. There's kind of an unwritten noncompetition clause we all follow. You know, 'cause it's not a big town."

"I see. I'll have to keep that in mind. I wouldn't want to step on any toes. Come on, let's go over there, sit in the reading chairs, and relax. I don't know about you, but my feet are killing me."

Serena stuffed one of the sandwiches into her large hobo bag and followed Addie to the chairs by the window. "It was crazy busy this morning. I think everyone was out and about. Speaking of crazy" — she swallowed a bite of her bun — "I had the weirdest customer this morning."

"How so?" Addie covered her mouth. "Sorry, don't mean to be rude, but I'm starving."

"Remember the lady pacing, waiting for me to open? Well, she wanted something to put her husband to sleep with. At least, she said it was for her husband, who hadn't slept well lately and needed some 'knockout' tea, but she said it had to be odorless and tasteless."

"What?"

"I know! Well, my mouth must have

dropped open, because she jumped in quick and said he'd tried some herbal mixes that were all flowery or tasted like dirt and hated them, so he wanted something that tasted like water."

"Is there such a thing?"

She shook her head. "Not in my business — at least nothing that's legal."

"What did you tell her?"

"I told her I blend tea. That I don't concoct potions, and if that's what she was looking for, she should try an herbalist or a naturopathic doctor, or even a witch, but not a tea merchant."

"You didn't tell her to consult a witch. You're joking, right?"

"No kidding, I did. I have a mind to call Marc and report her. I got a really weird vibe from her. You know, kind of snooty and hoity-toity. I wouldn't put it past her to be trying to knock off her husband or someone else."

"Wow. That is strange. Have you ever seen her around town before?"

"No, and I know most people living here. She would have to be an outsider, because everyone knows I don't practice herbology or do magic hocus-pocus potions — just teas." She got up, putting her sandwich wrapper in the garbage can by the counter.

"That's that, I guess. Lunch break over. I'll let you know if she comes back so you can come in and check her out and tell me if I'm nuts or if there's really something off with the woman."

"Sounds good." Addie wiped her mouth with a napkin. "Yes, I guess that was lunch. See ya." She waved.

Her brow furrowed. She thought about Serena's customer and her odd request, and then decided Serena probably had an even more vivid imagination than she did. After all, Serena had mentioned she loved to read murder mysteries, and Agatha Christie's trademark was — Addie bit on her lip — murder by poison.

As Addie pulled her newer red Mini Cooper into her driveway, her thoughts were focused on her evening ahead. Tonight she had dinner to make and a couple of hours of sorting through boxes ahead of her. Fifteen minutes later, the spaghetti sauce was simmering on the stove, and fresh coffee was steaming in her cup. She slipped into the living room to check her emails on her laptop, which she'd forgotten in her rush out the door this morning. She sat on the sofa, her legs drawn up, her laptop across her knees, sipping her coffee — but one look at her empty inbox, and her heart sank. It had been over three weeks since she sent some of the books she'd discovered in the attic to the library in Boston, for Jeremy to appraise.

She gnawed on her bottom lip and scrolled through all her past messages in case there was one she'd missed, but found nothing from him. She snapped her laptop closed and set it on the coffee table, shook her head, and got up to close the curtains, but stopped short when she reached the window. A car with its lights off sat parked at the dead-end loop that led into her driveway. There was no reason for anyone to stop there, as the loop only led down to her house. She squinted in the dim light, but couldn't work out the make or model, only that it appeared to be a dark color. She reached for her cell phone in her jacket pocket and tried to enter her pass code, but only got a black screen before realizing the phone was dead.

She wished now she'd had the landline connected. She chewed on her bottom lip, trying to think what to do. Her charger was upstairs in her bedroom. Dashing up the steps, she snatched the charger and stumbled back down the stairs, charger dangling by its cord. Breathless, she plugged it in and laid her hand over her heart, which was drumming an erratic rhythm. She glanced up repeatedly to keep an eye on the car and to scan the dusky yard for signs of an intruder.

An alarm screamed. She jumped. "Shoot." She'd forgotten about the sauce cooking on the stove. She ran through the smoky hallway to the kitchen, seized a towel from the rack, wrapped it around her hand, grabbed the red, hot handle and tossed the blackened, smoking pot into the sink. She waved the towel under the smoke detector, but it wouldn't turn off. Frantic, she tossed the towel on the counter, grabbed a chair, climbed up and pulled the cover off the smoke alarm to yank the battery out, only to discover there wasn't one. It was hardwired in and there was no off button.

The kitchen filled with heavy black smoke, she glanced at the pot still smoldering in the sink and saw the towel she'd tossed aside had landed on the hot burner and was consumed in flames. She jumped off the chair, grabbed a knife from the counter top and pushed what was left of the towel into the sink dousing it with water. Against her better judgment, she forced open a window. Aware that at any time the trespasser from the car might be out there waiting for just this opportunity to get in, but she knew there wasn't a choice. It was either face the intruder in the house or be struck down by toxic fumes and smoke. Besides, maybe a neighbor would hear the incessant screeching and call the fire department.

Sirens wailed in the distance. They grew louder, and she dashed back to the living room window just in time to see two fire trucks barrel down her driveway.

To her relief, the dark car was gone, and she was grateful to her small-town neighbors.

The firefighters stormed the house and told her to go outside and wait. Addie stood shivering in the cool fall evening. Her eyes focused on the commotion she could see through the open front door as firefighters made their way from room to room, checking for signs of a blaze. Someone placed a jacket across her shoulders. She snuggled into its warmth.

"You do know how to cause a commotion, don't you?" Marc looked down at her, an amused glint in his eye.

"I guess I do." She shook her head and laughed. "I tried to tell them there's no house fire — it was just my dinner and a kitchen towel cooking."

"Is this a testament to your cooking skills?"

"Not usually." She frowned, then chuckled. "I'm a very good cook when I'm not busy trying to figure out why a car is parked at the top of my driveway and my cell phone's dead and I can't call for help."

"A car?"

"Yes, a dark-colored one, as far as I could tell."

"Hum, anything else you noticed about it? Make, model, license pl—"

"No, the light wasn't good enough."

Marc withdrew a notepad from his jacket's inside chest pocket and began making notes. He asked a few more questions, then went to his car. He returned moments later, his face grim.

"What is it?"

"It appears an alarm just came through from your shop. My men are on their way there now."

Addie's heart dropped to the pit of her stomach like a rock.

Chapter Five

Flying through town lights flashing and sirens blaring would have been exciting if it hadn't been her shop they were en route to. The rock in the pit of her stomach was now all caught up in the knots growing inside her. She jumped out onto the curb before Marc brought his cruiser to a complete stop and gasped in anger at the shattered glass door.

"It might look worse than it is." Marc's boots crunched through the splintered glass on the sidewalk. "You stay out here," he called over his shoulder. "I'll go in and see what they've found."

Addie choked on the acid rising in the back of her throat. She couldn't believe this was all happening to her. A group of curious onlookers was forming on the sidewalk, despite the biting shore winds, and she scanned the gawkers for a friendly face. A tall man and woman standing near the back of the growing crowd caught her eye. She wasn't certain she'd seen the man before, but there was something eerily familiar about the woman. Unfortunately, her fur-trimmed jacket collar was drawn up, covering the bottom portion of her face. Addie took a step closer to try to get a better look, but as more people pushed in to catch a view of what was going on, she lost sight of them.

"You poor thing."

Addie spun around. "I'm so glad you're here. You wouldn't believe what's happened tonight." She hugged Serena.

"Judging by the way you look, I can make a fairly good guess."

Addie ran her hand through her hair and laughed. "I must look like a ratty mess."

"Not as bad as your shop does though."

"You should see my house."

"What? Your house was broken into again?" Serena cried.

"No. Smoke damage. I was cooking dinner." Addie shrugged and looked down at her feet.

"I see. Well, I don't really, but you can tell me about that later. What happened here tonight looks bad though."

Marc came out of the shop and strode over to them. "It's better than we first thought." He smiled. "Nothing inside appears to have been touched. I figure the alarm scared off whoever it was before they got in."

"Well, that's good news," said Serena.

Addie nodded. The rock lodged in her stomach softened. She took a deep breath. "What now?"

"I need you to come inside with me and see if anything was disturbed, and then I'll fill out the report, and we take the investigation from there."

"What about the car watching my house this evening?"

"That's already in my repo—"

Serena grabbed Addie's arm. "You're kidding? What car? Was it the same one as before?"

Without replying, Addie looked at Marc. "But what do I do now?"

"You'll stay at my place tonight," Serena butted in. "I insist you shouldn't be alone. You can fill me in on the details later."

Addie sighed and nodded.

"Good, that's settled," said Marc. "I was going to suggest that. Best if you do stay with someone, at least until you can install a home security system."

"I never thought I would need one, living here." Addie's bottom lip trembled.

"The good thing is that you paid for the upgrade to have the fire alarm go directly to our dispatcher."

"I did?" Addie's mouth fell open. "But smoke alarms go off all the time. Surely the fire department doesn't come running for every piece of burned toast?"

He tossed his head back and laughed. "No, not usually. In this type of fire and security system there's supposed to be a control pad that can be turned off in those cases, but you don't have one. Which seems strange? It tells me your aunt only installed part of the system." His brow knit. "Why would she only have the basic fire alarm capability, which obviously works on its own, but not have the whole package that includes the controls and home security features?"

"Hmmm, I wonder." Addie looked up at him. "She lived alone in that massive house. You'd think it would be something the fire alarm installer would have recommended?"

"You'd think so," Serena said, "especially given her age and failing health."

"Well" — Marc jotted something into his notepad — "you'll need to get your doors and windows alarmed, too, like you have here at the store."

"You're right. It appears that crime

doesn't just occur in the big city."

"Cheer up. You're still doing better than most of the merchants in town." He flashed a smirk at Serena. "They're still under the impression this *is* a sleepy little village and don't even have an alarm system on their shops."

"Not since the town raised the costs," snapped Serena. "You try paying for it on what I make a month and see if it's worth it."

"I think this incident is proof enough. It's worth the few dollars a month, *and* it still costs less than a private security company charges." Marc glared at her.

"Maybe we should go inside and take a look, Marc?"

"I'll wait out here." Serena crossed her arms.

Marc's brow rose. He frowned at Serena and followed Addie through the door.

When they returned to the street a few minutes later, Serena was in a discussion with a group of people, mostly merchants Addie had met when she had delivered her store flyers.

"I tell you, there was no trouble in this town till that, *that* woman got here."

Addie cringed. She recognized Martha's

shrill voice rising above the other mutterings.

Serena ran over to Addie and Marc. "The area merchants have called an emergency meeting for tomorrow, eight a.m. at my store."

"Why?" Marc squared his shoulders.

Serena shot Marc a sideways glance. "As you can hear, Martha has made it sound like there's a major crime wave sweeping town and has gotten everyone riled up."

Addie gave a nervous laugh and shifted her feet.

"I think you should join us." Serena smiled at her friend. "After all, you are a member of the founding family of the town, and they might listen to you explain what a real crime wave looks like. You know, being from the city and all."

Addie's lip stiffened. "Why is Martha trying to turn the whole town against me? Is she trying to force me into leaving town for some reason?"

"No." Serena's face paled. "Why on earth would she do that?"

"I don't know." Addie shrugged, not meeting her eyes. "It's just a feeling I have."

"Well, don't worry. There's no reason for anyone to run you out as far as I know, and a few break-ins don't make for a crime wave, so ignore her — everyone else does. She's just being her miserable old self."

Addie thought for a moment, but noticed Martha's voice growing louder and more animated as the crowd around her grew. "It seems they're not ignoring her tonight."

"Everyone's just upset tonight. They'll calm down soon enough. Please come. At least it's a chance to defend yourself against *her.*"

"Obviously, I should be there." Addie watched the faces of Martha's captivated audience.

"*And* you can't let her get away with this or try to make things worse, can you?"

"You're right." Addie nodded. "What time did you say? I have a lot to do tomorrow with getting this door fixed and getting my house back in order."

"I've already called Brian," Marc said. "He's on his way right now to shore up the door, and he promised me he'd have it replaced tomorrow. You go to your meeting, and *good luck.*" He shook his head and glared at Martha before walking to his police cruiser.

Brian arrived shortly after Marc left and secured a sheet of plywood over the door. He assured Addie that he'd be back first thing in the morning to properly fix it, and then he left.

The crowds dispersed, and the police cruisers had long since gone. Addie and Serena stood on the now-empty street. They crossed the road to Serena's car. She was chatting on about something, but Addie's mind was replaying the evening's events, and she wasn't listening. Out of the corner of her eye, she glimpsed a flash. The streetlight reflected on the windshield of a dark car, parked halfway down the road. She stopped in the middle of the street, clenched her fists at her sides and marched toward it.

"Wait," Serena called. "Where are you going?"

"To get some answers."

The car's engine revved, and it sped directly toward her.

"Are you crazy?" Serena grabbed her arm and pulled them both out of its path to the curb.

Chapter Six

Addie shivered. The morning air was unpleasantly chilly, and Brian was struggling to fit her new shop door. She tapped her foot and scanned every passing vehicle to see if there were any dark sedans lurking about. Although Marc's words and voice had been soothing and reassuring last night after he'd taken their statements about the near hit-and-run, when he left Serena's, concern was clearly written all over his face, and it made her feel even more on edge.

He'd assured them both that the car coming close to hitting her was more than likely a coincidence. He noted the streetlamps in the square didn't keep the area well lit. It seemed the town council opted years ago to just switch the original gas lamps over to electricity. Then something about integrity and tradition — *Blah, blah, blah,* Addie thought as she continued scouring the streets for villains in evil black cars. He'd also pointed out that the car didn't have its headlights on, so maybe the driver hadn't seen her walking on the road. Even though he'd said all the right things, she couldn't shake the image of the look on his face when he left. Little did he know that wasn't her first near miss with a black sedan on the road.

Brian finished and handed her the new door keys. She placed them on her ring with her house and car keys and threw them into her handbag. She was already running late for the eight a.m. meeting at SerenaTEA and dashed off as Brian was telling her he'd meet at her house at noon to replace her back door.

"Great, thanks, I'll see you then," she called back from Serena's shop entrance.

Her hand was on the latch when the door swung open. People, most of whom Addie recognized as business owners, began spilling out onto the sidewalk. "Isn't this the Town Square merchants meeting?" She looked blankly at the faces streaming onto the walkway.

"Yes, it was. Meeting's over, and none too soon," snapped a rather tall, middle-aged gentleman Addie didn't recognize.

"So soon?" She checked her wristwatch.

The man's eyes narrowed. "Soon enough

for those of us who aren't too high-and-mighty to show up." He sneered and walked away.

She watched as his long strides took him quickly to the street corner and wondered if he was the tall man she'd seen standing at the back of the crowd the previous night. Since he was apparently a shop owner, it would have made sense that he would have been there.

She found Serena humming in the storage room.

"What happened? The meeting was called for eight and it's not even half past. I missed it?"

Serena jumped. "Addie! You scared the life out of me."

"Sorry, but I'm shocked the meeting's over so soon. Who was that tall guy who just left?"

"That's Blain Fielding. You know, of Fielding's Department Store on Main."

"No, I didn't get to meet him when I stopped in there yesterday to deliver a flyer, but just now he didn't seem impressed with the meeting or with me. I guess Martha's rumblings haven't died down yet."

"Don't mind him — although he did his best to rile everyone up again, parroting Martha's mutterings." Serena shook her head. "That is, till I put an end to it. I told them all off."

"Really? You did that for me?"

"Of course I did. He thinks he runs the downtown business district, and obviously feels threatened by someone else in town whose name holds more influence than his does."

"It's nice to know the police chief's sister has that kind of influence." Addie winked.

"What? Me? No, he's not feeling threatened by me." Serena burst out laughing. "It's you, you silly girl. You have no idea of the power the Greyborne name has in this town, do you?"

"No, I guess I don't, and it worries me, since it appears that I've managed to make yet another enemy this week." Addie slumped onto a counter stool. "I'm getting a distinct feeling that someone is trying to run me off at all costs."

"Naw, I don't think so. They're just small-town people who gossip a lot and take a while to warm up to newcomers. Blain, well, he's just a bit of a control freak anyway. He's probably mad because he didn't call the meeting and someone else might have a good idea or two. You'll get used to them and him, eventually." She snickered.

"I hope so. I guess that's one of the

disadvantages of living in a small town; people can be pretty territorial, and everyone has their own niche and place."

"You just have to create your own, and with your family name, it should be no problem. Unfortunately, since your aunt became such a recluse due to her health in her later years, it allowed people like Blain to think they were more important in town than they are."

"I just don't want any more trouble." Addie reached for a scone from the covered plate display on the counter. "Aside from the name, what was so important about my great-aunt? Did she contribute anything else to the community?"

"Only anything and everything to do with arts and culture. Didn't you know anything about her?" Serena slid a plate toward her.

"Thanks. No, I told you, I didn't even know she existed."

"Well, your aunt Anita sat on every cultural and arts committee board in town. If there wasn't one she believed in, she'd start it. Like the Arts Festival Committee — they plan and organize four big festivals in town every year, and they've been doing that as long as I can remember. She was a major donator and contributor to the library, creating a foundation that's taken it from a small one-room building to the three-story one you see today."

Addie's eyes widened and she leaned in closer.

"She also set up a free lunch program in the elementary school and donated to the high school's arts and music departments. As well as paying for their new library extension, which is named after her. You might say she was a very prominent, contributing member of the community. on top of the Greyborne name."

"Wow. I have a lot to live up to," Addie said, biting into her scone.

"There's more, but you'll hear all about her soon enough, I'm sure."

Addie wiped the crumbs from her lips and stood up. "It's almost nine. I guess I'd better go open. Who knows what adventures are in store for me today?"

"I've got lots of food left over from this morning's *very* short meeting, so come by for lunch and help me eat it."

"Sounds good. You can fill me in on what happened at the meeting then. Have a good morning. See you at lunchtime." Addie closed the door behind her.

When she opened her door, she sighed and mentally added another thing on her growing to-do list: get the sign back on the door. The coffee cup graphic was also lost . . . right along with her initial excitement about owning her own store.

She pushed the door open and slapped her hand to her forehead — how could she have forgotten that Brian was meeting her at the house at lunchtime? She dashed back to tell Serena she'd have to take a rain check on lunch today. When she walked back to her shop, a stooped, gray-haired woman was just approaching her door.

"I'm here," Addie called and ran up behind the woman.

"Oh. Hello and good morning. Aren't you open yet?"

"Just opening; please come in."

"I can come back later if that's a better time." The woman smiled.

"No. Please tell me what brings you in today?" Addie stood holding the door open for her to enter. "Are you looking to purchase a gift or something for yourself?"

"I'm really not sure, dear." The woman shyly smiled. "Do you mind if I just browse awhile and see what catches my fancy?"

"Not at all — make yourself at home. Would you like some coffee while you browse?"

"No, thank you. I prefer tea and think I'll stop at that charming little shop next door when I'm done here."

"Tell Serena, the owner, I sent you, and to charge your tea to my bill, unless you'd like me to go and get you one now to enjoy while you browse?"

"No, no, don't bother yourself, dear. I'll just take a look around and be off."

"If you have any questions, I'll be right here."

Addie noticed the woman watching her as she took her keys from her handbag and put them in the drawer under the cash register. "Do you have a question?"

"No, no, dear, I'm just admiring your wee shop."

"That's nice. I'm glad you like it."

The woman walked past the front of the cash desk toward the curio shelves by the window. She examined a few of the glass pieces, but then walked back to the book section, all the while smiling and nodding over her shoulder at Addie. "You have such a lovely store. I'm meeting my daughter later for lunch. It's her birthday soon, so I'll pick her brain about what she'd like for a gift, and then I'll be back. I just know after seeing everything you have here that there's going to be something perfect for her."

"Yes, please do, and bring her back with you if you think it will help."

"I want it be a surprise. I just love surprises, don't you?"

"Yes, and birthday surprises are the best. I hope to see you later."

"You will, dear. I promise. But it's time for a nice cup of tea, so I think I'll pop into the shop next door now. I'll be back this afternoon." The woman's lips arched up into a half smile, and she left.

Addie strolled over to the display cabinet in front of the window to reorganize the venetian wineglasses the woman had been examining. She peered out and noticed the woman standing outside her door. A tall, younger woman came out of Martha's. She met up with the older one and they turned and walked in the opposite direction of SerenaTEA. Addie leaned into the bay window for a better look as they hurriedly walked toward Main Street.

Addie shrugged and took a step back. Martha then appeared on the sidewalk brandishing a broom. She turned and saw Addie in the window, sneered at her, and began sweeping the debris from her sidewalk onto Addie's doorstep.

Addie shook her head. Martha had definitely declared war.

Chapter Seven

Addie raced her Mini Cooper up her front drive and skidded to a stop. Brian's van was parked out front and he was sitting in one of the white wicker chairs on the porch, gazing down at his cell phone.

"Sorry, Brian," she panted, patting her chest. "A customer came in just as I was closing for lunch. I got here as soon as I could."

"That's okay." He looked up at her. "I just got a text from Marc." He flicked his sun-bleached blond hair out of his eyes. "He says you want a home security system installed, too?"

"He did, did he? Actually, I was going to ask you about it when you finished fixing the door," she said, leading him back to the kitchen.

Brian repaired the frame that had been damaged by the crowbar. He also attached a metal lock plate and strip along the length of the door. "Since you're looking at getting a security system, I'll have the guys install a new lock then, one that can be coded to the alarm keypad. This lock will do for now; it doesn't appear damaged."

"I'm sure it's fine for a day or two. Those metal plates have at least made it harder for someone to jimmy the door open again."

"All done here." He closed his toolbox. "Wanna tell me what kind of system you're thinking of?"

"I don't really know. Marc suggested having the windows and doors alarmed. But that sounds like a big job. There are a lot of windows in this house."

"Might not be as bad as you think. Let's take a look."

They spent the next hour going from room to room. He didn't say much. He just took window measurements and jotted down notes as they went. When they finished, he snapped his notebook closed.

"I'll have to do up a quote first. If you have any questions, you can call me or ask me when I drop the quote off. I don't think it will be as bad as you thought it would be though."

"How long do you think it will be? You know, until you can install the system."

"Once you give me the go-ahead, I'll book

it with a company I deal with in Boston. It'll depend on them as to when it happens."

"Okay." She frowned and bit her lip.

"I can see you're worried, and I don't blame you. You've had more than your fair share this week. So tell you what I'm gonna do."

"What? Make all the bad guys disappear?" She snickered.

He laughed and picked up his toolbox by the door. "I'm gonna put a rush on this, get the quote done up today, and if you agree with it, I'll light a fire under the guys in Boston. We'll get this done within the week."

"That sounds good — relieving, actually. Thank you." She smiled up at him, and their eyes locked. She hadn't noticed before, but he had the most amazing pools of sea-blue eyes she'd ever seen. As his gaze lingered on hers, she felt heat rise from under her collar and creep up across her cheeks.

His lips curved up into a wide smile. "I'll call you later," he whispered.

"All . . . all right," was all she could manage to stutter.

"To give you the quote." He chuckled and got into his van.

He'd just brought her back to earth. She went in and slammed the door.

"Silly girl, he probably has every woman in town drooling over him." She laughed at her vulnerability, grabbed her purse, and headed back to the store.

When she parked in her space behind the store, a red head popped out of Serena's back door, disappeared, and reappeared again. Serena ran toward Addie carrying a small box.

"Here. I packed a lunch for you, didn't think you'd have time to eat. I hope I'm not wrong?"

Addie laughed. "No, you're not wrong. I am starving. Thank you, you're a lifesaver." She gave Serena a hug.

"Don't you girls ever work?"

They turned in unison to see Martha standing at her back door.

"How anyone can make a living with the hours you two keep, I'll never know." She huffed and stormed into the bakery.

The two women burst out laughing.

"We have our own store police," choked Serena through the tears streaming down her cheeks.

"Hilarious. I can't believe small towns," gasped Addie between fits of laughter.

The white head reappeared out of the bakery door. "Just in case you do want *any* customers today, Miss *Greyborne,* I thought you ought to know there's a group out front waiting for you to open. That is, of course, if you're finished playing out here," she snapped, then disappeared back inside.

Serena giggled. "Oooh, we're in trouble now."

"Well, I have been gone longer than I planned, so she is right," chuckled Addie. "I'd better get in there. Thanks again for the food."

"No problem, see you later."

Addie unlocked the door and went to punch in the alarm code, but it was already flashing yellow for "standby." She shook her head. Had she really forgotten to set it when she went out? With no time to berate herself over her apparent memory lapse, she rushed to the front, tossed her keys in the drawer under the cash register, and raced for the door. A group of six women were perusing her window displays, and their faces lit up when she flipped over the "Closed" sign and held the door open for them to enter.

Her shop quickly filled with even more customers. She hadn't had this many in her store at the same time yet and was run ragged making certain everyone was looked after, and purchases were paid for. If this kept up, she'd have to hire some part-time help, and much sooner than she'd planned.

She had just finished answering a woman's questions about how her used-book consignment worked, and she glanced around for the next customer in need of her assistance. There was a tug on her jacket sleeve, and she spun around, almost knocking over the older woman from this morning.

"Oh, I'm sorry." She grasped the petite woman's shoulders to stop her from tumbling over.

"I'm fine, dear." The woman smiled up at her. "I've come back and think I'm going to need your help, if you're not too busy, that is?"

Addie glanced around at the myriad of customers. "No, never too busy." She tucked a wayward strand of hair behind her ear. "What can I help you with?"

"It's back here." The woman walked toward the rear shelves of the book department.

Addie looked back over her shoulder — she hated leaving all the shoppers unattended — and then she spotted the tall woman she'd seen the older woman with that morning. She was standing at the curio displays by the cash counter. She kept looking over her shoulder at the counter and then would walk over to the coffee maker, and then back to the display cases, all the while glancing over her shoulder. Addie thought she appeared to be looking for someone to help her, but the petite woman kept tugging on her jacket sleeve and didn't stop until they were in the "Politics, Philosophy, and Spirituality" section in the far back corner of the shop.

"It's here. I saw it this morning." She pointed to a book on the top shelf. "I'm afraid I can't reach it though. I think it's one my daughter would like, if you don't mind?" She smiled up at Addie.

"Of course I don't mind. That's what I'm here for. Is your daughter with you now?" Addie stood on her tiptoes to reach the book the woman had pointed to.

"No, she couldn't make it this afternoon. No, it's not that one. It's that one." She pointed with her twisted, rheumatic finger.

Addie stretched on her tiptoes for another one.

"No. Not that one, the one with the blue cover."

Addie reached up and stopped. "There are three here with blue covers. Which one is it?"

The woman grimaced. "I'm not sure now. Best take them all down, and I'll look."

Addie sighed and retrieved the first of the

blue-covered books. "*Birth of the Chaordic Age* by Dee Hock." Addie handed it to the woman. "Is this the one?"

"I'm not sure now. No. I don't think so. I think it's the one next to it. Do you mind?"

"Of course not." Addie's lips tightened, but she forced a smile while looking over the woman's shoulder. There was a line at the cash desk. She hated to, but knew she'd have to leave the woman and go. She grabbed another blue-covered book. "Here's another one. You can look at it while I run to the front for a minute. I'll be right back."

The woman grasped her arm. "Oh dear, I'm so confused now. I'm just not sure." She sobbed.

Addie stopped. She couldn't leave her in this state, but when she looked up front again, she could tell the other customers were getting annoyed waiting. She couldn't see the taller woman anymore and was curious to get a better look at her. She could swear it was the same one she'd seen come out of Martha's, who had then met up with this older one.

She turned back to the petite woman, but she was gone. Addie dashed back to the storage area, thinking she may have gotten turned around since she had seemed rather confused, but it was empty. She made her way to the front, searching over and around the bookcases as she went, but there was no sign of the woman.

When she got to the front of the store, she was kept busy apologizing for the delay in service and ringing in sales. She knew now for certain that she was going to have to hire some help. Another day like this would kill either her or her business.

It had been a long afternoon, and with the last shopper gone, she flipped the sign and leaned her throbbing head against the cool glass door. There was a rap at the window. She jumped and snapped her eyes open. Directly in front of her was the beaming face of Serena, who was waving a key ring in her hand. Addie blinked and then blinked again. Wide-eyed she opened the door. "Those are mine. How did you get them?"

"I found them out here in the corner, behind the door. You must have dropped them when you opened after lunch."

"Impossible — I came in the back. I threw them in the drawer, ran up here, and turned the dead bolt. I don't remember using them on the door lock. I think I forgot to lock it with the key when I left. Just the thumb-turn dead bolt was in place." She frowned and rubbed her forehead.

"They didn't walk out on their own, did they?" chirped Serena. "And guessing by the number of people you sent into my store — thank you, by the way — I'd say you were pretty busy this afternoon, so no wonder you don't remember."

Addie stared down to the spot Serena had indicated she found them, mentally retracing her steps. "I know I'm exhausted, but I'm certain. I put them in the drawer and just opened the dead bolt after lunch."

Serena's face turned ashen. "But how? Who?"

Addie shook her head. "I don't know." She rubbed her throbbing temples. "Maybe I'm just losing my mind, but I'm positive I put them in the drawer."

"You're not losing your mind." Serena's face softened. "You've been through a lot and you're just tired and need food. Come on, let's go eat. I know the perfect place to unwind."

Addie looked back into the store and frowned. "I wonder . . ." She chewed on her bottom lip.

"Wonder what?"

"The two women? No, it's nothing," Addie shook her head. "You're right. I'm just tired and hungry. Let's go eat."

■ ■ ■ ■

Addie took a deep breath when they stepped onto the street in front of the restaurant, feeling full and satisfied. "It's a nice evening for walk, isn't it? I love the fall. The crisp air's so fresh."

"I don't think there's anywhere else I'd want to be but here this time of the year."

"Me, too. I'm glad I moved to Greyborne Harbor," sighed Addie.

"I'm glad you came, too." Serena looped her arm through Addie's as they strolled toward their shops.

"And I'm so pleased we had dinner tonight. It was a good break for both of us, plus we got to know each other a little better." Addie squeezed her arm.

"I feel like we've been friends forever. Are you sure you've never been here before? Maybe we met when we were kids?"

"Nope, pretty sure I wasn't. My dad was though, I guess, since he was killed not far from here, but he never said a word about the place to me. I didn't know it even existed."

"Oh no. The breeze from the water's picked up." Serena tugged her poncho tighter around her shoulders. "Doesn't feel like such a short walk right now." She laughed. "Now, where were we in our dinner conversation? Oh yeah. Your mysterious keys — if you didn't drop them, how else would they have ended up outside the door?"

"Well, I've been retracing the afternoon in my mind all evening, and the only thing that makes sense is that the old lady took the keys out of the drawer. She watched me put them there this morning, so she knew where I kept them."

"But you said you were with her at the back of the store?"

"Well, my gut tells me it was her or the tall woman I told you about. The one I know I saw her with this morning. I think she was her accomplice, because the more I think about it . . . she seemed more interested in the cash desk than in looking at giftware or books, and the old lady seemed intent on keeping me busy at the back, and then they were both gone."

"But why? It doesn't make sense. Maybe it was a coincidence with the old woman. You were busy; it could have been anyone. Or maybe you did drop them when you opened the door after lunch."

"No, I'm positive I didn't use them. Just the dead bolt was locked. The alarm wasn't set, and it was on standby, I guess because I hadn't locked the front door with the key when I rushed out to meet Brian."

"I don't understand what she'd want with your keys."

"Maybe she hoped there would be larger bills in the drawer but only found the keys and thought she could get back in later to rob the cash register. Who knows?"

"Maybe she's a kleptomaniac, you know someone that steals compulsively." Serena's eyes widened. "Or the poor dear has dementia. You did say she seemed confused."

"Or maybe that was an act because her accomplice up front hadn't done her job yet, and she was buying her time?"

Serena shook her head and shrugged. "People. Who knows what goes on in their minds? I hate to think some old lady is running around Greyborne Harbor committing thefts though. But who would suspect her? So I guess it's a good cover. Here we are — hop in. I'll give you a ride around to the lane to get your car."

"Don't be silly. I'll cut through my shop. It's faster than you driving around the two blocks to get to it."

"Are you sure you don't want me to drive you around?"

"No, I'll be fine. Good night."

Chapter Eight

The next morning flew by, and Addie was exhausted. Lunchtime had long since come and gone. She knew she'd earned a break, but still didn't feel right about locking the store again in the middle of the afternoon. However, this couldn't be helped. Blain Fielding's assistant, Elaine, had called and said he wanted to meet with her this afternoon. She crossed her fingers, hoping this would be an opportunity for her to figure out if he was involved in her recent turmoil.

With a heavy heart, Addie turned the door sign to "Closed." She was more certain than ever that hiring part-time help now was essential, or soon she wouldn't have a business to worry about at all. She stepped into the street and locked the door. Serena dashed out of Martha's bakery, clutching a paper in her hand. She turned left toward Main, not back to her shop. It was all Addie could do to catch up to her sprinter's pace.

When she managed to, it wasn't until she reached the corner that she was close enough to tug on Serena's sleeve.

"Wait up. Hey, what's the hurry?"

Serena spun around, her cheeks flaming, her eyes swollen and red.

"You've been crying? What's wrong?"

Serena sniffled and wiped her nose on the back of her hand. "It's noth . . . nothing."

"Nothing? You're upset."

"I'm fine."

"Serena, what happened? Did Martha say something to you?"

"I have to go." She dashed off, crossing against the "Don't Walk" light, turned right, and ran into the entrance of Fielding's Department Store.

Addie darted to the crossing lights, which were still flashing the pedestrian warning, and stepped off the curb. A delivery truck squealed right around the corner, forcing her to jump back. Clenching her fists, she tapped her foot, trying to figure out what could possibly be wrong that Serena was in such a state and had run off to Fielding's at the same time she was to meet with Blain?

When it was safe, she bolted across the street. Two women she recognized as having been in the shop earlier spotted her and stopped, blocking her way on the busy sidewalk.

"Well, hello again, Miss Greyborne." One of the women pressed her lips into a half smile. "Funny to see you out and about in the middle of the afternoon, Hilde and I were just talking about how much we like your shop and saying we should stop in there now."

"That would be lovely. I'll look forward to seeing you later." Addie smiled, trying to skirt around the women.

"May I ask what hours you keep?" The corners of the second woman's lips curled upward, but her eyes took on the look of a Cheshire cat.

Addie sucked in a deep breath and matched the woman's Cheshire grin. "You know, I'd love to stop and chat, but I'm already late for an appoint—" The sound of sirens filled the air. Addie turned just as Marc ran into the door of Fielding's. "I have to go, sorry." She turned away from the two women.

"Well, I never," one of the women gasped. "How rude."

Addie fled, not daring to look back at the two women she'd left with their mouths hanging open.

When she reached the entrance to Fielding's, the street was a sea of flashing red and blue lights. Addie tried to move to the front of the quickly forming crowd, but as more people crushed in, she was pushed back and couldn't see what had caused the commotion. She boosted herself up on the raised base of the old gas streetlamp post.

A woman's shrill shrieks pierced the air. Whispers and sobs rippled through the crowd.

"What is it?" Addie grabbed the shoulder of a man in front of her.

He looked up at her, his eyes wild. "Blain Fielding's been murdered."

The back of Addie's throat tightened.

A collective gasp carried through the onlookers as Marc ushered Serena to his patrol car, handcuffs glimmering in the sunlight.

Addie jumped down from her perch and forced her way through the crowd. "Marc, wait. What's going on?"

Marc pushed Serena's head down, ushering her into the back seat, and slammed the door. He looked at Addie, his eyes full of pain, but he only shook his head, got into his car, and drove over to the police station across the street.

Addie raced across the road, weaving around the police cars and bystanders, and ran through the front entrance of the station. "Where's Marc?" she shouted at the desk sergeant. "I need to see him now." She slapped her hand on the desktop.

Another officer came out from behind the desk, his hand firmly grasping the top of his side holster. "Is there a problem here?"

"Yes, there is. Where is he, and where's Serena Chandler? Get the chief. I need to talk to hi—"

Marc came out of the back room as the second officer was unclipping his gun from the holster. "It's okay, Jerry. I've got this."

"You sure, Chief?"

"Yes, I'll be fine. Addie, come in." He waved her past the desk and motioned toward his office door.

They went in, and he slowly took his cap off, placed it on a coatrack by the door, and took a seat behind his desk. "What can I help you with?" He folded his hands on the desk.

"What can you help me with?" She leaned across his desk. "I just heard Blain Fielding was killed, and then you arrested Serena, and I want to know why."

"I'm sorry. I can't discuss an ongoing investigation with you. Is there anything else?" He looked down and shuffled a stack of papers on his desk.

"Anything else?" She gasped. "Anything else?" Her voice rose. "Yes, an explanation."

He glared at her, stood up, met her stance, and leaned toward her across the desk. "Sit down, Miss Greyborne."

She crossed her arms across her chest and huffed.

"Now."

His hot breath lashed across her cheek. Her eyes widened. She opened her mouth to speak. His neck muscles bulged, and she slithered into the chair across the desk from him. "Okay, I'm sitting."

He sat down and raked his hands through his hair, his face tense.

Her heart lurched out to him, but she bit the inside of her mouth, pressed her nails into her palms, and took a deep breath. "I know this is hard on you. She's your sister and all, but" — she leaned forward, her voice softening — "she's my friend, and I need to know what's going on. Where is she?"

"She's being processed in lockup."

"But why? On what charge?"

He picked up the pile of papers again and flipped through them, then threw them across the desk, sending them scattering across the floor.

Addie took another deep breath and

clenched her teeth. "What's the charge?"

He swiveled his chair around and stared out the window.

"Marc, please. What's going on?"

"Murder." His voice cracked. "Maybe even murder one."

"Murder?" Addie echoed. "Of who? Certainly you don't think she killed Blain?"

He sucked in a deep breath.

"But, but that's impossible."

"I only wish it was." He turned and looked back at her. Tears moistened his dark eyes.

"No, no, I don't believe it. It's not possible." Her thoughts reeled. Disbelief clutched at her chest. "Serena wouldn't. She couldn't, no, never."

Marc pursed his lips. "I'm afraid the circumstantial evidence is too strong at this point to disregard it."

"Circumstantial evidence? What evidence could you possibly have on Serena?"

He shook his head. "I can't discuss it with you."

"But she's your sister, and I'm her friend. I want to help if I can. I saw her just minutes before you arrested her. She couldn't have had time to kill anyone." She leaned closer to him. "Please. This is Serena we're talking about. What evidence do you have?"

His brow creased, and his eyes narrowed. "Someone will take your statement later, but for now, she's booked on the . . . the evidence." His glassy gaze turned toward the door.

"But Marc, if I can prove she couldn't have done it, then you can't hold her." She winced. "Can you?"

"We can and will unless there's overwhelming evidence to the contrary proving she couldn't have done it."

"But I can prove it."

"I'm afraid anything you have to say would have to be substantiated by someone else . . . who isn't a close friend. Otherwise, a good prosecutor could argue that you're covering up for her to give her an alibi." He sighed and rubbed his chin. "Anyway, bail will be set in the morning. Until then, there's not much we can do." He got up and walked to the window.

"I don't believe that. She's your sister, and you're the police chief."

"And that's exactly why I can't ignore the *evidence.*"

She walked around the desk and laid her hand on his arm. "Then let's go and find some witnesses, question everyone on the street and in the store. There has to be someone who saw her when she went in, and then you'll see the timeline doesn't work."

He shrugged off her hand and moved over to a file cabinet on the opposite wall. "Are you trying to tell me how to do *my* job?"

"No, of course not. We just can't give up."

"I'm not giving up. She's my sister, for God's sake." He scowled at her. "Now, if you don't mind, Miss Greyborne, I have police work to do." He pulled open the top file drawer.

Addie marched over and slammed the file drawer closed. "Stop it, Marc. Talk to me."

He snapped his hand back; the drawer had barely missed catching his fingers.

"It's probably just a matter of being in the wrong place at the wrong time. What possible evidence could you have on Serena that a few questions wouldn't clear up? Tell me." She grabbed his arm and spun him toward her.

Marc glared at her and stepped back. "She — she was found by Elaine and was standing over his body with a bloodied paperweight in her hand."

Chapter Nine

Tender fingers lifted her hair, readjusting the cold cloth on the back of her neck. She took deep, slow breaths and tried to stop her head from spinning.

"You worried us. I think you may have blacked out for a minute," Marc murmured. "Feeling better?"

"Uh, I think so." She sat upright in the chair, struggling to focus. "Thanks for catching me before I hit the floor." She weakly smiled up at him standing over her, concern written across his face. "Your reflexes are amazing though."

"Just goes with the job, I guess." He took the cloth off her neck.

"No, seriously, I noticed it before when I slammed the drawer closed. God, I could have broken your hand. I'm sorry."

"You were upset, and I was, well, I was being a cop and not a friend. It's me who should apologize."

"No, you were only doing your job and, and . . ." She frowned. "Can I please see Serena now?"

"I'm afraid not." He shook his head. "No visitors in the cells — especially not one who's a witness and hasn't given an official statement yet."

"Then let me give it and then let me see her. She must be scared stiff."

"I imagine she is, but rules are rules."

"You are so frustrating." She flipped her hair and straightened her shoulders. "Every time I think I see a gentler side of you, you have to go all RoboCop on me." She huffed. "Take my statement, then let me go see her." Her eyes pleaded with him.

His face flushed and he leaned across the desk and hit the intercom button. "Jerry, can you come in here? Oh, and bring a notepad." He clicked the phone off and stood back, his hands on his hips. "Okay?"

"Okay." She smiled shyly.

Jerry came in with a yellow pad and sat across the desk from her, taking notes. She was aware of Marc's expressionless eyes, which never left her face the entire time. However, when she stressed the short time Serena had been inside Fielding's, she did notice his jaw tighten. When she had finished, read over the statement, and signed it, Marc waved Jerry out of the room.

"Feel better?" he asked.

"Do you? Now can you see there is no way Serena could have had time to kill anyone?"

"Well, we have to see what any other witnesses have to say. Remember, it's not my job to judge; I just follow the evidence and present facts."

"Can't you just take off your cop hat for once?" She leaned back and grasped the chair arms. "This is your sister we're talking about, not some hardened, murderous criminal."

"I'm well aware of that, which makes it even more important for me to be impartial to all the evidence presented." He raked his fingers through his hair. "I'm trying, Addie. I really am."

"I know you are." She dropped her head and took a deep breath. "I'm sorry. What can I do to help now?"

"Nothing. Officers are out collecting witness statements and examining the crime scene. So we wait and see what they turn up."

"Does that mean there's still a chance she can be released tonight?" Addie rose to her feet. A slight smile curved the corners of her lips.

"Well, not really. The circumstantial evidence is pretty strong, so unless something really contradictory surfaces, she's here at least until the morning hearing."

Her face fell and she sat back down. "Then what?"

"We present all the evidence to the DA's office, and they decide based on that if they're going to follow through with the initial charges."

"And then what?"

"And then if they do . . . she goes to trial and is judged based on that." He shrugged and leaned heavily on the desk.

"But she's not guilty," she cried.

"Then we have to prove it, and the only way to do that is to find enough evidence establishing, without a doubt, that she couldn't have done it *or* find the person who did in the meantime."

"Then let's get to work." She beamed.

He laughed. "Addie, you're not a cop. Let us do our job."

She scowled at him.

"Trust me. I won't let my sister down. I'll turn over every rock till I find out the truth."

"I know you will, but I can be of some help. My dad was a cop in New York City before my mom died, and David, my fiancé, was an antiquities insurance investigator.

It's in my blood, and I lived it."

Marc's brow creased. "I thought Serena said your dad was a purchasing agent or something for private art and book collectors?"

"He was a reclamation agent. It's like a detective or bounty hunter of art and artifacts, you might say, but that wasn't until after I was about two when my mom got really sick. The shift work of an NYPD detective, and being so far from my grandmother in Boston, wasn't conducive to raising a little girl on his own. So he quit and transferred my mother to a Boston care center, and we moved there so my grandmother could help him with me. His first love had always been art, so he changed careers then for me."

Marc scratched his head. "Seem likes two opposite ends of the spectrum, the art world and police work, but I guess if he was happy . . ."

"He loved it. In his job he had to use all his detective skills to research and track down the artwork or rare books. I grew up with dinner table discussions about who, where, and how. Lots of times he was dealing with fraud and, well, let's just say some pretty shady types. He often told me it was the best of both worlds for him."

"But you were so young — didn't he have to travel with work like that?"

"At first he worked in local galleries, and trips were short. We lived with my nana, and she took care of me until she passed away. It wasn't until I got older that he took on the position with the international firm, and then he was away a lot of the time."

Marc sat on the edge of the desk. "That must have been hard on you even when you were older."

"I met my fiancé through him." She shrugged. "They had worked together on an a few art fraud cases and Dad thought we might hit it off, and we did." She smiled, and then her face crumbled. She looked down at her hands, sitting lifeless in her lap.

Marc cleared his throat. She looked up at him. Her eyes stung with tears she dare not release and she bit her lip. "The only reason why I told you all that was so you could see that I do know a thing or two about detective work. It was also part of my job as an acquisitions assistant. I researched, tracked, and put clues together. I know I can be of some help."

Marc got up, walked over to the file cabinet, and pulled out a large manila envelope. He leaned against the drawer and just stood there.

"What is it, Marc? You look shaken."

He took a deep breath and turned toward her. "Hearing what your dad actually did makes me wonder now, too, if there wasn't something else behind his accidental death."

"What are you talking about?"

"I hope you don't mind." He cringed. "But Serena mentioned that you had a lot of unanswered questions about your father's accident, so I thought it wouldn't hurt to take a look at the state police records myself — you know, fresh eyes on it and all." He looked sheepishly at her.

"No, of course I don't mind. Thank you, I appreciate it. What did you find?" She leapt to her feet and reached for the envelope.

He pulled it away. "Sit down. Please."

She flopped back into her chair, her eyes filled with questions, but Marc just stood there fumbling with the envelope in his hand. "You said the state police ruled it an unfortunate accident, which they did, but that they also brushed off some burning questions you had at the time, and that's not in their official report."

She nodded. "I wouldn't expect those to be. They didn't take me seriously."

"No, you're right. And after reading the report and looking through the accident scene photos, I also had some questions for them, but the investigating patrol team brushed me off, too, and said it was all in the report."

"Like what? What questions?"

He pulled photos out of the envelope, laid them across the desk, and leaned over her shoulder. "Like the angle at which the car broke through the guardrail, and this second set of skid marks alongside your dad's." His finger stabbed at a set of three road photos. "See how both sets drift sideways, and then here's the smashed guardrail, and the inside ones skid off by themselves. And this piece of metal — probably part of a bumper." Excitement built in his voice. "But a different color than your dad's car, by the way, here." He pointed to another picture. "*None* of this was considered part of the investigation. They said the skid marks didn't prove anything and could have been made anytime because it's a well-traveled highway. Worst of all, they'd already ruled it an accident due to heavy fog and the speed he was traveling. They said he just lost control on the sharp curve." Marc sighed heavily.

Addie stared at him and then back at the pictures. Her stomach churned as her eyes floated over the images in front of her. "I had . . . had no idea." She gasped and picked up one of the photos and looked up at him. Tears streamed down her burning cheeks.

Marc's face turned ashen. "You haven't seen any of these before, have you?"

She shook her head.

"I'm sorry. I just assumed."

"No, I'm glad you showed me. I always questioned their findings."

"I hate to speak poorly of fellow officers, but my gut tells me this was a pretty shoddy investigation from the start. They didn't even really investigate as far as I can tell."

"That's what I said, but they said there was no evidence to prove any foul play, so it was obviously an accident."

"Did you tell them what kind of work your father did?"

"Yes, but I couldn't tell them why he was on that highway or prove any dealings had taken place before the accident. They did discover he had just left my great-aunt's, but they didn't feel it was important and showed no motive for anything other than what they ruled it as."

He stroked his chin. "If you don't mind, I'd like to take a drive out there in the morning and see the scene for myself."

"Of course I don't, but what about Serena?"

"It's best I stay as far away from her case

as I can. I can't afford to do or say anything that might jeopardize the case and cause a mistrial."

Addie slumped down in her chair.

"Don't worry. I've got good men and women on it. She'll be fine." He patted her shoulder reassuringly.

"If you say so — but I'm going with you tomorrow."

"I thought you might say that." He winked.

Chapter Ten

Addie jumped when Marc's police car pulled into her driveway honking as the tires screeched to a halt. She dashed into the kitchen to grab the fresh cups of coffee she'd made and raced down the front steps. Travel mugs in hand, she stood at the passenger door and waited for him to open it. When he didn't get out or even reach over and open it from inside, she bent down and peered through the window. The car was empty.

She heard his muffled voice behind her and turned around, but couldn't see him. She walked to the side of the house and peeked around the corner. He was on his phone pacing back and forth on the sidewalk near the rear of the house. She couldn't hear what he was saying, but his body language was tense, and he waved his free hand around like he was poking someone in the chest.

Addie retreated to the car to wait for him. When he came back, his face was crimson and beads of sweat had formed across his brow. He opened her door, and she silently slid into her seat before he got in his side and slammed the door shut. His knuckles whitened as he gripped the steering wheel.

They sat in silence for a few minutes until he let out a deep breath and released the chokehold he had on the wheel. Her hand trembled as she passed him a travel mug. He looked at it as if he'd never seen one before, and then he looked at her. A light sparked in his eyes, and he took the cup from her hand and drank a long sip.

"What's wrong? Anything you can tell me about, or should I mind my own business?"

He turned toward her, his face twisted in anguish as he fought back tears. She reached for his hand and stroked it gently. It tore at her heart to see him in so much pain.

"That call," he choked.

"Yes?" Her eyes fixed on his.

"It was Jerry. The DA's office just called the station." He took another long sip.

"And?"

He sucked in a deep breath. "They're going to be charging her with second-degree murder and request bail to be set at two million."

"What? No. They can't."

"They can," he croaked. "They have proof that Serena intended to kill Blain when she went to see him." His hand quivered as he brought the cup up for another drink.

"But how? What evidence could they possibly have showing intentional murder?"

His jaw tensed. "It seems our friend Martha made a statement about something Serena had said to her in her shop that afternoon just before she was found standing over Blain's body."

"What did she say?"

"I don't know. I'm going to the station now to read the witness statements and try to figure this out." He scoured his hair with his hand. "I'm sorry, Addie." He started the engine. "We'll have to go to Pen Hollow another day. I've gotta go."

"Of course, no problem, but I'm coming with you." She fastened her seat belt.

He nodded and pulled out of the driveway. They drove in silence to the station. Addie's mind reeled, trying to put the pieces of what happened into some kind of perspective, but nothing made sense. Why would someone like Serena utter words that led to her being charged with murder? She was one of the most happy-go-lucky people Addie had ever met. She swallowed the lump growing in the back of her throat.

Marc glanced sideways at her. "I told you, no rock unturned; we'll get to the bottom of this."

She nodded, fighting the tears stinging her eyes.

He clasped his hand over hers on her lap and gave it a gentle squeeze.

She took a deep breath and clutched her other hand over his.

Jerry greeted them at the back entrance, a file folder in his hand. "I thought you'd want to see this, sir. I'll bring you the crime scene reports soon. They're just about finished running the fingerprints."

"Thanks, Jerry." Marc grabbed the folder and swept past him into his office.

Addie followed on his heels and closed the door behind her. Marc stood beside his desk, pushed his cap back off his forehead, and opened the file. His eyes scanned the pages, his head slightly nodding, but then he frowned. Her heart raced. She opened her mouth to speak but closed it and clenched her teeth.

He looked up from the report. His eyes filled with outrage and slammed the folder on the desk. "Shit."

"What . . . what is it? What do they have?" Her eyes locked on his.

He flopped into his chair and scrubbed his hands over his face. "It looks bad right now — really bad." His shoulders slumped.

She reached for the file, but he closed it and pulled it away. "I can't let you read that. It's police business."

"Don't do this to me again. Don't shut me out. You know I can help."

"Yes, but . . . but you're named in the report."

"Me? How? You mean my statement?"

"Yes, and a few other mentions I'd rather you not see now."

"What? God, I'm so confused. Please let me see it."

"I'll give you an edited version." He picked up the folder.

She plopped into the chair across from him and folded her hands in her lap. As the seconds ticked by, she could feel her palms sweating, and she discreetly wiped them on her jeans. Her jaw and neck tensed, and she squirmed to release the aching and took a few short, deep breaths, but his eyes continued to scan the pages in front of him. After what felt like an eternity, he pursed his lips and laid the folder back on the desk.

"Long story short, your statement, along with two others, isn't being taken seriously by the DA's office."

She raised her eyebrows and opened her mouth.

His hand flew up in a "stop" motion. "There were two other people who also saw Serena enter Fielding's, but none of you could verify the exact time, and the DA feels *guesses* aren't indisputable proof of innocence. But to be honest, his doubts probably center on the fact that it's well known in town that you and Serena have become friends . . . and he just doesn't consider you to be a reliable witness. It's their fear that you could be covering for her."

"But if other people saw her enter the store, shouldn't the DA be able to see I wasn't covering for her in any way?"

"You'd think so, but they feel that because no one can give an exact time they saw her enter, none of it establishes her innocence. Plus" — he fumbled with the folder — "there are the other matters you're named in later in the report that he feels brings your credibility into question."

"Which are?" She glared at the folder. "What have I done that would question my character and credibility?" She leaned across the desk and reached for the file.

He pulled it away. "Not now."

She slumped back in her chair and shook her head, gnawing on her bottom lip.

Marc looked at her and smirked. She stopped chewing her lip and straightened up in her chair.

"Well, what about Elaine, Blain's assistant? Surely she must have been in the office and can testify what time Serena arrived?"

"Nope, she was on her coffee break." He shook his head. "And when she returned, Serena had a paperweight in her hand and was standing over the body on the floor in front of the desk."

Addie tapped her foot and drummed her fingers on the arm of the chair.

"You've got that look. What are you thinking, Addie?"

"I'm thinking either there was someone else in the office when Serena went in, or they had just left and she might have seen who it was. You need to question Serena right away."

"Paula . . . umm, Officer Shire already did. Serena didn't mention seeing anyone coming out or in the hall or in the staircase leading to the second-floor offices."

"Then ask her again. Maybe she saw something and can't remember because she was already upset about something when she went to see him. There had to have been someone else there, or just there, and she hasn't put it together in her mind yet."

Marc nodded and wrote something on a notepad in front of him.

"Unless . . . there's another entrance to the office? Is there a back stair —"

Jerry knocked and flung the door open, rushed over, and handed Marc another file. He nodded at Addie, shrugged his shoulders apologetically, and backed out of the room, closing the door.

Marc flipped the file open and read. His jaw tensed. "Well, it appears Serena's prints were only found on the paperweight and the doorknob on the outside of the office door."

"That shows right there it couldn't have been second-degree murder." Addie leapt to her feet.

"In what way?"

"If she had *intent* to kill him when she went in, she would have closed the door behind her, so if her prints were only on one side of the handle, then the door was left open. Wouldn't she want privacy if she had murder on her mind?"

"Yes, but the DA can argue that they had a heated argument and things got out of hand."

"True, but that doesn't make sense."

"Why not, you said she was upset when

she went to see him?"

"I did but you said his body was in front of the desk, not behind it." He nodded, "which means that he was standing up when he got hit and not sitting down." Marc's eyes narrowed. "So they'd have to have been face-to-face, or at least close enough for her to grab a paperweight out of anger and strike him, as the DA's claiming. But Blain is twice her height. She would have had to pull a chair over, stand on it, and then whack him in the temple. Which is where I assume the fatal injury occurred, since it sounds like he died immediately?" Addie noticed Marc's jaw tense. "Think about it. She couldn't possibly have done all that before she hit him. He'd have wrestled her to the ground long before, don't you think?"

Marc nodded and stroked his chin.

"Not to mention putting the chair back in place while still holding the bloodied paperweight before Elaine came back." She scowled and rubbed her forehead. "But what I don't get is why she picked up the paperweight in the first place."

"She said she was in shock when she saw him on the floor in front of the desk. She saw the paperweight covered in blood and picked it up because she couldn't believe what she was seeing, and then . . . well —"

"Oh, Serena, no." Addie scrubbed her hands over her face. "Why, why did you have to be so careless?"

"People don't always think clearly in traumatic situations." He shook his head.

"Well, I hope the DA takes that into consideration."

"I doubt it. The fingerprint evidence and the fact that she was found standing over the body is all they need right now." He closed the folder, staring at it and tapping his pen on the desk, and then jumped up and grabbed his jacket. "Come on. We're taking a little ride."

Chapter Eleven

Marc pulled the cruiser up in front of Fielding's. Addie grimaced and glanced sideways at him. "What are we doing?"

"I have to take a look myself. As you've pointed out, there's just too many unanswered questions."

"Yes!" She fist pumped the air, jumped out and dashed into the store behind Marc, raced through the glass foyer, and turned left up the stairs leading to the second-floor offices. They slipped under the police tape, opened the glass hallway door at the top of the stairs, and entered the outer office. The lights were on. Marc flung his hand back, halting Addie at the door. He drew his gun, made his way across the outer office, and peered into the interior office.

"Police," he called, "anyone here?"

Addie scanned the small room. There were a desk, a computer, a large triple-drawer file cabinet against the sidewall, and a silk plant in the corner by the window.

"It's all clear. No one else is supposed to be in here, so the crime team must have left the lights on." He turned back to her, clipping his gun in its holster.

"How long has Elaine worked here?"

"Umm, probably close to fifteen years, I think."

"That long, hey?"

"Yeah, why?"

"Just that there aren't any personal touches. So I'm guessing Elaine's already left her job, which seems odd, since Blain just died yesterday."

Marc surveyed the room and looked at her. "Yes, that is odd."

"I know," she whispered. "You'd think there'd be lots of details to look after today. I wonder who's in charge now."

"I am. Can I help you?" Addie jumped at the harsh voice behind her and spun around on her heel, staring into the chest of a very tall, dark-haired, younger-looking version of Blain.

"Hi, Andrew," said Marc. "You've stepped into your father's shoes already, have you?" He leaned around Addie and shook Andrew's hand. "Congratulations, I guess."

"It was always planned that I would take over Fielding's one day." He shrugged his wide shoulders. "I just didn't expect it to be so soon."

Addie stepped forward and offered a handshake. "My condolences, Andrew."

He glanced down at her and put his hands on his hips, looking over her head. "So, Chief — I hear that's what they call you now." He raised his eyebrows.

Marc nodded.

"What can I do for you today?"

"This is still an active crime scene, and I see Elaine's office has been cleared out. Are you aware that's interference with an ongoing investigation?" Marc crossed his arms and stared at Andrew.

"Oh, I thought you had Dad's killer in custody? Didn't think it was still a problem."

"There is a person of interest in custody, yes, but as long as the notice is posted on the door and crime scene tape is in place, it's considered an active scene."

"I heard the case was pretty open-and-shut. The killer was found with the weapon standing over his body."

"We don't make assumptions in my line of work; we look for facts." Marc's eyes bored into Andrew's tense face.

"Oh, yes." He mirrored Marc and crossed his arms over his chest then rocked back on his heels. "I think I remember hearing your *person of interest* is Serena, your sister, isn't it?"

Marc's chest puffed out. "I'll examine the scene now, Andrew. I'm sure we've kept you long enough from your *new* duties," he said between gritted teeth as he turned toward the rear office, but then he stopped and looked back. "Tell me, Andrew, how was your trip to Europe? When did you get back?"

Andrew glared at Marc and stormed out of the office, his footsteps echoing in the stairwell as he went.

"Wow," gasped Addie. "What was that all about?"

Marc adjusted his gun belt on his hips. "That . . . was Andrew Fielding. The biggest ass ever born, and one I hoped this town was rid of for good."

She grimaced. "I take it there's some history there. You can tell me all about him later."

Marc glared at the door Andrew had disappeared through. "There certainly is."

Addie rubbed her hands together. "Where do we start, Chief?"

Marc laughed and shook his head. "You do have a way with changing the subject, don't you?"

"Not changing it, just lightening up the

mood a bit." She smiled. "And . . . we have to figure out how we can prove Serena's innocence, so one thing at a time. You can fill me in on Andrew later."

"Deal," he chuckled.

They walked around the plush interior office. Like Marc, she wore gloves. He said they were a precaution, in case she had the urge to touch anything and contaminate the crime scene more than Andrew had already. For all the sparseness of the outer reception area, this was definitely a contrast. Addie's eyes wandered to the paintings hanging on the walls and the antiques displayed in cubbies on the wall-length bookshelf. She ambled over to it, awestruck by the elaborate scene, and casually browsed through the book titles, and then gasped.

"What? Did you find something?"

"He was a rare book collector. Some of these titles are first editions. See, here's *The Three Musketeers,* and it's one of the first 1846 English editions. And this one. It's the 1937 print edition of Tolkien's *The Hobbit.*

Marc came up beside her. "Are you sure? There's not much security for that kind of collection."

Addie pulled a heavy book from the shelf and looked at the inside copyright page. "Yes, and this is the 1954 print edition of

The Lord of the Rings," she said, taking books from the shelf and glancing at the copyright pages. "Here's *The Fellowship of the Ring* and *The Two Towers.*" She scanned the shelf. "Funny — Blain doesn't have a copy of the 1955 first edition of *The Return of the King* to complete the set?"

Marc peered more closely at the bookcase and then ran his fingers around the frame. "Nope, nothing here to indicate some kind of laser or high-tech motion security system."

"It appears there might be a couple of books missing."

Marc stood back beside Addie, her eyes examining the alignment of the books. "Yes. See how these have fallen over onto the books beside them. They're not as orderly as the other shelves are." She pointed.

"Rare books, with no security, here in a department store office?" His brow furrowed. "This doesn't make sense."

"There seem to be lots of things lately that don't make sense." She frowned, but then spotted an abnormal contour in the oak paneling on the wall surrounding the bookcase. "Have you seen this?" She ran her fingers around an outline, and then pressed into the center of the panel, popping it open.

"Stand back." Marc reached his arm in

front of her and slipped his flashlight out of its hip case, shining the beam through the opening. "Well, I'll be."

"What? What's in there?" Addie whispered, following him through the doorway.

He flipped a light switch on beside the door. She stopped. The room was filled with books and antiquities. Her heart pounded against her chest wall. She struggled to catch her breath. It was like the first day she had stood in the stacks at the British Museum.

"This is amazing," she uttered.

"And maybe a clue as to why Blain was killed." His eyes widened. "This goes way deeper than Serena being upset about some stupid little petition, I think."

"Petition? What petition?"

Marc's face turned crimson. He turned and stepped away from her.

She grabbed his jacket sleeve and spun him toward her. "What petition? Is that what she had in her hand when she left Martha's?"

"You saw it?"

"No, she didn't show it to me. What's the petition for?"

Marc shook his head. "Please don't press this. It's nothing."

"It has something to do with me, doesn't

it? Tell me — and I want the truth."

He placed his hands on her shoulders and stared into her eyes. "Promise me you won't get upset."

"I can't do that till I know what you're talking about."

"Fair enough." He sighed and took a deep breath. "Apparently, Blain started a petition with the other merchants to try to force the town council to revoke your business license."

Her eyes widened, and she opened her mouth. He pressed his finger against her lips. "Hear me out."

She nodded.

"He said you had only been granted the permit because of your family name and no one had done a background check on you, and he was concerned there were *irregularities* in your past."

Her eyes bulged.

"He felt you had been involved with some criminal activity in Boston and that it followed you here, which, according to him, caused the sudden increase in our crime rate."

"That's insane!" she shouted. "How dare he. I'll sue."

Marc nodded. "Yes, it is insane. But don't worry. Only a few busybodies like Martha believe him."

Addie felt the color drain from her face. "Is that what Serena was so upset about and why she was going to see Blain?"

"Yes, and now you know why the DA isn't very interested in your statement."

She nodded and sniffled.

"They can't take the risk of you lying to cover for Serena when you might have put her up to the murder, or at least given her the idea. Of course, Martha's statement about Serena saying, 'Addie won't stand for this, and neither will I. Blain has to be stopped,' before she ran off to his store didn't help much either."

Addie hung her head.

He tilted her chin up. "It'll be okay. I told you, no rock left unturned, and I think with this room, we've turned over a boulder today."

She laughed. "Yes, maybe. It sure puts a different spin on Mr. Blain Fielding and gives other motives for someone wanting him dead."

He stood back, hands on hips, and surveyed the hidden storage area. Addie followed his eye scan, gasped, and bolted to the far end of the long, narrow room.

"Will you look at that," said Marc over her shoulder.

He reached around her and pushed on the center of another wall panel. It clicked open.

Chapter Twelve

"It's a staircase." Addie stepped forward.

"Stop." Marc grabbed her elbow. "Don't contaminate this area. Andrew did enough of that in the other offices."

"Right."

"I'll call the station to send the crime team back over to take photos and prints." He dialed his cell phone. "Damn, no reception in here." He headed back into Blain's office.

Addie squatted in the doorway, squinting into the darkened stairwell. The only light came from the room behind her, casting her shadow across the small landing. In the gloominess, two darker shapes on the floor caught her eye. She leaned over to get a better look and teetered forward. A hand nabbed her collar and pulled her back.

"I thought I told you to stay out."

"I was trying, honest. Shine your flashlight there." She pointed to the darker shapes on the floor.

Marc crouched down beside her. "From here, it looks like it could possibly be blood streaks across the imprint of a shoe sole? We'll see if that's what it is when the equipment arrives, and if it is, we'll run a match with Blain's blood type."

"I guess we know how the real murderer might have gotten out without being seen by Serena," Addie said.

"Don't jump to conclusions. We have to prove how long that's been here, and if it is blood and a match first." Marc stood up. "Look Addie, your keen eyes and rare book expertise has helped to shed a different light on things and has been helpful, but . . ."

Her eyes narrowed. "What are you saying?" She stood up and looked at him.

"The guys can't get here for about an hour. They've got the equipment out at Mrs. Crawly's place."

"Another break-in?"

"Possibly, but probably not. She's our local cat lady, and every once in a while, she gets it in her head someone's tried to break in and steal her cats."

"Oh."

"Anyway, when they get here, I'd rather you weren't . . . here." He flinched. "If you know what I mean."

"Yes, I understand." She laughed. "After all, how would it look for the chief to have the friend of the *person of interest* working the case with him?"

"Working the case? I wouldn't say that."

"Well" — she smirked — "assisting him, then. You know, like a partner."

His mouth dropped. "Partner?"

She winked. "I need to get to the shop anyway. I hope I haven't lost all the customers I managed to gain this week." She turned to go and stopped. "But promise me, as soon as you find out anything, let me know?"

"You'll be the first to hear. I promise, *partner.*" He choked out his last word.

Addie slowly worked her way back through the hidden chamber, inspecting books as she passed by them. One by one, titles jumped out at her, causing her to pause. When she reached the end of the long row of shelves, she stopped and turned back to the last section and pulled a brown leather-bound book from the shelf.

"Marc, come here for a minute."

He looked up from his notepad. His brows raised. "Did you find something else?" He walked toward her from the stairwell door.

"I think I might have. I've been looking at some of the titles here and the condition of the books."

"And?"

"Well, a few of them I recognize as being on my father's list of books to retrieve."

"Really?" He looked over the top of the book she was holding. "Is this one?"

"Yes. It's *Tamerlane and Other Poems* by Edgar Allan Poe. It was the first book he ever published, and it was under the name 'a Bostonian.' It's very rare — only about fifty copies were printed. I'm positive Dad was trying to track it down. A collector reported his copy stolen to the insurance company. And this one." She pulled another book from the shelf. "It's a first edition of *Don Quixote.* I'm fairly certain it was stolen from the library in Barcelona last year. It was on our watch list."

Marc took the book in his gloved hand. "Are you sure? This one?"

"It's easy enough to find out. Every museum and library gets an updated list of books and relics reported stolen or missing. Part of my job was to keep a lookout for them."

He turned the book over in his hand. "You're sure this one was on your list?"

"Fairly sure. I have some older lists on my laptop from when I worked. I can show you."

"There's a big market for this type of crime, isn't there?"

"Oh yeah, smuggling antiquities, books, art, you name it. Anything of high value that can easily be moved and sold; it's global. Part of David's job was to track down stolen property and see who was showing stronger than usual interest in acquiring it. He broke up a lot of crime rings during his career, as my father did."

Marc stoked his jaw and stood back, surveying the shelves of books. "We'll have to check these out, but it sounds to me as if this case just got a whole lot bigger."

Addie made her way back to her shop, her head down against the wind. Even though the sun was shining, the strong gusts blowing off the harbor had a bite to them, and she pulled her coat tighter around her chest. When there was a lull in windblasts, she managed to look up. Martha was in front of her bakery, sweeping the sidewalk free of blowing leaves and papers.

Martha stopped sweeping when Addie came parallel to her. She leaned her chin on her hand at the top of the broom handle and stared as Addie passed.

"Hello." Addie smiled at her. "Looks like a losing battle today with this wind."

Martha glared at her. Her eyes never wavered as Addie made her way to her shop door.

Addie glanced over her shoulder and felt the stab of Martha's icy stare as she unlocked the door. When she stepped inside she noted Martha was back to her thankless sweeping.

"Wow, how uncomfortable." She shuddered, and turned on the lights. "Guess I won't be on her Christmas card list." She chuckled, picking the mail up from the floor in front of the post slot.

She dropped a pod in the coffee maker, and while a cup brewed, she sorted through the mail. Junk went directly into the recycling bin, and bills were tossed in the top drawer under the register. On the bottom of the stack, she came to a postcard. The image was of an ornately cast gold key set on a red silk cloth.

"Beautiful," she whispered, turning the card over in her hand. The only message scrawled across the back was *Be careful.* She shivered. "Thanks for the warning." There was no name or postmark — not even a stamp. She turned it over again, frowning. The door chimes behind her rang. "Well, I'll have to figure this out later." She tossed it into the drawer.

Soon the store was filled with shoppers, including a group of three nosy locals she overheard whispering and snickering behind their hands. They'd apparently come in to have a look at the *murderer's* friend.

She turned toward the three, heat rising up from under her collar. "Alleged murderer," she said between clenched teeth. "Now, ladies, anything I can help you find? Are you looking for something for yourselves?" Her eyes glanced at each of them. "Or a gift for a *friend*?" She flashed a tight-lipped smile. They hurriedly shuffled out of the store without even a backward glance.

A darker-haired, middle-aged woman watching from the far side of the bookstore began to laugh. "Well done." She walked toward Addie. "I'm surprised you bit your tongue as well as you did." She beamed, holding out her hand. "Hi, I'm Catherine Lewis. Your aunt and my mother were close friends."

"Catherine Lewis? That name sounds familiar."

"Perhaps your aunt mentioned me or —"

Addie shook her head. "Not my aunt. I never knew her."

"You don't remember, then?"

"I think I've heard the name, but I'm sorry, I can't remember from whom. Anyway, I'm Addison; call me Addie."

"I know exactly who you are." She grinned, her cheeks flushing.

"Well, it is a small town, and I guess most people know who I am, even if I don't know them." She smiled and shrugged. "After all, with my last name, anonymity here seems impossible."

Catherine cupped Addie's hand in hers, tears glistening in her eyes. "You've turned into a beautiful young woman. It's a pleasure to see you in person again."

Addie stepped back. "Again? You've met me before?"

The woman nodded, stepped toward her, and tucked a wayward strand of hair behind Addie's ear. Her fingers lingered on her cheek. "Yes." She smiled and looked deep into Addie's eyes.

Addie recoiled.

"Ah, well, it was too much for me to hope that you'd remember. You were so young then." She pulled a tissue from her pocket, dabbed her teary eyes, and rushed out the door.

Addie fell back against the counter. Who was this woman who made her feel like someone was walking across her grave?

Chapter Thirteen

The afternoon flew by with a steady stream of shoppers. More people seemed to have discovered the pleasure of browsing through her bookshop with a coffee in hand and reading while they snuggled into one of the comfy leather chairs. She felt fulfilled knowing her vision was coming to light.

Brian finally dropped by to give her the quote on her home security system, stating it couldn't be installed for another week. He was most apologetic, but she was frustrated. This kind of haphazard service wasn't something she was used to. His quote was already two days later than promised, and now he tells her that the installment is delayed, too? However, even with the distractions and her annoyance over the news, Addie's thoughts kept returning to Catherine Lewis and the strange things she'd said. When Marc pulled up outside just as she was closing the shop, she was relieved to finally have someone to ask about Catherine.

He leapt out of his car and bounded toward her door, a grin flitting across his face.

She raced out the door to greet him. "What? A major break in the case?"

His eyes darkened and dropped. "Well, no." He fumbled with his cap in hand.

Her heart sank.

"But I do have great news." He looked up, eyes sparkling. "Umm, don't turn around," he mumbled through closed lips, "but Martha's watching us from her window. Let's go inside." He placed his hand on the small of her back and ushered her toward the door.

"She's watched me all day," she whispered. "When I got back, she stood on the walk with a broom in her hand, staring at me until I got inside. I couldn't help but think how much like a witch she looked." Addie smirked and glanced sideways at Martha.

"I know she's really quite harmless," Marc said, following her into the store, "but I don't trust her right now. She's riled a lot of people up with this petition thing and is probably looking for more evidence to try to use against you with the town council."

When safely away from prying eyes, Addie spun around toward him. "Okay, partner, what have you got?"

He sauntered past her over to the coffee machine. "Want one?"

"No, I don't want coffee. I want to know what's got you grinning like the Cheshire cat."

"Everything in good time." He dropped a pod into the machine.

She stood back and crossed her arms, tapped her foot, and glared at the back of his head. He was silent as his coffee brewed. She opened her mouth to speak, but shut it when he slowly tore open a sugar pack and poured it into the steaming paper cup. Believing he was done, she opened her mouth again. Without turning around, he raised his finger to silence her and picked up a spoon, methodically stirring his coffee. By this time, her cheeks were burning and beads of sweat were forming inside her collar. When he was finished, he placed the spoon on the counter, took a long sip, stretched out his rigid shoulders, and sighed. Her jaw tensed. She took a step toward him. He spun around, a sly grin across his face, and then he burst out laughing.

"Darn you." She stamped her foot. "Stop

with the teasing."

"Ah, but it's so much fun."

"What has you in such a great mood?"

"Well, *partner*" — he winked — "it seems we found enough evidence today to place reasonable doubt on Serena's charge of second-degree murder."

"What?" she cried, jumping up and down, clapping her hands. "So she's off?"

"Not exactly . . . but . . . the charges have been stayed *for now,* pending further investigation, and she's being released as we speak."

She bound toward him, threw her arms around his neck, and gave him a tight squeeze. "That's wonderful. We have to go see her."

"Not so fast. She's staying with our parents tonight and is really tired. She hasn't slept a wink, as you can imagine."

Addie frowned, her lips pursed.

"She told me to tell you she'd be by first thing tomorrow."

"Good, I can't wait to see her." She beamed. "Other than tired, is she doing well — you know, keeping her spirits up?"

"Yes, I think what the DA's office said this afternoon really helped."

"What did they say?"

"Well, I managed to cast enough doubt

on Serena's guilt by showing proof of Blain's possible involvement with smuggling and perhaps acting as a fence or middleman for a larger operation. So they're going to be checking all his associates and travels over the past few years to see what they can dig up."

"That makes sense. International travel on store business would have put him in all the right places to make his black-market buys."

"That's the thing. As far as I ever heard, he only went on short department store buying trips to Boston and New York. I'm not sure if you know, but Blain's wife was killed in a plane crash a number of years ago. He was booked to be on the same flight, but had to cancel at the last minute because of business, so she went on ahead. He was supposed to meet her the next day." Marc's lips tightened. "He hasn't flown since and hired a purchasing agent to take care of all the long-distance buying trips."

"No, I didn't know." She rubbed her neck and frowned. "But then that means if he is involved in anything shady, he was most likely the middleman, right?"

"Which of course got me thinking about Andrew spending the last ten years in Europe and took me back to where his and my problems began." He cocked his brow, and the corners of his lips curved up. "After high school, he got in with a bad crowd and was drinking a lot. They started pulling some robberies around town. I was a rookie cop back then and caught him in the act. In the end, Blain got him off without jail time, because he was good friends with Chief Ryan, but the condition was that Andrew was to leave town and not come back, at least not under Ryan's watch."

"And?"

"And so, with all that . . . I managed to pose enough questions to the DA implying Andrews's possible involvement . . . that . . . he will be investigated, too."

"Brilliant."

"It's not enough to charge anyone with at this point, but it does show the DA that there's a lot more to it than an open-and-shut case against Serena and that it does warrant further investigating. He feels that with the new evidence uncovered, it sounds like it goes deeper than a merchant's petty squabble. And there you have it." He shrugged.

"Well, that's the best news I've had all week. I'm so relieved."

"I'm glad you went to Blain's office with me. Without your keen eyes, it might have been a while until we uncovered the hidden chamber, and by then, who knows where Serena would have been."

"You would have found it. You're a great cop."

"You're forgetting that the investigating team had already processed the scene and I went out of curiosity after vowing not to get involved. So, no, if you hadn't had me questio—"

She pressed her finger to her lips. "Shhh, we just made a good team today." She smiled and dropped a pod into the coffee maker. Marc hovered beside her, fidgeting with his coffee cup as hers brewed. It was clear to her that there was something else he wanted to talk to her about. "Well, are you going to tell me?"

"Am I going to tell you what?"

"What else is on your mind?"

He took a sip and placed his cup on the counter. "You picked up on that, did you?"

She grinned at him and winked.

"Well, I was talking to Serena, and . . . it's just that she doesn't have many close friends."

Addie grimaced and shook her head. "She really is a character. I find it hard to believe she has so few friends."

"It's her own doing. She's very particular

about who she lets past her walls."

"That's sad."

"It's her choice. The only person she was ever really close to left town abruptly without a word to her, and it really hurt her. So until she knows a person better, she keeps most at a safe distance. But she does think of you as a friend now, and . . . well . . . she cares about you and what happens to you."

"Even with all that's happened to her in the past two days?" Addie's brow knit. "I'm the last person she should be worried about, but she's amazing and has been to me since the moment we met. So what are you getting at?"

"Well, it's because she does care."

Addie nodded. "And . . ."

"She told me about the black car." He cringed. "And . . . please know she feels really bad about breaking your confidence and hopes you'll still be friends, because she was sick about it when she discovered that I didn't know."

"You didn't know what?" Addie felt a shiver race up her spine.

"Well, through one of her interrogations she let it slip that . . . it seems you've had more run-ins with it than you have told me about — like the first day you opened your shop?" His brow raised, his eyes locked on hers.

Addie bit her lip. "It's just that black sedans are so common, and . . . well, I'd already been so much trouble."

"You haven't asked for any of this, and we need to get to the bottom of it. Anything would be a lead right now."

"I know." She leaned on the counter. "It's just that I'm new in town, and people are already seeing me as a troublemaker. I don't want you to think that, too." She looked up at him. "It's probably nothing; maybe a prank to chase me off. Serena said Blain Fielding felt threatened by me. Maybe it was him and he just wanted to scare me away."

"I knew Blain my whole life. He could be an ass, but I don't think he would have resorted to anything so threatening."

Addie drummed her fingers on the counter, gnawing on her bottom lip.

"You have a tell, you know." Marc smirked, taking a sip of his coffee.

"A what?"

"A tell. It's something people do as a reaction to something else, and it gives away how they're really feeling no matter how hard they try to hide it."

Her eyes narrowed.

"Like a twitch of the eye or cheek when they lie or are trying to hide something."

"It's only been a few days, but I've already noticed that Serena's freckles pop out whenever she's feeling the least bit flustered or embarrassed or excited about something but tries to hide it?"

"Exactly. That's a tell."

"I didn't know I had one, too. What is it?"

"You bite your lip when you're upset or thinking."

"I do not."

Marc chuckled and shook his head. "Yes, you do."

"Interesting. You're pretty observant."

"It goes with the job." He took another sip, keeping his eyes on hers.

"I guess I shouldn't play poker with you, then?" She held his gaze.

He laughed. "No, probably not, but it might make it interesting, 'cause I suspect you are pretty observant, too."

"Well, I have noticed one thing."

His jaw tensed. "What's that?"

"Exactly what you just did." She beamed at him. "When you're trying to hide your true thoughts or feelings about something, your jaw tightens. Like you're gnashing your teeth together so you don't say anything."

His eyes widened, and she saw by the

strangled look in them that he was fighting the impulse to clench his jaw, but then he broke out in laughter instead.

"See?" She pointed at him, chuckling. "You do, don't you? Admit it."

He shook his head, his face flushed.

"And you can tell Serena not to worry. We're still friends. It's just her brother that I'm not sure about." She stuck out her tongue teasingly, dodging his half-hearted swat at her arm.

Chapter Fourteen

Addie nearly danced into her house that evening. She hummed while she flipped on the foyer lights and made her way from room to room, snapping on light switches. When she got to the kitchen, she sucked in a deep breath — until the security system was installed she wouldn't be able to completely relax — and was relieved to see the door was tightly closed.

She put a kettle on to prepare a cup of an herbal tea that Serena had given her to try. It was supposed to help with relaxation at bedtime, and after the day she'd had, she knew she'd need it. And of course, she thought as she smiled, a nice long soak in her beloved claw-foot tub wouldn't hurt either. While she waited for the water to boil, she started her laptop. She still hadn't heard from Jeremy and decided that if there was nothing tonight, she'd call the library during the day to make sure he was okay.

When her emails loaded, there wasn't one from him, but another one caught her eye.

Dear Ms. Greyborne,
I would like to take this opportunity to congratulate you and thank you once again for the outstanding contribution you made to the acquisitions department during your work exchange here at the British Museum. As you know, the book you discovered in the stacks was a very rare and valuable piece and one we are most happy to have in our possession, so it is with great pleasure I am writing to inform you of an exciting opportunity that has become available. As we understand, you are no longer in the employment of the Boston Public Library. It is our hope that I might convince you to consider working with me on a contract basis as a museum representative in retrieving lost and stolen manuscripts believed to be presently located in the United States.

I will be in your area in a few weeks and hope that we may discuss this opportunity at that time. I arrive in Greyborne Harbor on the 24th and have arranged lodgings at the Grey Gull Inn for two nights. It is my hope to meet with you at your earliest convenience upon my arrival.

I look forward to speaking with you again.

Kindest Regards,
Roger Moore

Stunned by the offer, Addie reread the email, grabbed her tea and headed upstairs. She couldn't believe it. The curator of the Antiquarian Books Acquisitions Department of the British Museum was actually offering her a position to assist him in retrieving books for them? She only worked there for six months and didn't even know him that well, and besides, they had trained teams of specialists on their payroll already who did just that. So why offer her a contract? She shrugged shaking her head.

Roger's odd request would have to wait. Right now, her skin prickled at the anticipation of soaking in the deep claw-foot bathtub. The banging pipes were the only slight annoyance as she lit her favorite candle, placed her teacup on the chair beside the tub, and lowered herself into the bubbly bathwater. Warmth rushed through her, and it didn't take long for the music pumping through her earbuds to lull her into a total state of relaxation. She jerked with a start when her chin dropped into the now-frigid bathwater. She shivered and took out the earbuds, setting them next to her phone on the chair. It had been a long time since she'd relaxed enough to drift off in the bath, and judging by how cold the water had become, she must have slept for a while.

She stepped out onto the bath mat and rubbed the soft cotton towel over her goose bump-riddled skin. The ceiling above her head creaked. It was followed by the sound of a dull thud. She froze and strained to listen, but the rush of blood moving from her pounding heart into her ears drowned out all other sounds. She held her breath and swallowed hard, trying to relieve the lump growing in the back of her throat, while reaching for her cell phone.

The old clock downstairs in the study began to chime. She jumped. Her phone slipped from her fingers and skidded across the damp wooden floor. She crawled on hands and knees to retrieve it, counting out the number of chimes. There were nine before the house went quiet again. A loud thud downstairs sent prickles across her skin. She leapt to her feet, grabbed her pink silk robe hanging from the back of the bathroom door, and slipped the hook latch into the eye hole. She wasn't sure how secure it would be for keeping an intruder out. This was an old house, and the glass doorknobs had never been fitted with proper locks, but that was all she had right now between them and her.

Legs wobbling, she made her way back to the side of the tub and sat down. Fingers trembling, she pressed Marc's number. Her breaths came short and fast, and her head spun. She put it between her knees and waited for him to pick up. "Marc, where are you?" She gnashed her teeth. Finally, an out-of-breath voice answered. "Marc," she whispered. "It's Addie. I think there's someone in my house. I'm upstairs locked in the bathroom."

"Stay there. We're on our way. And don't hang up the phone."

"I won't," she whispered. She heard rustling sounds in the background, and his voice shouting orders, then an echo over what sounded like a police radio. Then all went quiet and stayed quiet. "Marc, are you still there?" No answer, but she could still make out muffled background noise and knew the connection hadn't been lost.

The minutes ticked by, and terror snaked its way up her spine. Finally, his voice crackled through the speaker, and she took a deep breath, not aware she'd even been holding it.

"Can you make it downstairs to open the front door? Don't worry, we've got the house surrounded, and there's no sign of a break-in."

"Are you sure?"

"Yes, I think it's safe for you to open the front door. Just be quiet about it."

She clenched her fists at her sides and took a deep breath, grabbed her curling iron from the countertop, and brandished it over her head as she tiptoed downstairs in the dark and unbolted the front door.

The door flung opened. Marc pulled her out into the cold evening air. Goose bumps erupted over her skin beneath her light robe. Another officer placed his arm around her shivering shoulders, ushered her to a warm cruiser, and then joined the others inside. Marc eventually came out, got into the driver's seat, and glanced sideways at her, but didn't say anything.

She drew her thin robe close around her throat. "What did you find?" Her lip quivered.

He looked at her and took her hands in his. "There's no sign of forced entry — not the windows, the doors, nothing."

Her eyes widened. "Nothing? It was just my silly imagination?"

He shook his head. "No, unless your idea of good housekeeping is throwing stuff on the floor. There's no question that someone was in your house tonight."

Marc accompanied Addie through her inspection of each of the twenty-three rooms, plus the three large ones in the attic. He took notes as she commented on the contents of the drawers or cupboards that had been rifled through. As far as she could tell, nothing appeared to be missing, but to be sure, she'd double-check with the lawyer in the morning, since he had a full inventory, completed prior to her taking over the estate. If anything of value was missing, it would be on his list. When they finished the inspection, Marc had her go back to his cruiser to wait for him while he got reports from the officers still on the scene.

She was grateful that before they had started the arduous task, he'd escorted her to her bedroom and stood guard outside while she changed into a pair of jeans and a warm sweater, but as she sat alone now in his patrol car, she was freezing. Numb from head to toe, she replayed Marc's words — "no forced entry" — over and over in her mind.

He slid into the seat beside her and handed her a steaming cup. With trembling fingers, she grasped it and took a sip. It was coffee, and it burned as it trickled down the back of her throat, but she didn't care. It was good to feel something right now.

"I know you're upset and tired, but I have to ask you a few more questions. Are you up to it?"

She nodded and took another sip. "Yeah, I'll be fine. I needed this coffee though, thanks."

He nodded. "Me, too." He clinked his cup to hers. "Well, it's clear to me that our room by room inspection determined the whole house was searched. Do you have any idea what the intruder or intruders were looking for?"

"No, it's like the last times. Nothing seems to be missing, which makes me suspect that they're looking for something specific and think I have it."

"Any *idea* what that might be?"

"None. If antiques or books were missing, then we'd have a clue they were looking for valuables, but with nothing standing out as having been taken . . . it just doesn't make sense. Unless . . . it isn't a robbery attempt, but a scare tactic to try and run me off?"

"I doubt that. This goes beyond someone

trying to put a scare into you. No, it's definitely someone looking for something." He flopped his head back onto the headrest and closed his eyes. "Next big question is . . . who else has keys to your house?"

Addie shook her head. "No one I can think of."

"What about the lawyer, Raymond James?"

"No, when he gave me the keys, he said it was the only set and advised I get copies made."

Marc sat up and looked at her. "Did you?"

"No, I haven't had time." She swirled her coffee cup.

"Well, so much for that theory." He leaned his head back again.

"Serena?"

"No."

"Brian?"

"No, he didn't replace the lock — he said we'd do that when they installed the new security system."

Marc sucked in a deep breath and forced it out through puffed-up cheeks. "Well, I'm at a loss."

"Me, too." She gnawed on her bottom lip.

"Stop it." He playfully nudged her arm.

She laughed. "Sorry — habit, I guess."

Addie's attention was drawn to the stream

of officers going in and out her front door. She rested her forehead on the cool window glass and closed her eyes, lost in her thoughts.

Marc patted her knee. "You look beat."

"I'm okay. They should be finished soon anyway, shouldn't they?"

"No, it'll probably take most of the night — lots of area to sweep for prints."

Her shoulders slumped.

"Besides, I don't think it's a good idea for you to stay here until the security system's in place. Someone definitely used a key to get in."

"I've racked my brain and I don't know of anyone. Unless . . . ?" Her eyes narrowed.

"Unless what — or should I say *who*?"

"What do you know about Catherine Lewis?"

"Catherine? Why would she have a key?"

"I'm not saying she does, but she stopped by my shop and introduced herself. It was really weird. She said something about meeting me when I was little and how happy she was to see me again in person, all grown up."

"Did you meet her in Boston sometime?"

"Not as far as I know, but she made it sound like it was here, and she said her mother and my aunt had been good

151

friends."

"They were, if I remember correctly. What's weird about that?"

"Nothing, now that I say it out loud, I guess. It was just a feeling I had at the time."

Addie pulled her key ring out of her pocket and turned it over in her hands, trying to get a mental picture of who might have a copy. "If they were close friends, wouldn't it stand to reason her mother might have a key? You know, in case of emergencies or something? People do that with friends."

He took a sip of coffee and rubbed his neck. "Well, yes they do, and your aunt was old and living on her own, so maybe her mother, Ruth, did have a key. But why would Catherine be breaking in and ransacking the house or the store? She's a nice lady and well respected in the community."

"Maybe she thinks there's something of her mother's here, and she wants to get it back?"

"Then why wouldn't she just ask you for it? No, I'm not even going to investigate that one." He shook his head.

"I don't know; ignore me right now. I'm just tossing out possibilities." Addie leaned her head against the glass.

"Okay." He tossed his empty cup into a

trash bag on the floor by her feet. "Time to get you checked into the hotel. Buckle up." He started the engine.

"Were Catherine and Blain friends?" she asked, sipping her coffee.

"They knew each other. It's a small town. Why? What are you thinking?"

"Just wondering, that's all. I'm trying to see if there's a connection. Remember, I told you the whole conversation with her felt weird."

"I think you're tired, and your mind is going overboard with all this. I'm sure Catherine wasn't . . . isn't involved with Blain or Andrew's antiquity smuggling. If, in fact, that's what they were doing."

"Just think about it, will you? For me." She smiled coyly in the dim light. He glanced at her, the headlights of a passing car revealing amusement etched onto his face. "Oh, and one more little thing . . ." she added, cringing.

He groaned and glanced sideways at her.

"Please, just indulge me for a minute?"

"All right," he sighed. "What now?"

"Raymond has a list of all the estate holdings."

"As he should, being the executor."

"Right. And this is a small town and there are not that many lawyers."

"Where are you going with this?"

"Well, it stands to reason —"

"Wait. You're not suggesting Raymond James, the most ethical lawyer I've ever met, is behind this, are you?" He shot her a side glare and the car swerved.

She grabbed the dash. "No, no, but what if Blain or Andrew or even Catherine used his services, and one of them got ahold of the list or found it sitting around on his desk and saw something on it that they wanted to get their hands on?"

"You're getting carried away now. I'm sure he's not about to leave one client's file out when there's another sitting in his office."

"Mistakes happen, don't they?"

"Yes, but now you're really stretching, don't you think?"

"Maybe. I don't know." She tightened her lips and stared out the window as the flashing hotel sign came into focus.

Marc stood in the open doorway while she settled into her room. After placing her overnight bag, which he had insisted she pack when she left the house, in the closet and her makeup bag on the counter in the bathroom, she walked over to the door to thank him. His finger tilted her chin up, and he smiled down at her. She liked the way the corners of his eyes crinkled when he smiled. A wave of tremors swept through her, and she steadied herself by leaning into his hand.

"Remember, no rock left unturned. That goes for your case, too," he whispered. His warm breath swept across her cheek. She stared up into his soft, brown eyes, as he leaned in closer. Her heart raced. She arched upward. Her eyes closed, and his velvety lips brushed across hers.

Her eyes flew open. She pushed him away and gasped. Her head thudded back against the door. His eyes widened. Hurt and confusion crossed his face. She shook her head. Tears burned at her eyes as she darted behind the door, shutting it quickly, pressing her forehead against it. Her heart pounded, making it hard for her to catch her breath. "What did I just do?" Her palm slapped the door.

Chapter Fifteen

The morning alarm rang far too early for Addie. She'd tossed and turned half the night, thinking about Marc and what had passed between them. She vowed never to let it happen again. He was a friend and couldn't be anything more. She still loved David and always would. The other half of the night was filled with distorted dreams of running from shadowy faces floating in and out of book covers. She pulled the comforter over her head, wishing it would all go away. How would she be able to face Marc again? She moaned.

Her eyes closed, and she snuggled in under the warm duvet until she remembered Serena was dropping in to the shop today. Addie didn't know what to expect for business on a weekend, but as foot traffic into her shop had grown all week, she feared it could get busy fairly early. She hoped Serena would drop by ahead of time so they'd have a chance to talk before the Saturday-morning shoppers started their rounds. Only half seeing, she headed in the direction of the in-room coffee maker, started a pot, and then quickly showered.

The hot water refreshed her, and she ran over her mental to-do list, adding *post the "Help Wanted" sign* she had purchased a few days ago and had forgotten about in all the recent chaos. When she got out and dressed, the bedside clock said it was eight. Marc had told her he'd pick her up at eight-fifteen to give her a lift to the store. She wondered how he'd react seeing her today. "Darn it. I wish I had my own car; then I could avoid seeing him all together," she muttered, pouring a cup of coffee, then crossing the room to stand at her third-floor window, which overlooked the main entrance and parking lot.

Her room provided an amazing view of the town, nestled at the bottom of the hill on the harbor. Dispersed throughout the scene was an array of foliage in various shades of fall colors. The sight tugged at her heart. It was no wonder the tourist business boomed this time of year. Growing up on the East Coast had spoiled her, and she couldn't imagine having to go on a tour bus, like the people she was watching below boarding theirs, just so they could enjoy the same scenery that she was lucky enough to witness every day.

She studied the tourists — a mix of shapes, sizes, and ages. Some appeared excited as they embarked, ready for their day ahead. Others looked like she felt: half asleep and in need of another coffee. One tall woman stood apart from the group and paced along the sidewalk. Addie couldn't make out her features, because she wore a large scarf draped over her head and shoulders. But there was something about her that didn't fit with the rest of the tourist group. Addie had a gnawing feeling that she knew her and leaned forward to try to get a clearer look.

A black Honda sedan pulled up behind the bus. The woman hurried over, tossed a suitcase into the back, then hopped into the passenger seat, and the car pulled away. A cold chill rushed across Addie's shoulders. She grabbed her purse and bolted from her room slamming the door behind her. She pressed the elevator button repeatedly, but the lighted floor indicator above the door didn't move from the third floor. Spotting the stairwell exit, she dashed to it, burst through the door, and bounded down the steps. Breathless, she shot out into the lobby and ran directly into Marc.

"Whoa, whoa, whoa." He steadied them both by gripping her shoulders. "What's got you in such a rush this morning?"

"Did you just drive up?" she cried.

"Yes. Why? Am I late?"

"Did, did you see it?"

His forehead furrowed. "See what?"

"The, the car, the black car?" She pulled away and stepped toward the door.

"Hey there. Slow down a minute and tell me what's going on?" He clutched her jacket sleeve. "Look at me." He spun her toward him.

"A black Honda sedan. Did you see it when you pulled into the parking lot?"

"Yes, well . . . I think so, but I wasn't —"

"We have to go find it. It can't have gotten far."

"Do you think it's *the* car?" He trotted to match her pace.

"I'm sure of it." She stood beside his cruiser and tapped her foot, waiting for him to unlock the doors. When she heard them click, she jerked the door open, plopped into the seat and fastened her seat belt. "Let's go — hurry."

"Let me get in first." He adjusted his seat belt. "Did you see which way it headed?"

"No, the bus was blocking the driveway,

ut I'm guessing into downtown. The other way leads to the riding stables, and the woman who got in didn't look like she was dressed for horseback riding."

"What woman?"

"The woman I saw on the walk out front who got in it. I know I've seen her before. There's something really familiar about her. The way she walked and held herself. I just can't place her though. Maybe it was the tall woman from my store who was also in Serena's? Oh, I don't know, but hurry."

"Did you get a look at her face?"

"No, she was wearing a scarf, but there's something. I know it. I can feel it."

Addie closed her eyes and concentrated on the hazy image of the woman's features. Her eyes shot open. "She was at the store the night it got broken into."

"You saw her? In the store? Why didn—"

"No, she was at the back of the crowd watching. She was with a tall man . . . oh God. It was Andrew."

"That doesn't mean they were guilty of anything."

"No, but it proves they know each other, and she could be part of everything that's happening. Does Andrew drive a black Honda?" Her eyes scanned down every side street they passed.

"I don't know. I'll check it out though." He pulled up in front of her store.

"Can we drive around just a bit longer, please?" she asked, her eyes pleading with him.

"It's almost nine, and judging by the traffic down here already, you're in store for a busy day." He winked. "I'll drive around a bit and see if I can locate it. You go to work. This is *police* business, after all."

"You can be so, so, so" — she clenched her fists and shook — "frustrating." She got out and slammed the door.

He rolled down the passenger window. "Addie."

"What?" She spun around.

"Have a good day." He smiled and pulled out into traffic.

"Argh." She stamped her foot. Taking a deep breath, Addie straightened her shoulders, smoothed out the upturned hem on her slacks, looked up, and came face-to-face with Martha.

Her brow cocked. "Humph, first y'er friends with a murderer, then you show up first thing in the morning with *him* — chief of police, no less. What're you up to, girlie?" Her lip curled.

"Good morning." Addie nodded, held her head high, and strode to her door.

"I got my eye on you," Martha called out.

The fine hairs on Addie's neck bristled, and she could feel Martha's eyes boring into her back. Heat swept across her cheeks. She didn't dare turn around to acknowledge her any further.

Addie fumbled with her door latch, cringing at the thought of how the whole town, through the gossip grapevine, would soon hear about the police chief driving her to the shop this morning, and she dropped the keys. She scrambled for them, aware that Martha was still drilling holes into her back. Then an equally sickening thought struck her: it wouldn't take long for someone from the hotel to add their tidbit in, mentioning the fact that Marc had also checked her in to the hotel last night. She mentally put on her big-girl pants, puffed her cheeks, blew out a deep breath, and finally fit the key into the lock, pushing the door open and sliding inside without so much as a single look back at Martha.

She took a deep breath, then steadied herself by pacing up and down the rows between the bookshelves. When panic over the possibility of further gossip about her subsided, she felt ready to start the day. The first thing she checked off her to-do list was placing the "Help Wanted" sign in the bookshop window. Then she sat down at the counter and called Brian on the store phone, flipped on the speaker, and began readying the cash counter for the morning start.

"Look," he said. "I've just hung up with Marc and already told him I'd call the company in Boston again today and upgrade the work order to urgent. Aside from that, there's nothing else I can tell you."

"That's great —"

"Yeah, whatever, talk to the chief. I've already told him it's out of my hands now."

"Oh, okay, I didn't' realize, I —"

"Tell me something."

"Sure, what?"

"Tell me, why's Marc taking such a special interest in your personal affairs?"

Addie's elbow slipped off the counter and slammed onto her thigh.

"It's out of character for him. Usually, he's detached and impartial to a case. So what's up with you two?"

"What do you mean?"

"Well, either he thinks you're a complete ditz who can't look after herself, or —"

"Or what?"

"Or . . . nothing, never mind."

Words failed her. She mumbled something incoherent, clicked off the call, and blew out a sharp breath. Although she had to admit to herself that earlier in the week, she'd been irritated with Marc, too, when he'd called Brian on her behalf, except since then she'd put it down to her being friends with Serena or to it being a part of the small-town lifestyle she didn't understand — but now? A virtual stranger telling her that this wasn't the case made her think twice. She drummed her fingers on the countertop. Did Marc actually think her incompetent and not able to look after herself?

She chewed on her bottom lip and stared out the window, recalling the day that she'd decided to set up her own business and had started scouting available locations near the town center. Her first choice had been Main Street, but when she saw this double bay window space for rent, and only half a block off Main, she couldn't resist. She knew it was still a good location for foot traffic because of the way the Town Square shopping district was designed. It was an actual square of streets around the municipal buildings, with parkland behind them. Main Street, from what she could tell, was only called that because it faced the front entrances to the civic buildings. But here, she had the full view over the park, and she was happy with her decision, but now? Between Marc's apparent doubts about her competency and the fallout from any damage Martha might invoke, she wasn't certain that she'd even be here in another month to enjoy it. The door chimes jingled, and she jumped. The clinking jerked her from her thoughts and announced the beginning of another workday.

Chapter Sixteen

The store filled up early, and there was no sign of things slowing down as lunchtime approached. Addie's feet ached, and her stomach rumbled. She'd gone nonstop. It seemed the flames of Martha's rumor mill hadn't been lit yet, and she breathed a sigh of relief. Marc she would take care of when she had time to think, but now she could kill for a five-minute coffee break.

She'd just finished wrapping an early edition of Margaret Mitchell's *Gone with the Wind* and explaining to the woman how her book consignment system worked: 30 percent to Addie and 70 percent to the customer. The woman appeared happy with the pay division and left promising to return soon with her books. A meek woman with curly blond hair slid a sheet of paper across the counter toward her. Addie tried to focus. It was a résumé. She looked up, smiling at the young woman in delight. Addie was ready to hug her and hand her the keys to the store right then and there. However, she did manage to control the urge and quickly read through the woman's short work history.

"Well, Paige, this looks good. A degree in comparative literature from Brown — excellent; and some previous retail experience — perfect." She smiled over the paper at the pasty-faced girl, who appeared to be growing paler by the minute. "Are you okay? Would you like to sit down?" Addie pointed to a counter stool.

"No," she whispered. "I'm fine."

Addie shrugged, but kept one eye on the girl as she continued to scan her résumé.

"It says you graduated two years ago, but then there's no work history after that? Did you take some time off?"

"Yes." Paige's head drooped, and she clutched at her purse with both hands. She looked up, tears filled her dull blue eyes, and she sniffled loudly.

"What's wrong?"

Paige shook her head.

"Okay. It's none of my business anyway, and I don't have a right to ask, but I am concerned. The store can get fairly busy, and I can't be here all the time. So I really need someone who can step up and take over some of the workload. Do you think you're up to that?"

Paige nodded quickly. "Oh yes, yes, I can do that." A timid smile crossed her lips. "Just give me a chance, I'll show you."

Addie rubbed her chin and glanced back at the résumé in her hand. "I also see there isn't a local address or phone number. It says at the top here — Boston?"

Paige bit her lip and shuffled her feet. "I've just moved and haven't found a place to live yet," she mumbled. "But I will soon."

Addie studied the distressed young woman standing in front of her. She sucked in a deep breath. "Okay. When can you start?"

"Really, I got the job?" Paige squealed. "Oh, thank you, you have no idea what this means to me. I promise I won't let you down."

Color returned to Paige's ashen face, and Addie decided she must just be the nervous type and might take some work yet, but she was desperate and willing to take a chance on the girl.

"You're welcome. I'm happy you walked in here today; you have no idea how much I need help."

Paige scanned the shop. "It looks like business is booming."

"Yes, it is. What's a good day for you to start?"

"Umm, well." She fidgeted with her handbag. "Monday?"

"Do you think you'll be able to find a place to live by then?"

"If I have a job to go to, then it's easier to rent a place. I'm sure something will come up today."

"Where are you staying now?"

Her cheeks flushed. "I'm okay. I have a place to sleep."

Addie eyed her closely, but Paige offered no further clues. "All right, as long as you're not stuck living on the street, it's none of my business."

Paige's shoulders relaxed, and her face softened.

"Monday sounds perfect." Addie shook her hand.

After Paige left, Serena poked her head over the top of a bookcase, her eyes wide. "Don't tell me you just hired Paige Stringer?"

"I did, why? Do you know her?"

"She didn't tell you, then, did she?" Serena walked around to the counter.

"Tell me what?"

She scowled. "I just knew it. Those two are up to something."

"Hey, slow down. Two who?"

"Them." She motioned her head backward.

"You're not making any sense."

Serena leaned against the counter, shook her head, and took a deep breath. "She's Martha's youngest daughter."

Addie felt the color drain from her face and slumped onto the stool beside Serena. "No, she never told me," she whispered. "What do I do now? I hired her."

"Well, the only good thing is, as rumor has it, she and Martha had a major falling-out a couple of years ago. Word was it was over an affair that Paige was having with one of her professors, and when they got caught, he was fired, and they moved to Boston. Gossip was then that she got pregnant, and he apparently had a bad gambling problem. I heard that Martha wouldn't send her money. She said she didn't pay for a fancy education just so she'd end up like Martha had, and . . . I don't even know for sure if it's all true. It was just what was going around in the town rumor mill. But I guarantee Martha's behind her working here." Serena huffed.

"And if it's not true, maybe she's embarrassed by the gossip, and that's why she seemed to be hiding something." Addie glanced down at the résumé. "She just seemed scared and alone. Not vicious or conniving."

"Well, don't trust her. She was probably sent here to work as a plant for Martha and her gang, to gather more fuel for that stupid petition. Look what it did to me."

"I know, you poor dear." Addie threw her arms around Serena and hugged her tight. "I've been worried sick."

"I'm fine, now that I'm not number one on the most-wanted list anymore." She smiled. "Oh, I have something for you." She reached into her large handbag.

"No, I should be giving you a gift. After all, you are the first jailbird I've ever known," chuckled Addie.

Serena swatted her arm. "It's not really a gift, but I figured you'd be hungry, so . . . voilà, lunch. I hope you like it."

"I don't even care what is. I'm starving," Addie shrieked. "God, I could kiss you."

A woman browsing through the curio cabinet behind her laughed, and a few other customers snickered. Addie turned bright red, then laughed and shrugged her shoulders. "It's amazing what I'll do for food."

A man sporting a black, Boston baseball cap piped up. "I'll have to remember that the next time I want a kiss."

The shoppers howled. Addie was shocked when she realized how many people were actually in the store. She stood up and announced. "I hope no one minds, but a girl's gotta eat," which was met with cheers and encouragement. She took a bow and sat down.

Serena almost slipped off her stool, laughing as she handed Addie a homemade roast beef sandwich and then pulled out a plastic container. "And this," she sputtered between giggles, "is dessert."

"Ah, you are so thoughtful. I don't know how to thank you." Addie smiled and squeezed her hand. "You're my rock."

"Nonsense," said Serena. "You're mine, and I have to thank you for springing me out of the big house." She pushed stray wisps of hair from her eyes. "Marc told me that if it hadn't been for you, he'd never have found that door or room. Thank you."

Addie's cheeks warmed, and she cast her eyes down. "He would have eventually found it. I was just in the right place at the right time." She shrugged. "Do you want half?"

"No thanks, I ate before I came. You know, you can take more credit than you're giving yourself for the discovery."

Addie waved off her comment and bit into

her sandwich.

Serena shook her head and eyed the shop. "It looks like business is good. That's great, since you've only been open a week."

"I couldn't be happier — although it does help being the only bookshop in town."

"How are sales for this stuff?" Serena motioned toward the curios.

"Not as good, but I'm still hoping. The oils sell well, and the candles, but the knick-knacks — pfft. Not so well."

"Yeah, there's Mildred's Emporium and Gifts over on Main. I think that's where people are used to going."

"I was in there, and she does have some nice things, but I can't compete with her low prices."

"They're all knockoffs, you know, made-in-China stuff. Yours are the real deal."

"I know, but her prices are so good." Addie took another bite. "If that line doesn't pick up, I might look for a distributor in Boston. I can't let them go for the prices it would take to sway people in town my way."

"Good idea. I've got some contacts there. Let me know if you're ever interested." A sly looked appeared on Serena's face.

"What?" Addie opened the plastic container. "Oh, turnovers, yummy, thanks." She smiled up at Serena, who still had a teasing look in her eye. "What? Do I have food stuck in my teeth?"

Serena laughed. "No, but speaking of 'interested' . . ."

"Yes?" Addie's eyes narrowed.

"How are you and Marc doing — or should I say, *what* are you and Marc doing?" She smirked.

"What? Why? Did he say something to you?"

"Don't worry, he's very professional and all, but I know my brother. I've never known him to take such a keen interest in a case. I'm thinking that there's something more happening between the two of you. Come on" — she leaned toward Addie, her arms propped up in her lap — "tell me everything."

Addie felt the heat creep up her neck to her face. She brushed her cheek where his warm breath had caressed it last night and she touched her finger to her lips, but then she shook her head, remembering he thought her to be, in Brian's words, "a complete ditz." "There's nothing to tell. I got broken into again, and he's on the case, and you were charged with murder and —"

"This is strictly business and all professional-like, then?"

"Yes, it is. Besides" — she tossed her head

back — "he thinks I'm a complete idiot and can't take care of myself."

"No, he doesn't. Quite the opposite, I think."

"What?"

"He's always asking about you." She grinned and slyly glanced at Addie out of the corner of her eye.

"He's just keeping tabs on me. He thinks I'm involved with a crime syndicate or something."

Serena's eyebrows twitched. "I don't think so." She wagged her finger and broke into a grin.

"There's nothing else to it. I'm just a case." Addie's lip quivered as she stared down at the last piece of turnover in her fingers and swallowed hard. She could feel Serena's eyes burning into her.

"Okay, if you insist that's your story and you're sticking to it, but I'll get it out of you somehow. I know there's something going on between you and my brother. Just call it little-sister instinct. He likes you. I know he does." She nudged Addie's knee. "And you like him. I see it in your eyes."

A cough rattled from behind Serena's shoulder. Addie's gaze shot up. Serena jumped and spun around on her stool.

"Well, speak of the devil."

Marc rocked back on his heels, his face flushed. "Well, I see you two are catching up, so . . . so I'll . . . I'll just drop by later." He fumbled with his cap as he retreated backward out the door.

Addie let out the breath she didn't even know she'd been holding.

Serena erupted in laughter, and the man in the Boston ball cap smirked and winked at Addie.

Chapter Seventeen

"Look, I'm sorry, Addie. I had no idea he was standing behind me."

Addie shot her a sidelong glance and proceeded to lock the front door, sliding past Serena, who was hovering beside her, and then made her way to the back room.

"So, that's it." Serena trailed after her. "You're not going to say anything? Will you ever speak to me again?"

Addie stopped, folded her arms and studied Serena's crumbling face. She felt a stab at her heart and huffed. "Serena, I'm just, just so . . ."

She pulled at her hair and spun away.

". . . mortified."

"I know. It was bad taste and timing on my part." Serena tugged at her sleeve. "But we don't know how much he overheard. Maybe he'd just walked in and didn't know what we were talking about?"

"That might have been the case until you

said 'speak of the devil.' Darn you. I'm so embarrassed — again."

"Again? Why, what else happened?"

"Nothing," she snapped.

"Okay." Serena's brow arched. "But if it helps," she continued, a crooked smile crossing her lips, "I think he likes you, so it's not all bad if he heard us talking about him. Is it? After all, it might help the two of you get —"

"Stop." Addie's hand shot up. "It matters because we're just friends, and there's going to be enough rumors spread by Martha and her posse."

"Martha? What does she have to do with anything?"

"She saw him drop me off first thing this morning and let me know her thoughts about it." She winced. "It's just that I hate gossip." Addie grabbed her purse from the countertop. "Let's go eat."

Serena's face lit up. "So we're still friends?"

"Of course we are."

"Good." Serena heaved a sigh. "After all," she said, stepping back, "I'm thinking you're going to be my sister-in-law soon, and —"

Addie jostled her with her shoulder. "Stop it. Marc and I are just friends and business partners."

"But Marc doesn't have *business* partners," she snickered.

Addie locked the alley door behind them. "Just get in and drive." She slid into Serena's passenger seat.

Serena got into the car and looked at Addie sideways, arched an eyebrow, and gave her a wicked wink. "You do like him. Don't you?"

"What? No, he's the police chief, and *your brother.*"

"So?"

"So, nothing." She straightened her shoulders, plonked her purse on her lap, and stared ahead through the window. "It's strictly business."

"Well, let's just say, theoretically of course, if it *were* more than police business —"

"Yes?" Addie frowned, her eyes fixed forward.

"You'd have my blessing."

"Let it go, Serena. I have enough on my plate right now. Besides . . . I'm not ready."

"Okay." She grinned. "But I'm just saying." She shrugged and pulled out of the back parking spot and headed down the lane. "Where do you want to eat? Mario's on Main?"

"I'd rather not, if that's all right with you. I want to go someplace we can talk and catch up. There wasn't much chance of that today in the store."

"There's the restaurant in your hotel?"

"No, it's filled with tourists these days."

"I know." She bounced in her seat. "The Grey Gull Inn; it has great food."

"I've heard about that place. In fact, I know someone who's going to be staying there in a couple of weeks."

"The restaurant's probably packed though, since it's Saturday night. But there's a great rooftop patio that'd be perfect. They have heat lamps out there, and it should be quiet."

"Sounds good."

They drove in silence down the winding road toward the harbor. Addie marveled at all the shops and cafés that were scattered along Marine Drive, which overlooked the seawall. "I had no idea it was as booming down here as this."

"You've never been down here before?" Serena glanced at her.

"No, I haven't had time. Wow. It's like its own little village. I love it." She craned her neck, trying to take it all in. "Too bad everything's closed for the night. I'd love to explore."

"Tomorrow's Sunday. Town Square's closed, and so are you, but this area is hopping then. We should come back. You'd love some of the quirkier shops down here." Serena pulled into the Grey Gull parking lot.

"I'd love to." Addie unclipped her seat belt. "Oh, but I'll have to see how it goes. I'm really behind on sorting the attic. It's kind of been a lost week."

They entered the foyer of the dining area and Addie's heart sank. As Serena had feared, it was packed. The bench seating around the entrance way was filled, and a crowd stood waiting at the hostess station. "Should we try someplace else?"

"No, we'll get in. Wait a minute." Serena pushed through the crowd.

Addie followed, weaving her way to the front behind Serena. "Sorry, sorry, sorry," she repeated when she nudged too close to startled patrons. When she caught up to Serena, she was chatting with a pretty, young blond woman. Addie clutched her purse in front of her and leaned forward to hear their discussion. The man behind her edged closer and huffed in her ear, his hot breath gusting across the back of her head. She turned and flashed an apologetic smile, but he returned it with a fixed stare.

Addie shuddered and turned back to Serena. The hostess gathered two menus and asked them to follow her. Addie twisted around toward the man behind her.

His cheeks puffed out and his lips pursed until the hostess announced loudly, "We can turn on the heaters on the rooftop deck for you. It should be warm enough." His taut features relaxed.

Addie smiled and nodded at him and trailed after Serena.

As they passed through the dining area, Addie scanned the large, beautiful room. The far wall was made of floor-to-ceiling windows that gave a perfect view of the harbor stretched out before it. Serena started up the steps leading to the upper deck. Addie took one more fleeting glance around the dining area and paused midstep.

She grabbed Serena's coattail and tugged. Serena's foot wavered, and she started to tumble backward. Addie thrust her arms up to stop her friend's downward spiral.

Serena turned to her, eyes wide. "What was that all about?"

"Sorry, I didn't mean to pull so hard."

Serena squared her shoulders. "What's so important?"

"See, over in the corner table?" Addie whispered. "Isn't that Andrew Fielding?"

"Yes, so what?"

"Who's the woman with the brown, tightly

permed hair he's with?"

"Elaine. Why?"

"No reason." Addie gnawed her lip. "Just wondering."

"That's why you almost sent me tumbling down on top of you? Sheesh." She shook her head and trotted up the stairs.

Addie's hand lingered on the bottom of the railing. She couldn't help but wonder why Andrew would dismiss Elaine and then have dinner with her just days later. She shrugged it off and took a step up, but her eyes remained fixed on their table. Her foot was hovering over the next step when Andrew reached inside his jacket pocket, pulled out an envelope, and slid it toward Elaine. She picked it up, slipped it under the table, peeked inside, nodded, and tucked it into her handbag. Addie's breath caught at the back of her throat as Elaine got up and walked toward the door.

She swallowed hard and dashed up the stairs. Serena was seated at the only occupied table on the very chilly patio. A propane heater had been placed beside it, and she sat sipping a glass of water, browsing through the menu.

Addie plunged into the chair across from her. "You aren't going to believe what I just saw."

Serena flinched and dropped her menu. "Andrew just paid Elaine off."

"What? How do you know that?"

"He gave her an envelope, and I'm sure by the look on her face it was full of money, and then she got up and left." Addie took a sip from her water glass.

"Oh, Addie, Addie, Addie." Serena shook her head. "I think this week's gotten to you. You're seeing —"

"I know what I saw."

"I'm sure you do, but how do you know it was some sort of payoff and not something completely innocent?"

"Like what?"

"Like a severance payment. Maybe he felt bad about dismissing her after fifteen years of working for Blain and wanted to make things right. Who knows?" Serena leaned forward and patted Addie's hand. "Now let's order. I need some food."

"Maybe you're right." She let out a heavy sigh. "But I have a feeling there's more to it than that." She propped her chin in her hand and gazed out over the harbor.

"You're not going to let this go, are you?" Serena closed her menu.

"How can I?" Her eyes softened when she looked into Serena's drawn face. "I guess we've both been through a lot this week."

"Yes, we have." Serena's head dropped.

"We just have to figure it out and get to the bottom of it all, and then we'll both feel better and carry on with our normal lives."

"You're right," sighed Serena. "I guess I just wanted to forget about it all for a few minutes."

Addie picked up her menu. "I know that was selfish of me. I do tend to get too wrapped up in things sometimes, and this is *supposed* to be dinner to celebrate your freedom."

Serena laughed and picked up her water glass for a toast, but then set it down and frowned. "We can't really celebrate though, can we?"

"Why not? Umm . . . I think I'll have the steak sandwich. What are you going to have? My treat, anything you want."

"Thanks, but . . . I don't think we can celebrate until the real killer's caught and your break-ins come to an end. I can't help but think they're all related."

Addie sighed and put her menu down. "I do, too, but there's so many unanswered questions, and as hard as I've tried, I can't get all the pieces to fit together yet. We're missing a big one, as my dad would have said, and once we find that piece, the rest will fall into place."

"Maybe we should tell Marc —"

"No. Don't you dare."

Serena cringed. "Not even about the envelope exchange you saw tonight?"

"Pfft." She shook her head. "It's too early. Besides, I don't want to be made a fool of again by the police." She set her water glass down. "Like you said, it could be something completely innocent. We need more proof that something else was behind it."

"Okay." Serena pursed her lips and looked questioningly at her. "If that's how you feel, then . . . ?"

"It is. Let's eat, and then I'm hoping you can drive me to my place so I can pick up my car? I hate not having it."

"Sure, no problem." Serena closed her menu and signaled for the waiter hovering in the warmth at the top of the stairway. "Yes, I'm hungry — especially for him." She giggled.

Addie took a sip of her water from the goblet on the table and choked.

Serena's brows furrowed, and she glared at Addie. "What? What's so funny?" She smirked, then broke out laughing.

"Serena, *you're* too funny. Now I see why you *really* wanted to come here. You're just a flirt." She lifted her water glass in a toast. "Cheers, but he is kind of cute," she whispered behind her hand as the waiter approached their table. "You go girl." She grinned.

"No, no, no, it's not what you think. I just need a bit of a pick-me-up."

"Yeah right, that's what it's called, is it?" Addie snickered.

Serena tucked a wayward strand of hair behind her ear and beamed up at the handsome, chiseled-featured waiter, her eyelashes fluttering like frenzied butterflies.

Addie groaned from behind her menu.

Chapter Eighteen

A pounding noise woke Addie with a start. It took her a few seconds to figure out that she was in the hotel room. She turned to the bedside clock. Red digits glared *7:00 a.m.* She moaned and rolled onto her side, cuddling under the duvet. The banging sound continued. She opened her eyes and listened closer and realized the clatter was coming from her door. She fumbled for her robe at the foot of the bed and staggered toward it. A red head appeared on the other side of the peephole.

"What is going on," she muttered and flung the door open. "Do you have any idea what time it is — on a Sunday morning, no less?"

"Good morning." Serena's freckled face beamed back at her.

Addie looked at the steaming cups of coffee she held in each hand. "Okay, come in." Her face softened. "But to what do I owe the pleasure of this early-morning awakening?" She inhaled the coffee. "Mmmm, smells perfect."

"I knew a good cup of coffee would get me past the door." Serena stepped inside. "We're going to the harbor today, remember?"

"What I said was . . . I *might* be able to go, but I have a lot to do, and this is my only day off."

"Look, we've both had a rough week." Serena sat on the end of the bed. "A day off to have some fun is exactly what we both need, right?"

Addie heaved a deep breath. "I guess. But it's only seven." She pointed to the clock. "I'm sure the shops don't open till nine or ten at least."

"They open at nine, so you have plenty of time to shower and get ready. I wanted to catch you before you raced off to your musty old attic."

"Definitely not a worry at this time of the morning."

Serena's bottom lip quivered.

"All right." Addie yawned. "Just let me wake up a minute."

She showered and dressed, and they were out the door and driving toward the harbor by quarter to nine. A Sunday morning sleep-in and a leisurely coffee with an eleven a.m. start would have suited her better, but Addie had a gnawing feeling that Serena was up to something this morning. However, Serena was right; it had been a tough week, and they were both due for a bit of fun. She sat back and smiled when the seawall came into view. She rolled down her window and took a deep breath.

"See, you can feel the tension release already, can't you?" Serena pulled into a side street off Marine Drive and parked at the curbside. "Besides, any later and parking would be an issue. It gets pretty busy down here on Sundays."

"I never thought of that."

"Yeah, any later and we might as well have parked at our shops and walked down."

The morning flew by. Serena made certain they stopped into every shop along the drive. She said it would not only give Addie a glimpse into what treasures could be found in the unique shops down here but was also a great way to network and meet other merchants outside the Town Square.

Addie had to agree. They had fun exploring the souvenir, antique, and vintage clothing stores, and of course there was no shortage of bars and quaint restaurants along the seawall. It would be well worth her time to market around this area during the summer high season, because as far as she could tell, there weren't any bookshops.

Serena checked the time on her cell phone and grabbed her stomach. "My, oh my, just look at the time."

Addie eyed her. "Your stealth mode button must be malfunctioning. What's going on?"

"Nothing. My tummy is just signaling it's time to eat, and I know the perfect place." She pointed toward a sign that simply read "Fish 'n' Chips."

Addie stayed quiet, although her inner BS radar was beeping and whirling.

Serena bypassed a lovely table for two with a harbor view and chose a table set for four, near the back.

When the server brought their clam chowder and fish sampler platter, Addie motioned to the two other place settings. "You can take these if you like." She didn't miss the sly look that passed between Serena and Miss Dimple Cheek.

The waitress's dimple winked from her right cheek. "I'll just leave them for now."

"Are you waiting for someone?" Addie blew on her chowder, her gaze held steady on Serena. "This is the tenth time you've looked over my shoulder." Addie glanced behind her, trying to see what Serena was looking at, but nothing stood out. Giving up trying to understand her friend, she continued to eat.

Spoon halfway to her mouth, Serena's face lit up, and she waved. "I hope you don't mind, but . . ."

Addie twisted around in her chair. "Marc?"

"Hi, I took the afternoon off and hoped . . . well . . . thought, maybe you might still want to take that drive to Pen Hollow with me after lunch?" He twisted his ball cap in his hands.

Addie turned toward Serena, who was beaming like the Cheshire cat, and glared at her.

"Won't you join us?" Serena pointed to the empty chair beside Addie.

"Well, I wouldn't want to impose."

"Nonsense." Serena waved her hand over the platter. "We have plenty."

"Go ahead." Addie motioned to the open spot next to her. "After all, it's Serena's party and I'm just along for the ride, *apparently*."

Serena waved the server over to take Marc's drink order as he made himself comfortable.

Addie took a sip of her water. Her hand

remained gripped around her glass as she placed it back on the table. Marc reached for a scallop from the platter. His hand grazed over hers. She felt the heat rising up under her collar and creep across her cheeks.

"Well, I do hate to eat and run," Serena piped up, her eyes gleaming with mischief. "But you two have an excursion to make, and I should get home and finish my laundry since I'm back to work tomorrow." She tossed a twenty-dollar bill onto the table and left.

Addie's lips creased to a thin line. So she *had* been set up, just as her gut feeling had warned her earlier. She shifted in her chair to look directly at Marc. "Let's get on with this. It seems that you and your partner in crime have gone to a lot of trouble to make this *chance* meeting happen." Her eyes stung with tears she was fighting to hold back. Tears of embarrassment about their kiss, about what he might have overheard in her shop yesterday, tears of the loneliness she felt and the fears that had haunted her since David died. David, who was the love of her life — or so she had thought, until now. She was so confused, and she bit the inside of her mouth to keep her tears in check.

"I'm not sure what I've done to get you so hostile toward me. But —" For a brief moment, his face softened.

How could she tell him she wanted nothing more than for him to hold her in his arms and kiss her again? For a fleeting moment, she almost relented, but then she caught herself and hardened her heart.

Marc stirred his uneaten food around his plate. "It's not what you think, it's only that I —"

"Really? Then you tell me just what it is that *I'm* thinking," she snapped, straightening her shoulders.

He shook his head, let out a throaty sigh, pressed his hands against the table edge and shoved his chair back. Addie's heart sank. She knew she had pushed him too far this time.

Chapter Nineteen

Silence filled the car on the drive to Pen Hollow. Addie glanced at Marc occasionally, longing to talk about what had happened between them, but she couldn't find the words, because she wasn't sure what had actually taken place or why she had responded the way she had, or why he was really here, or why . . . there were too many unanswered questions. His eyes remained steadfast on the traffic and the road, and she sensed that he wouldn't be receptive to a discussion right now anyway, so she bit her tongue.

She did notice his attire for the day and inwardly approved. It was the first time since their initial meeting that she'd seen him out of uniform, and she decided she liked his casual look of denim and a T-shirt. He definitely could fill out a pair of jeans nicely — something his bulky police issue hid.

At the summit of the Pen Hollow Highway, he pulled his Jeep Cherokee to the side of the road at the switchback curve that had been the scene of her father's accident. She started shaking. He turned to her, his eyes filled with tenderness.

"Do you still want to do this?"

She looked at him, took a deep breath, and nodded.

"Good." He placed his hand gently over hers and squeezed.

His touch ran up her arm. She quivered and withdrew her hand.

His eyes dropped. "I'm sorry."

"No need to apologize. I'm . . . I'm just jumpy right now."

He reached into the back seat. His hand grazed across her shoulder. Electricity raced through her, and she grasped her tightening chest.

"Are you okay?" He pulled a briefcase from the back.

She nodded. Her mouth went dry, and the hold on her chest twisted. His eyes narrowed and he studied her face.

"If this is too much, I understand."

"No, it's not . . . no . . . this is something I have to do." She smiled weakly. How could she ever explain that she was reacting this way because of him, and not so much because of being at the scene of her dad's death? Or, maybe it was all of it, mixed up together. She put her hand on the door handle. "I'll be fine. Where do we start?"

He took the envelope of pictures out of his case. "Follow me," he said. "We'll try and retrace the accident as best we can based on the photos."

She got out. Her eyes scanned the repaired guardrail, and her shoulders slumped. "Can you tell where his car actually went through?"

"I'm sure there are welding seams if we look close enough." He came around to her side of the Jeep and kneeled in front of the barrier. He pulled a photo out of the envelope and placed it across his knee. He studied it, stood up, and stepped back. His eyes darted back and forth between the picture and the rail. He took a few steps to his right and stopped.

"This looks like the same angle, if I'm not mistaken." His eyes narrowed, and he peered back at the photo, then at the guardrail. "Yes, I'm sure of it. What do you think?" He held out the photograph.

She leaned in for a look and nodded her head. "I'd say so. Where's the one of the skid marks?"

"Here." He pulled out another picture.

"So, this is where . . ." She stepped back and looked down at the asphalt. "The inside car skidded against his and sent him careening through the rail?"

"By my calculations, I'd say so." Marc stroked his chin and gazed down the highway. "I'm going to try and re-create in my mind when this all started. I'll be back in a minute."

The top of his head quickly disappeared behind a ridge in the twisting decline of the narrow highway. Addie studied the photo she was still holding in her hand and tried to picture what exactly had occurred that night. Judging the point of impact by the calculations they'd made, she went over to the rail and peered down. Her head spun. It was a good three-hundred-foot drop down the side of a sheer cliff to the rocky bottom.

Her heart thudded against her chest wall, and she clutched at her collar. Her breaths came short and fast. Her knees buckled. She grabbed on to the guardrail for support. "Oh God, Dad, how horrible for you." Sliding to the ground, she leaned her head against the cold metal railing, struggling to fill her lungs.

She didn't hear Marc return, but when arms wrapped around her, she knew his feeling and the musky scent of his aftershave.

"Oh, Marc, it's so awful. I can't believe he ended up down there. He never stood a chance."

He pushed strands of hair from her face and tucked them behind her ear. "I know. It must be rough on you to finally see this."

She scrubbed her hands over her face. "It is, but I need to, because I had a hunch this wasn't a single-vehicle accident, and I needed to see it with my own eyes." She sat up straight and looked into his pinched face. "What did you find? . . . Is there anything of use back there?"

He took a deep breath. His eyes never wavered from hers.

"Well? What did you find? Were the state police right, or —"

He shook his head. "I don't think so. I think it's just as you suspected from the beginning." He turned away and stared off into the distance.

"You mean . . . he *was* murdered?" The words caught in the back of her throat, and she leapt to her feet. "Crap! Now, six months later, how on earth are we supposed to catch this . . . this murderer? Why couldn't they have just listened to me in the first place?" She pounded her fist against the top of the guardrail.

"I can't and won't make excuses for fellow officers, but my guess is that they had no evidence of foul play and filed their report based on his apparent speed and the road and visibility conditions at the time."

"But the skid marks should have been enough proof that there was foul play, don't you think?"

"Maybe, but as they said, it had been foggy, and the rubber marks could have happened anytime. There have been a lot of near misses on this curve, and . . . some that weren't lucky, like your father."

"I know, but —"

"The best I can calculate, the other vehicle sped up behind him and followed side by side, nudging him onto the shoulder in a couple of spots where I found faint signs of skid marks. By the time they reached the top of the incline, here" — he pointed to the shoulder in front of the repaired guardrail — "they must have been traveling pretty fast. I'm guessing your father was trying to get in front of him but didn't know about the switchback at the top. Then, right here, two skid marks appear to collide, and, well . . . that's where it looks like your father's car left the road."

Her face crumbled, and tears stung her eyes.

"Come on, let's head back. There's nothing more we can find here. It's been too long for any evidence of proof to survive. We'll" — he cleared his throat — "*I'll* just have to do it the old-fashioned way."

"What way is that?"

"Put in some footwork and find the evidence elsewhere." He offered a weak smile and held her door open.

"You're not getting rid of me that fast, mister." She frowned up at him as she settled into her seat.

She heard him chuckling as he closed the door and walked around to his.

"Look, Marc. If you think for one minute that I'm going to let this go . . . well . . . well you've got anoth— What? What's so funny?"

"The look on your face." He snorted. "You are the most confusing and stubborn woman I've ever met."

"Yes . . . so I've been told." She folded her arms and glared at him.

He smirked and shook his head.

The return trip to Greyborne Harbor was quiet, but the air was no longer filled with uncomfortable tension. Addie stared out the window, lost in her thoughts, and tried to put all the pieces of her father's death into perspective. Her mind darted from one recent occurrence to the other. When they pulled into her hotel parking lot, she turned to Marc.

He glanced sideways at her. "What?"

She opened her mouth to speak, but shut it.

"If you want to say something, then please just say it. The tension between us has been unbearable, and I can't stand it anymore." He parked and turned off the ignition.

"It's just that . . ."

"Come on, you can spit it out. I've never known you to hold back before."

"Okay . . . here goes. Tell me if I'm nuts." She chewed her bottom lip.

He hung his head. "Not exactly the direction I was hoping this would go, but — go on."

She took a deep breath. "Okay . . . how did my aunt Anita die?"

"Your aunt? Why?"

" 'Cause . . . I'm wondering now if it's all related."

His eyes widened, and his mouth dropped open.

"You know. My break-ins, Blain's murder, my father's?"

Marc leaned his head back and frowned

but didn't say a word.

"Well, what do you think?"

"I'm thinking, and I'm not sure what I think. I guess I haven't thought your aunt's death might be related." He turned his head toward her. "What on earth made you think it could be?"

"It would make sense if it were." She excitedly leaned toward him. "Think about it. My father had just left her place, and he was run off the road and killed. A week later, she dies. I inherit her complete estate and now I'm plagued with break-ins. So it appears that someone is looking for something they think I'm in possession of now."

"But what? So far nothing's been missing in these break-ins. It's all so random."

"I know, and at first I thought it was someone trying to run me out of town for . . . well, who knows what reason . . ." She waved her hand. "None of that matters now when you look at the whole picture."

"What picture? Your dad dealt with some shady types. It could have been any of a hundred people. Your aunt was old and sick —"

"I know, I know." She waved off his excuses. "But when you consider all the links and start connecting them, doesn't that tell you there might be more to a few random break-ins than first thought?"

His eyes narrowed, and he straightened in his seat. "But are they connected?"

"I think so, yes. Everything that's happened here . . . maybe isn't as random as it appears. I think, given everything, someone is looking for something specific — and has been for a while now."

His lips tightened into a thin line. "I don't think I can agree, because as far as I know, your aunt died of natural causes. Her doctor was there. And after all, she'd been sick for years and was in her late eighties. That can't be a link to anything else."

Her cheeks puffed out, and a loud, exasperated sigh escaped her lips. "Was an autopsy done?"

"No, I don't believe so. No need, given her age and declining health."

"So no one looked for anything suspicious?"

"No, her physician just signed the death certificate. That's usual in these cases."

"Hmmm."

"I know that look. You are nuts if you're thinking what I think you are." He sat upright and stared at her.

"I am her only surviving relative, and . . . yes . . . I guess I am."

He slapped his palm to his forehead.

"Really? You want me to get a court order to exhume her body and have an autopsy performed?"

"Yes."

"Oh, Addie, Addie, Addie, what am I getting int—"

She jumped when his cell phone rang.

He reached over and looked at the caller ID. "It's the station. I have to get this, sorry."

"I'd better go anyway. Thanks for today," she murmured, then closed the door and headed for the hotel entrance.

"Addie, wait." He called through his open window.

She turned around and he waved her back.

"What?" She leaned forward and gripped the partly open window edge. "What is it, Marc? Another break-in?"

He shook his head and looked up at her, his face ashen. "Raymond James was just found dead."

Chapter Twenty

"What? Raymond's dead?" She swayed and grasped the side of the car.

"He was found by the weekend cleaning staff at his office tonight."

"I can't believe it. But how?"

"Don't know yet, but I've gotta go."

She nodded and bound around the front of the Jeep to the other side.

"Hey, where do you think you're going?"

She flung the passenger door open and popped her head in. "With you, of course."

"No, no way."

"Why not?"

" 'Cause I can't take you to an active crime scene, that's why."

She pursed her lips. "Well, okay. I guess you're right, but promise you'll call me as soon as you get any details."

He nodded. "Will do."

"Thanks." Her brow furrowed as she watched him pull away.

When she entered the lobby, her mind was on what she knew about Raymond James, which wasn't much. He had been her aunt's lawyer for many years and was the executor of her estate. Her gut gnawed at her. She knew this was somehow related to everything else that had happened.

She pressed the elevator button, stood back to watch the overhead light indicator, and waited for it to reach the main level. She tried to refocus her thoughts on the fact that her new employee would be starting in the morning and she'd have to be ready to train her. A familiar voice echoed across the lobby. She spun around in time to see the old woman who had been in her shop earlier this week. She and the taller woman who had been browsing that same day were walking arm in arm into the hotel restaurant, chatting amiably.

Addie's eyes narrowed. She took a deep breath, strode past the front desk, and looked up at the clock behind the clerk. It was past seven and had been a while since she'd eaten lunch with Serena. She stood on tiptoes and scanned the restaurant, easily spying the two women. She selected a table that was hopefully near enough for her to hear their conversation but stay concealed from their view by a large fake palm plant.

The server came over and took Addie's order for a seafood salad. When she left, Addie peeked around a palm leaf. Another woman had joined the first two. There was something familiar about her, but with her back to Addie, it was impossible to tell what. She strained to see better, but it was no use. There was no way to see the woman's facial features without putting herself at risk of discovery. She sipped her water, keeping her eyes on the three women. Although she was too far away to hear their conversation over the din of the other diners, she could tell by their body language that they were very familiar with each other.

A server approached their table, and the new woman held her menu to the side and pointed to something on it. The waiter wrote down her order, and took her menu. It was still no use. Addie couldn't see her well enough to identify her.

In exasperation, she took a big gulp of water, and then the server returned. He stood behind the woman and asked her something. She nodded and turned her head toward him to reply. Addie choked on her mouthful of water. "Catherine Lewis?" she sputtered, water spilling down her chin.

She set her water goblet on the table and

took a deep breath. She was certain the old woman had told her she was only visiting in Greyborne Harbor. Was it Catherine they were here to see? When she thought about it now, there was still the possibility that her initial gut instinct, which maybe she'd been too quick to dismiss had, in fact, been correct, and that the old woman, or the younger one, did take her keys from the drawer. Because right after that Catherine had shown up at her store, and tonight she was here having dinner with them. Could she be involved with whatever was going on, too?

Nonsense, she thought. Marc had told her Catherine was well known and liked in the community. She was bound to have friends outside Greyborne Harbor who would visit her. Besides, it was quite possible the other two women were innocent of her suspicions.

Her cell phone vibrated. Addie glanced at the call display.

"Addie? I can't say much right now," Marc whispered, "but we need to talk. I'll meet you in your room in about an hour," and then he hung up.

Addie stared blankly at her phone. He'd sounded so cryptic it sent a chill racing through her. She looked back at the three women and decided she wasn't going to find out anything else about them tonight unless she followed them when they left. But Marc was on his way, so that would be impossible now. Besides, it was probably nothing. She knew she needed to talk to Catherine soon and try to find out more about her and how she knew these women.

"Is this the person you were looking for?"

Serena's head appeared around the palm. "Yes, thank you," Serena said, nodding at the server, and she plopped down into the seat across from Addie. "I've been looking everywhere for you."

"I didn't expect to see you tonight. Is everything okay?"

"Yes, I just wanted to check in and see how your day went." Serena grinned.

"Would you mind sitting here?" Addie patted the seat beside her.

The server's brow shot up, but she took the menu she had begun to set at Serena's spot and placed it at the setting beside Addie's instead, then filled Serena's water glass.

"Okay." Serena switched chairs. "I'm not eating. Just a tea, please." She handed the menu back to the young server.

The waitress nodded and left.

Serena turned to Addie. "What's up with this cloak-and-dagger stuff?"

"I'm trying to stay hidden from a couple

of people in the dining room."

Serena frowned. "Anyone I know?" She leaned forward, peeking around the palm into the main room.

"Remember the old woman and her accomplice who I thought may have taken my keys?"

"Yes." Her brow creased as she scanned the room.

"They're by the window. See, the gray-haired one sitting beside the one with darker hair, with their backs to us, and the tall woman facing us who I thought was —"

Serena gasped. "The tall woman facing us is the woman who came in looking for the knockout tea."

Addie's mouth dropped open. "You're kidding?"

"No, I'd remember that face anywhere. She really creeped me out."

"Do you recognize the other woman they're with?"

"Not too sure. I can't see her face. Who is it?"

"Catherine Lewis."

"Catherine? How on earth would she know them?"

"You tell me. You said you'd never seen the tall woman before, yet here she is enjoying a friendly meal with one of the town's most upstanding citizens." Addie chewed on her bottom lip. "Curious, isn't it?"

"I'd say." Serena shrugged. "What do we do, phone Marc?"

"Not necessary. He'll be here in about" — she checked her cell phone's clock — "fifteen minutes."

"Wait, he's coming here, tonight?" Serena's eyes lit up. "I dropped by to see how the two of you got along today after I set you up" — she winced — "but I see it went very, very well."

"No, no, no, it's not what you think. It's business."

"Sure." She grinned. "If you say so."

"He has something to discuss about a case he got called to after we got back, that's all." She took a sip of water and stared straight ahead.

"If . . . it's that innocent, then why are you so defensive?"

"Can you please give it up?" Addie banged her glass down on the table.

Serena rolled her eyes. "If you insist."

"No, seriously, it's a case that might be linked to everything else."

Serena looked away and surveyed the room. "If you say so."

"Look, Raymond James," Addie said, her voice dropping to a faint whisper, "was found dead in his office tonight."

"What?" Serena shot around in her chair and stared at her.

Addie nodded.

"Wow, this is getting so weird."

"You'd better believe it. And I think it's about to get even weirder." She eyed the three women across the room.

Chapter Twenty-One

"I'm bored," Serena groaned and started flipping through all the television channels a second time.

Addie checked her phone's clock and sighed. "Well, he is an hour later than he said he'd be. If you want to leave, go ahead. Tomorrow is Monday, and we have to be up early for work."

"No, I'll wait. I want to hear what he has to say about Raymond's death."

"I know. The anticipation is driving me crazy." Addie gazed out the window into the parking lot below. "Oh, Catherine's just leaving."

Serena jumped up. "What color car does she drive?" She peered around Addie's shoulder.

"Looks like she's heading for that white or silver SUV. I can't really make out the color in the dark."

"Yes, no black sedan." Serena moaned and

flopped back across the foot of the bed. "Does any of this make sense to you? I know I'm lost."

"Me, too. There's too many pieces that don't fit."

"I know, like me being charged with murder."

"Don't worry, we'll figure out who and what's behind this and get your name cleared of any suspicion. I promise."

"I hope so. Even though the charge has been stayed for now, if they don't find any other leads, it still could come back to me. After all, I was furious with him when I went to his office, and Martha attested to that." Serena flung her arm over her forehead and moaned.

"I just know we'll figure this out. My gut tells me it's all related."

"But how? I'm not seeing it." Serena sat upright. "What could your break-ins have to do with Blain getting murdered, and now Raymond?"

"We don't know yet that he was murdered. He was older, and maybe he had a heart attack or stroke. We have to wait and see what Marc says."

"You're right." Serena flopped back onto the bed.

"Although, if it was natural causes, why

did Marc say we have to talk and want to speak in my room?"

"Maybe he has something else on his mind?" giggled Serena.

"Stop it." Addie playfully slapped Serena's foot.

"Ouch, you bully." Serena bellowed.

"Am not. You're just a pain." Addie smirked and checked the time. "I wonder where Marc is." She tapped her phone on the tabletop. An email alert pinged. "Maybe this is him." She checked her email. "No. It's from Suzanne, Jeremy's assistant." She read the message. "Hmmm, pretty vague."

"Did she say anything about the books you sent him to be appraised?"

"No, she didn't mention them." Addie shrugged and set her phone back on the table. "She said she just heard from him and he's been tied-up with *business*, but everything should be resolved shortly and he hopes to be back in Boston soon." She frowned and reread the message. "Weird."

"What is?"

"Well, when I called her the other day, she said he was called away on an emergency, something to do with his sister, but now she referred to it as business."

"That kind of thing does happen. What's weird about that? If Marc needed me, I'd be off in a flash."

"Except for the fact that he's never mentioned to me before that he even had a sister, and I've known him for over five years. Don't you think family would've been something he'd mention, at least once?"

"How close of friends were you? Maybe he's the type of guy who doesn't share personal stuff with the people he works with."

"We were friends. He helped me through a lot after David died, and I'm not sure I'd be half-sane today without his support at the time."

"Okay, but did you ever ask him about his family?"

"I'm pretty sure I did, because he said we were very much alike, alone in the world now."

"Maybe they weren't close. Some siblings don't have great relationships and only need each other in a crisis, like I need Marc now." Serena chuckled.

"Maybe, but you and Marc seem to have a great relationship."

"Yeah, but only when he doesn't pull the big-brother crap on me."

Addie chuckled and bit her lip, gazing out the window. She realized that she really didn't know much about Jeremy outside the office. Serena might be right. It was more of a comradely colleague relationship rather than a true friendship, as she had been thinking of it. Why would he discuss family with her? "There's Marc in the parking lot now." Addie leapt to her feet. "He looks upset."

"Should I leave? He said he wanted to talk to you. He might get more upset if I'm here."

"No, stay put; you're involved in all this, too." She patted Serena's foot as she walked past the bed toward the door.

"Okay, but if he gets mad, I'm outta here."

"That's fair. Let's see what he says first though."

"Hi." Addie opened the door. "Serena and I were just watching some television."

He peered into the room, rubbed the nape of his neck, and strolled inside. He stood near the foot of the bed, staring down at Serena.

She propped herself on her elbow. "Hi." She smiled timidly and waved.

He sucked in a deep breath. Addie closed the door and stood beside him. "What is it? You're as white as a sheet."

He slumped down on the bed beside Serena. She bolted upright. "What's wrong?"

He propped his elbows on his knees and

fumbled with the ball cap in his hands, took another deep breath, and stood up. He planted his feet squarely and looked down at his sister, a wave of regret crossing his face.

"As an officer of the law, I'm bound to ask you this." His voice cracked. "Where were you today between four and six p.m.?"

Addie gasped. Serena jumped to her feet.

"Why, what's going on?" Addie grabbed his sleeve and turned him toward her. His face was drawn and pale. He looked back at Serena.

"I have to know. Please answer," he barked. "Now."

"I . . . I . . . I was at Mom and Dad's for dinner. You can call them." She pulled her phone from her pocket, her hand quivering as she held it out to him.

"Thank God." He sighed as though he'd been holding his breath and leaned back against the television cabinet.

Addie placed her arm around Serena's trembling shoulders. "Marc, why on earth would you question Serena like that?"

Marc walked over to the window and stood staring into the parking lot. "Because of" — he slumped into one of the chairs — "of Raymond's death. At first, it appeared to be natural causes. The cleaners found him sitting drooped over his desk when they went in. There weren't any initial signs of foul play, but I detected the subtle scent of perfume in the air. The cleaning staff was all men, and none of them were wearing cologne. I called Raymond's assistant, Barbara, to see if she had been working today, but she'd been out with family. She did verify that it wasn't unusual for Raymond to work Sundays. He liked to prepare for the next week and catch up on billing."

"Okay, but what does this have to do with your sister?"

His jaw tensed and his lips pursed tight. He took a deep breath. "There was also a cup of half-drunk tea in front of him. When I picked it up and smelled it, the scent was familiar, but there was a slightly unpleasant odor to it. I couldn't make it out, but I found a recently opened bag of loose-leaf tea sitting on the side table. It had the same basic scent, but without the strange odor."

"So he had some tea, so what? Lots of people drink tea," Serena muttered.

"I know, but it was a brand from your shop and had your red label on it."

Addie seethed and walked over to him. "You're saying Serena poisoned his tea? That's crazy, and you know it."

"I know it is." His teeth clenched. "But

the perfume I smelled was the same one Serena wears." He glared at Addie and stood up.

Her cheeks burned and she looked away.

"Do you think I liked having to ask my sister where she was tonight when someone was murdered?" He stomped past her toward the door.

"I'm sorry, Marc. I shouldn't have questioned you."

"No, you shouldn't have." He stopped at the closed door and stretched out his neck and shoulders, turned around, and looked at Serena huddled in a ball on the bed. "I am sorry, Serena." He walked over to her and sat down, rubbing her back. "But I have to cover everything as a possible lead. I know you know that."

She looked up at him and nodded, sniffling. "It's just not fair that because of some common perfume and a bag of tea from my shop, I'm now on America's most-wanted list again."

He laughed and hugged her. "I'm so sorry. I know I didn't handle it well. I knew it would be hard on me to have to ask you that."

Addie slipped onto the bed next to him and smiled. "Why don't you start at the beginning and tell us exactly what you found? It sounds like you're pretty certain this early in the investigation that it was murder. Don't you have to wait for a coroner's report or something?"

"Yes, which is what delayed me so long. When I suspected the tea, combined with the perfume scent in the room, I called the coroner's office. They had someone they could send out, and he took samples of the tea and blood and ran them through a preliminary tox screen."

"They can do that?"

"It's not conclusive, and it takes a couple of days for the actual screen to be finished, but it showed enough irregularities in his system and in the tea for a preliminary finding of a toxic substance. We'll know in a few days exactly what it was."

"Did they do an air sample, too, to identify the perfume?"

"He did, but said it probably wouldn't be irrefutable, but . . . I do know it's the same as Serena's. I gave it to her for her birthday."

"I can't be the only person in town who wears it." Serena huffed and crossed her arms.

"I'm sure you're not." Addie leaned across Marc and patted her knee.

"Look, sis, you have a strong alibi for today, so there's no charge here now. I just had to ask."

She smiled weakly and nodded.

"Maybe . . . someone's trying to set her up," cried Addie.

Serena's eyes widened and she jumped to her feet. "Yes, that's it."

"After all, with one murder charge already against her, she'd be the perfect one to throw suspicion on, wouldn't she?"

Marc stroked his chin and looked at her. "You may not be far off with that theory, Addie."

"Yeah, and in the meantime, I look like a deranged killer on the loose." Serena clicked her tongue and strode to the window.

Addie looked at Marc. "What kind of tea was it?"

"The Heavenly Delight blend. Why?"

"Because I think there is something to that. With that other charge hanging over her, it would sure take the heat off anyone else."

"I sell a lot of Heavenly Delight, so that's not a lead. It's my most popular blend. Even . . . wow." Her mouth fell open.

"What?" Addie leapt to her feet.

"Even Catherine Lewis bought some a couple of weeks ago."

Chapter Twenty-Two

It was past nine and still no sign of Paige. She'd been asked to arrive fifteen minutes early so she could be shown the opening routine. As the minutes ticked by, Addie resigned herself to the fact that the "Help Wanted" sign would have to be posted in the window again. She hadn't seen this coming and had thought at least one of her problems had been resolved.

How she could have been so wrong about someone? What if her other instincts were off, too, and none of what was happening was connected, even though her gut told her it was? What would Marc and Serena think of her if she had been completely wrong about everything? Perhaps it was just as the Boston police had told her about David's murder and these were all crimes of opportunity, not linked to anything else.

Addie retrieved the sign from the storage room and took it back up to the window.

When she leaned into the bay window, she caught sight of Paige, who appeared to be having a heated discussion with Martha. Paige's arms flailed about her, and Martha stabbed her finger into Paige's chest, sending her tripping backward. Addie dropped the sign and rushed to the door.

It flung open before she could grab the handle, propelling her backward into the end of a bookshelf. The hanging sale rack crashed to the floor, and the books toppled onto her head.

"Oh, no," cried Paige. "I'm . . . I'm sorry." She leaned over to help Addie to her feet. "Are you okay?"

Addie took her outstretched hand and managed to stand up. She winced when pain shot through her butt cheek from landing hard on one of the rack's metal shelf edges, but she stretched her back and dusted off her slacks. She glanced at the undamaged rack behind her and returned her gaze to the sniveling girl hovering in the doorway, her eyes wide with fear.

Addie laughed. "Don't worry about it. I learned an important risk management lesson for the work site: don't place sale displays by the front door."

Paige's wild eyes darted from Addie's smiling face to the books strewn over the floor. "You're okay with this? I'm not fired?"

"Of course not; like I said, it's taught me an important merchandising lesson. Come on, let's get you freshened up and ready for your first workday."

Confusion crossed Paige's face as she strode toward the back with Addie.

"There's a lot for you to learn, as I expect I'll be called away from the store from time to time, and I'll need you to be able to take charge when I am."

Paige's brow furrowed, and she looked back at the shelf on the floor and then, again, at Addie. "I don't get it. First I'm late. Then I almost kill you. And you're not upset?"

"Hey, don't sweat it — unless, of course, it was all intentional?" She raised her brow and glanced at her.

Paige vigorously shook her head.

"Then there's no problem. Life happens." She shrugged and pointed her toward the small washroom in the back of the storage area. "I'll be out front when you're ready."

Paige heaved a sigh. "Thank you," she said, her voice a cracked whisper as she disappeared into the restroom.

When Paige returned, Addie had the mess cleaned up and was busy ringing in a customer sale. She glanced over at her and smiled. Paige was fresh-faced and appeared eager to start her orientation.

As the morning progressed, Addie found her to be a fast learner, even though there was really nothing difficult in the work itself. It was basically familiarizing her with the store and walking her through the different sections and rows, showing her how the books were displayed according to their genre. Paige caught on quickly, and Addie was relieved. The real time-consuming process was in teaching her the computerized cash system and showing her how to use the register's various program features. When it came to customer service, Paige was a pro, and Addie stood back and watched her take on her sales role as if she had been working there for months, not hours. She only required occasional assistance on issues like how to search for an out-of-print book a customer was looking for or how the book consignment system worked.

Addie noted her protégé sagging and checked the time. "Oh my, you must be starving." She slapped her forehead. "I got so wrapped up in showing you the ropes, I forgot to give you a break."

"That would be great. My head's swimming with information, and my stomach's growling. I hope none of the customers heard it?"

"I didn't, so don't worry, run along. Take an hour, and get some fresh air, too. It looks like a beautiful day out there."

Paige grabbed her bag from under the counter and headed for the door but stopped and spun around. "What about you? You're the boss. You should eat first."

The door chimes rang, and Serena bounced through the door, carrying two small paper lunch sacks.

"I think that problem's been solved." Addie beamed. "You go. See you in an hour."

Serena acknowledged Paige as she swept past her, but the expression on her face was none too friendly. "How did the spy make out this morning?" she whispered.

"She's not a spy, and she's *fantastic.*" Addie scoffed and took the bag lunch Serena held out for her.

Serena plopped on a stool at the coffee counter and tore into her lunch, glancing up through her thick eyelashes, her face grim.

"What's the matter? I know that look. What's on your mind?"

Serena puffed out her cheeks and heaved a deep sigh. "Nothing." She took a bite from her sandwich but kept her eyes fixed on Addie.

"I'm getting really uncomfortable with this. What is it you want to say?"

Serena slowly laid her sandwich down on the counter. "It's just that I'm afraid she's going to hurt you when you find out she's been sent here as a spy for Martha and her troop, that's all." She tapped her fingers on the counter.

"Don't worry." Addie reached across over and squeezed her hand. "I'm fairly sure that's not what's going on."

"But how can you be sure? Martha's conniving."

"Because I don't think she's happy about Paige working for me. That's how I know."

"Did Paige tell you that? Just be careful. It could just be to throw you off."

"No." Addie shook her head. "I saw something this morning."

Serena's eyes widened. "What did you see?" She leaned closer.

"Paige was late, like over forty-five minutes late, and —"

"On her first day? The nerve of her." Serena's mouth fell.

"That's what I thought, too, so I decided to put the "Help Wanted" sign back in the window, and that's when I saw it." Addie's eyes held a glint of the slyness she was feeling, and she took a bite of her sandwich.

"Come on, stop it. Stop teasing me. What did you see?"

"Well . . ." She swallowed and took a sip of her cold coffee and winced. "I really do need to make a fresh cup. Give me a minute, will you?"

Serena's hand grabbed hers. "Not a chance — tell me."

Addie laughed and sat back down. "Oh, Martha and Paige were having a huge argument out on the sidewalk in front of Martha's place. Martha actually thrust her finger into Paige's chest hard enough to send her flying backward."

Serena's eyes grew to the size of saucers and she leaned in.

"Then Paige came rushing in crying, really upset."

"Did she tell you what they were arguing about?"

"No, and I didn't ask."

"What? Why not?"

"Because it's none of my business, and if she wants to tell me, she will." Addie shrugged and took the last bite of her lunch.

"So that's it. That's what you're basing your assumption on. They were arguing about Paige working here and not something else?"

"Yup." Addie stood up. "Now can I make a fresh cup of coffee?"

"Pfft, and I thought you had an instinct for this detective stuff."

"I do. I have a *feeling* Martha isn't happy about Paige working for me, and that's what she was mad at her for this morning, so I think I'm safe from Paige spying on me."

"Yeah." She shook her head. "But only if Martha doesn't figure out first how to use Paige and her new position to her advantage."

"Then we have to make sure we wrap up this whole mess so she can see I'm not a bad person and am no threat to her before that *might* happen, won't we?" Addie winked.

Chapter Twenty-Three

Addie and Serena cleared off the counter after their lunch. A burst of excitement built in Addie's chest and raced up through her cheeks when Marc's smiling face appeared at the window. Her reaction didn't seem to go unnoticed by the prying eyes of her friend, who stuck out her tongue and giggled as he walked through the door.

"What? What are you two up to?" He glanced from one flushed face to the other smirking one as he tucked his patrol hat under his arm and planted his feet firmly in a stance commonly taken by police officials.

Serena shook her head. "Absolutely nothing, Officer." She winked at Addie. "Well, I should be off, got a business to run. Not all of us have *hired* help." She flashed a fleeting look at Addie and headed for the door.

Paige came in as Serena brushed past her. Serena gave her a wary smile, and then she looked back at Addie, her head cocked and brows raised.

Addie huffed. "See you later, and thanks for lunch." She shook her head, feeling impatient with Serena's incessant misgivings about Paige and her true intentions.

"You're back early. I don't think you've been gone even half an hour?" But her question was lost. Paige stood silent, her eyes fixed on the back of Marc's head.

He turned around and looked at her hovering near the doorway. "Hi, Paige." He nodded. "Haven't seen you for a long time. How's it going?"

She was speechless, and all she did was nod back at him. Addie thought she looked as though she were about to bolt. "Paige, do you know my friend Marc?"

"Your friend?" Her tense face appeared to relax somewhat.

"What? Is Addie such a horrible boss that you didn't think she could possibly have friends?" Marc chuckled.

"Yes, well no, of course not, but I thought . . ."

"You thought what?" Addie's eyes narrowed. She was curious to know how her employee viewed her.

"It's just that my . . ." She cleared her throat. "My mom said you were a troublemaker and were into some pretty bad stuff in Boston and now the troubles followed you here."

"That's nonsense," cried Marc.

"That's what I told her, too, but then when I saw you here, I figured . . ."

Addie took a deep breath. "You figured what?"

"Umm" — Paige's eyes dropped — "that maybe she was right. I'm sorry."

Addie shook her head and clicked her tongue. "No worries; we're all entitled to our own thoughts. I just feel bad that your mother has such a low opinion of me."

"I tried to tell her she was wrong, that you were one of the nicest people I've ever met."

"And what did she say?" Marc smirked, his eyes narrowing.

"She said you'd do nothing for me except to take me farther down with you." Her voice drifted to a whisper.

Marc huffed and shook his head. "Well, I think I've heard enough of this slander." He shifted his weight on his feet. "Addie, the reason I came by was because I heard you had a very efficient assistant working for you now" — he smiled at Paige — "and I was hoping I could steal you away for a few hours. There's something I want to show you."

"Of course. Oh, wait a minute." She looked at Paige. "Do you feel comfortable working on your own for a couple of hours, or is that asking too much on your first day?"

"If you think I can, then I know I can." She beamed.

"That settles that. It'll be a good test for you, and if you pass it with flying colors, I'll even throw in an immediate dollar an hour raise."

"Wow, that would be great. I promise, I won't let you down."

"I know you won't. I have faith in you."

"Thanks for trusting me. Wow, this is fantastic." She almost appeared to skip down the aisle as she headed toward the back of the shop.

Addie laughed and looked at Marc, who was shaking his head.

"What?"

"That's a big increase in one day, don't you think? But hey, you're the boss."

"She really proved herself today, and it's worth it. Plus if you keep dragging me out of here all the time, she deserves some extra responsibility pay." Addie retrieved her handbag from under the counter. "Paige, we're off," she called, heading to the front of the shop.

Paige came to the front of the store, a wide smile across her face. "I have your cell number. If I have any questions, can I call?"

"Yes, most certainly, don't hesitate. I'd be upset if I found out you needed help and didn't ask for it," Addie called back from the doorway and headed to Marc's car parked at the curb.

He opened his patrol car door for her, and she nodded her appreciation. She glanced at Martha's shop window and was met by an unmistakable look of contempt. She shuddered and turned to Marc as he fastened his seat belt. "What have I ever done to that woman to make her dislike me so much? I've just recently met her, and we've never really even spoken."

Marc peered down through her side window and was struck by the same look from Martha. He shrugged. "With her, it could be anything, but my guess is because you're an outsider and have now claimed the rights of the town's oldest family. She'll eventually get over it. I hope."

"I do too. I feel like I'm walking on eggs shells all the time with her." Addie glanced back at the now unoccupied window. "Where are we off to? I was so happy to have an opportunity to leave the shop and not have to close it down, I didn't even think to ask."

"You'll see." He smirked and flashed a sideways glance at her.

"Come on, can you at least give me a hint?"

He pursed his lips and frowned, opened his mouth to speak, and then closed it. Then he bit his bottom lip as though he was thinking. "Umm, well. Nope, don't think so."

She laughed and playfully slapped his arm. "Thanks for nothing. How do I know I haven't been kidnapped?"

He pulled over to the side of the road, shut off the ignition, and turned toward her. "If that was the case, then I'd have driven you farther away than two blocks." He winked and got out.

"What? We're here?" She slouched down and peeked up at the building they were parked in front of. "This is where we're going? Raymond's office?" She rushed to meet him on the sidewalk. "But why? I thought you didn't want me around here."

"I didn't, and you shouldn't be, but it's not an active crime scene anymore."

"But you said to leave investiga—"

He waved both his hands in the air. "I don't like it, but Barbara just called me and said she found something that might involve your cases, and you seem to be involved in everything one way or another anyway, whether I like it or not."

"You hate me interfering."

"Yes, I do. I'm not happy about it. Some things are better left to the police, but I've come to see that *maybe* you might be right about a few things." He winked and held the door open to Raymond's office for her.

"Marc, thanks for coming by." Barbara approached them from behind the front reception desk.

In contrast to Barbara's casual appearance on Addie's previous visits to the office, today Addie thought she looked exactly like a legal assistant out of a 1950s movie. Her graying black hair was pinned up in a tight topknot, making her birdlike features look more like those of a stern librarian type. However, her usual warm smile lessened the severity of her dour face today.

She cordially greeted Addie and led them into the back office. "I discovered the missing file this morning when I was trying to finish last week's billings and then pack them up for storage." She gestured to the half-emptied file cabinet. "I thought I better not touch anything else until you came and could check for more fingerprints or something."

"You're right. That was good thinking. I'll have to get the crime scene team back. I guess we cleared the area a bit too soon."

She wrung her frail white hands and looked over at Addie, who was making her way to the file cabinet. "It seems such a shame, dear. I don't understand it. Why you?"

Addie stopped and stared at her. "Why me what?"

"It's your file that's missing."

"Mine?"

"Yes, and I don't understand where it could have gone. I just worked on the latest billings to your account last week and Ray — um, Mr. James was going to review them along with those of some other clients yesterday. That's why he was working, so he could approve the account billings, and I could post them today when I came in. I know yours was here on Friday, along with some others. I put them all on his desk before I left for the weekend."

Addie stepped back from the cabinet and looked at Marc. She could feel the color draining from her face. He nodded a quick look of understanding and pulled a notepad out of his shirt pocket. He scribbled something into it and looked up at Barbara. "I'm afraid I'm going to have to restrict access to the offices again."

Tears filled Barbara's eyes, and Addie's heart ached for her. "You and Mr. James were close, weren't you?"

Barbara nodded and dabbed her eyes with a tissue she pulled from her sweater sleeve. "I worked for him for over twenty-five years."

Addie placed her arm around the woman's shoulders. "I know this is hard on you, but have you noticed anything else missing today? You know, since the police let you back in."

"Not really. I stopped looking when I found those missing files," she choked.

"*Those* missing files?" Marc interjected. "Did you discover other files missing?"

"Yes," she nodded. "Miss Anita Greyborne's is gone, too."

Addie's brows shot up.

"Your file was kept in front of it in the cabinet. When I couldn't find yours with the others on the desk" — she glanced at Addie — "I assumed Mr. James had mistakenly put it away, but I still needed to post it to the bank, so I looked for it and found your aunt's gone, too." She shook her head. "I've been in such a daze since I got the news. I'm really not sure what I'm doing." She sobbed openly.

Marc held her hand in his and gave it a gentle squeeze. "I understand Barbara. I think you need a few days off. Since I'm declaring this area an active crime scene again, it will give you some time to process all this."

The site of his tenderness toward this distraught woman sent Addie's heart racing. Except for the night they'd shared a kiss, she'd rarely glimpsed this gentler side of him.

"Addie, since this is again an active crime scene, I'm going to have to ask you to leave immediately."

Her mouth dropped open, but she looked at Barbara's tear-blurred eyes and closed it.

"You don't mind walking back to your store, do you?" He wrote something in his notepad.

She bit her tongue and nodded. "Barbara, please let me know if there's anything you need," Addie said, retreating out the door.

"Thank you. I will."

She heard Marc behind her asking Barbara a few more questions as she swept by the reception desk. A flash of yellow on the computer monitor caught her eye, and she stopped. She leaned over and peered at the sticky notes papered across the bottom of the screen and gasped.

"Barbara, can you come out here for a minute, please?" she called.

Chapter Twenty-Four

"Barbara," Addie said, pointing to the sticky notes, "is this your handwriting?"

"No, it's Mr. James's. Why? Is it important?"

Marc glanced at Addie.

"Yes, it might be." She bit her lip in thought. "But I'm not sure."

"What does this have to do with anything?" Marc leaned closer and read the notes. "I don't see anything written here that might be related to the case."

"Maybe not, but . . . would it be okay if I took one with me to check something out?"

"What are you thinking?"

"I don't mind if the chief doesn't. They aren't anything important . . . now." Barbara choked back tears. "Mr. James didn't like computers, so he'd leave me a note when there was something he wanted me to do for him." She blew her nose. "I'm sorry." She sobbed and turned away.

Addie patted her arm. "That's okay. I know this is hard for you. But I'd really like to take one." She looked hopefully at Marc. "It doesn't matter which one. You pick."

He looked at her, his mouth set. "I can't do that — everything, anything, could be evidence."

"Please. I'll give it back. I promise. You can even put it in one of those plastic evidence bags, and I won't touch it. I just really need to check something out."

He let out a deep breath and shook his head. "I guess it would be all right. I don't see anything there that would be of use to the investigation, but I want it back today, and . . . I hope you're going to tell me what you think it means."

"I will. Come by when you're finished here to pick it up." She smiled as he placed one of the notes in an evidence bag and handed it to her.

"Guard this with your life."

"I will, promise." She turned to leave, but a file on the desk caught her attention.

"Barbara, what's that folder?"

"It's just some invoices I still have to file in the proper client folders. I got a bit behind recently."

"Humm. Anything of mine in there?"

Barbara's forehead creased and she

opened the folder, flipping through the documents. "No, I don't think . . . wait. Here's one of your aunt's." Her brows knit. "I wonder how I missed filing this? It's from over a year ago." She pulled a page from the bottom of the stack and handed it to Marc.

He studied the paper and looked up at Addie. "Well, this answers the question as to why your house security system was never installed, only the fire."

"What?" She slid around beside him and peered down at the invoice.

He rubbed his forehead. "Looks like Raymond declined the home security install. See, he had to sign here" — he pointed — "stating he was aware of the risks associated and relieved the company from any liability should a break-in occur, and it's noted that the client insisted on only having fire protection alarms installed." He looked at Barbara. "Do you remember anything about this?"

She took the paper and studied it. "Yes." Her brow creased. "And at the time I thought it was strange, but Raymond said he didn't want Anita wasting her money."

"How would that be wasting?" Addie scratched her head.

"He said there was more chance of that old house catching fire than her being broken into in this town."

Addie shot Marc a look and opened her mouth to speak.

He flashed her a silencing look. "Makes sense." His eyes filled with an intensity that told her to be quiet.

She stepped back. "Yes, well . . . I'll leave you both to this. I'd better get back to the shop," she said and retreated toward the door.

The tension from Marc's face eased and his stiffened shoulders relaxed.

"I'll talk to you later Marc, and it was nice to see you again, Barbara. I only wish it was under better circumstances." She turned on her heel and prayed her steady walk would mask the confusion roiling inside her.

She made her way down the two blocks back toward her shop, then made a detour along the backside of Town Square and popped into the toy store. The shop was small but filled with learning tools and games, and when she spotted the object of her search, she grabbed it and headed for the checkout counter.

"You're in luck today," chirped the spiky-haired salesclerk. "That's on sale. We don't get much call for blackboards these days. Most everyone wants the new whiteboards. There's still one or two of those on the back wall if you're interested."

"No, this will be fine. It'll be perfect for my project." She paid and tucked the three-by-four wooden-framed board under her arm as best she could before she opened the door.

Addie stepped out onto the street just in time to see a black sedan speed by, make a U-turn at the far end of the street, and then swing into a parking spot halfway up the block.

She strained to see the make and model of the sedan, but it was impossible from this distance. Her awkward purchase made walking a struggle, and she slowly made her way in the direction of the black car, but the board kept slipping. She stopped to rearrange it, attempting to carry it in front of her, but the bottom frame bounced against her shins, and she switched it back to its previous underarm position. When she peered up at the sedan again, a familiar-looking woman hurried out of the travel agency office and darted across the street. She hopped into the sedan's passenger side. It pulled out and headed in Addie's direction. She squinted and focused on the far side of the car as it drew closer. When it was almost parallel to her, she had a clear view of the passenger. Her mouth fell open, and her breath caught at the back of her throat.

"Sheila?" The car made a sharp right turn and drove right past her shop to Main Street. "Arg, arg," she cried. "Why didn't I focus on the driver, too?" A man passing by her on the sidewalk glanced sideways at her, arched his brow, and chuckled at her outburst. She smiled meekly at him and hurried her pace back to her store.

Breathless, she struggled to open the door. Paige came running to her rescue and held it for her. "You're back early — and what's this for?" She picked up one end of it and helped her carry it to the storage area.

"It's for a project I'm working on," Addie said, smiling. "How did it go on your own?"

"Fine, great, I think. There were a couple of small book sales, and a woman came in with some books she wanted to sell. I told her you'd get back to her."

"Sounds good." Addie nodded her approval as they walked back to the front of the shop.

"And Catherine Lewis came in. She left a note for me to give you when you got back."

Addie took the small envelope, ripped it open, and read the short, hand-scrawled invitation for tea after Addie closed the shop today. She frowned and folded it up, sliding it into her jacket pocket. "So you didn't even miss me. That's good. It means I can sneak out more often." She laughed and dropped a pod into the coffee brewer. "Want one? You're due for a break."

"I'm actually a tea drinker."

"Then why don't you go get one from Serena's and take a break while you're at it?"

She shuffled her feet and grimaced. "Well, I'd rather not go into Serena's."

Addie stopped midway through the motion of retrieving her cup of coffee and stared at her. "Why on earth wouldn't you want to go into Serena's? I hope it has nothing to do with her murd—"

"That's not it. It's, it's just that, well . . . I don't think she likes me very much."

"Of course she likes you." Addie shook her head and smiled. "She likes you just fine. She's just had a bad go of it lately, that's all. Besides, she's my friend, and you're bound to see a lot of her around here."

The door chimes rang, and they both glanced up. "See, what did I tell you?" Addie chuckled. "Now go, shoo, take at least half an hour. You didn't take a full lunch break."

"That's 'cause I felt guilty about being so late this morning."

"Look, take what I'm giving you now. Some days it might be too busy for either of us to take any breaks."

"Hopeful wishing." Serena plopped down into one of the leather chairs.

"Don't get too comfortable; I've got something to show *and* tell you. Come to the back with me," she called over her shoulder, heading for the storage room.

She could hear Serena mumbling as she struggled out of the deep, comfy chair. "But I'm tired, Addie. I just want to curl up in a ball and go to sleep. What's so important?" She slithered around the corner into a rickety chair intended for the dump.

"Ta-da." Addie smoothed her hands around the edges of the blackboard.

A look of confusion flashed across Serena's face. "What's it for?"

"It's my crime board."

"Your what?"

"You know, a crime board, something I can use to keep track of all the suspects and try to establish links between them."

Serena yawned. "You watch too many police shows."

"Maybe, but I know my dad and David used them, and they were a great help in keeping track of who, what, where, when and why." Addie hammered a nail into the drywall. "Here, give me a hand hanging it."

"Now what are you two up to?" Marc's voice boomed from the storage room doorway.

Addie jumped and dropped her end of the board. "My God, you scared the life out of me." She pressed her hand to her pounding chest.

"You probably didn't hear me come in over all that noise. What's that for?" He jerked his head at the blackboard.

"This," Serena said, taking on the mannerisms of a game-show hostess, "is Addie's new detective tool."

"That's what I was afraid of," he groaned. "Don't you think you should let the real police do their job?"

"I'm not trying to do your job, honest. But there are so many unanswered questions. It can't hurt for me to try and put some of the pieces together, can it?"

He shook his head and glanced at Serena. "I suppose you're giving her your full support in this amateur sleuthing venture, and you know how dangerous it can be. Dad was a cop, me, your cousin Bruce?"

"Of course I know." Serena scowled at him. "But . . . maybe I am . . . yes, definitely I am." She moved beside Addie in a show of solidarity.

Addie peeled off the box of chalk taped to the side of the frame. "I was starting to lose track of who's who and what they might mean in my cases and to the murders, so I thought this little tool would help us . . . umm . . . me, keep track."

"You do know we have a whiteboard at the station and do the same thing there?"

"I know, but I don't work there and can't see yours, so I needed to make my own, because the list of players just got one more addition today." She wrote one word on the board and stood back.

"Sheila? Now I'm lost." Mark combed his hair with his hand. "That's not a name you've tossed around before. Who's she?"

Serena gasped. "Isn't she the woman you worked with in London?"

"Yup." Addie nodded smugly.

"But how? And why her?" Serena frowned, looking at the name.

"I don't know the answers to that yet, but when I left the toy store today, she was the passenger in the same black Honda sedan that tried to run me over and has been following me. The same one I saw at my house."

Marc stood back and stared at the board, rubbing his chin. "And you're certain this was the same woman you knew in England?"

"Positive. The car raced right past me and I caught a good look at her."

"Did you see the driver?"

"No. I was too focused on the passenger, because when I saw her getting into the car from a distance, I thought there was something familiar about her. Besides, I could only see in the front windshield. The side windows were tinted too dark."

"This car has been stalking you and tried to run you down. Why wouldn't they see you on the sidewalk?"

"I don't know. They looked like they were in a hurry, and they were talking and the blackboard was under my arm and might have shielded me — who knows?"

Serena moaned and rubbed her temples. "I guess we do need this board to keep track of the suspects. I know the list is growing too long for my little head to keep straight."

"That's how I feel. Everything has been happening so fast, none of us have had time to process any of it and look at how all of it's possibly connected."

"But if I may remind you two ladies, this is police business, and *if* there is a link, we will find it."

"But have you? Have you considered all

the suspects and what might link them to two and maybe even four murders and the break-ins?"

"Well, we haven't had time, and as you said, it's been happening so fast and seems pretty random at this point."

"Exactly my point. What if, like I said before, they're not random, and there is a link?"

"Well, it is possible." He looked at the board and shook his head. "I guess."

"What does it hurt to be proactive and look for means and opportunities and possible links on my own?"

"Because things like this are better left to professionals — and besides, what are you going to do with the information?"

"Give it to you, of course . . . if anything turns up, that is."

"Addie, this could be dangerous. There's already been two —"

Paige popped her curly head around the door of the back room. "Sorry to interrupt, Addie, but Brian's here to see you."

Addie looked at Marc, exasperation across her face. "Okay, thanks. Tell him I'll be right there."

"Will do." She disappeared back into the store.

"I hope he's got good news for me." She

looked back excitedly at Marc and Serena. "Not that the hotel is horrible, but it would be nice to get home."

Chapter Twenty-Five

Addie swept into the storage room. "Fantastic, the alarm system will be installed in the morning, so that means I should be sleeping in my own bed by tomorrow night." She stopped short. Her eyes darted between Marc and Serena. "What is it? Why do you both look so glum?"

"How about angry?" Serena glared at Marc.

Addie winced. "Okay . . . 'angry' is a good word for it. What's up?"

Marc turned away. Serena's eyes bored into his back. "He was just playing big brother again."

He spun around on his boot heel. "I am worried, Serena, that's all."

"I'm a big girl now, Marc. I'm twenty-seven and don't need you anymore to protect me or tell me what to do."

"In this matter you do." His eyes fixed, unwavering, on hers. "You are still the only suspect in Blain's murder. The charge has been *stayed* for now, not dropped, and going off and getting yourself involved with some half-baked amateur investigation is going to do nothing but put the spotlight back on you in the eyes of the DA's office."

"I would never do anything to put Serena in jeopardy." Addie stepped between them. "And that's exactly why I need to start looking at all the possibilities here and how there might be connections."

"Then let the truth come out the way it's supposed to, Addie. Let the system do its job."

"And what happens if the *system* doesn't come up with another suspect, or it takes years until it does, and the attention stays on Serena?"

Marc's face fell with exasperation. "It won't. The truth will eventually come out."

" 'Eventually'? That's the problem. What happens in the meantime? She remains a prime suspect the rest of her life?"

"That won't happen. Something will turn up soon."

"Good, but in the meantime . . ." Addie picked up a piece of chalk and stepped up to the board.

He shook his head. "You're determined to do this, aren't you?"

"Yes." She planted her feet firmly. "I promise no investigating on my own, *and* I won't involve Serena for anything other than an extra set of eyes and ideas." A sly smile curved the corners of her lips, and she peered at him through her lashes. "I swear. And we'll report anything we figure out directly to you."

The tension on Marc's face softened, and he nodded. "Promise, no actual investigating. Keep it to the blackboard?" His eyes pleaded with her. "After all, it's one thing if I share something with you at a crime scene, off the record, but completely another if you run off on your own to investigate it."

Addie held her fingers up in a Scout salute and nodded. "I promise, just looking at suspects, means, motives, and links."

He heaved a heavy sigh. "Then I guess I can see no harm in this. Carry on." He shook his head and chuckled. He sat down on one of the boxes of books and stared up at her attentively.

She straightened her shoulders and beamed at Serena.

"Well, go on." He motioned to the board. "I'm curious to see what pieces you've got and how you've put them together." His eyes twinkled with amusement. "Who knows, maybe you can teach the police how to do their job."

She ignored him and turned to the board, pointing at the name written there. "First question: why is someone I knew in London here in Greyborne Harbor?"

"Maybe she came to see you. After all, you said you worked together for six months and she started to get friendly with you just before you left. Maybe she missed you?" Serena piped in.

"But why wouldn't she have checked with me before booking a flight across the Atlantic Ocean?" Addie pursed her lips and studied the name. "And why is she traveling in the same car that's been stalking me and tried to run me over?" She shook her head. "Next question: who are the two women from the shop and why were they having dinner with Catherine Lewis, *and* how are they related to each other?" She wrote on the board, then turned to look at Marc and Serena.

Marc shrugged. "It's a small world, and it's probably not related."

"Okay, but they stay on the board until we can prove otherwise."

"Don't forget to put Blain down as a victim." Serena covered another yawn.

Marc stroked his chin in thought. "Well, I think Andrew is a person of interest, even though the DA has refused to follow that lead so far."

"Yes, and what about Martha?" Serena pointed at the board. "Add her; she seems to have it in for you."

"Well, we can put her name here as a suspect for the break-ins, maybe, but there's no way she killed Blain. She was at her store." The chalk squeaked as Addie added Martha's name to the growing list.

"But if we add Martha," Marc said, frowning, "we'll have to add half the townspeople who have had any dealings with Addie since she's been here. She can probably come off."

Addie nodded and erased Martha's name. "This doesn't give us much in the way of suspects so far. We have Andrew and the mysterious Sheila, and no connection." Addie tapped the board and added, thinking out loud, "Except Andrew did spend the last ten years in Europe."

"Maybe there is a connection we just don't know about." Serena jumped up, took the chalk from Addie's fingers, and drew a line between Sheila and Andrew's names.

Addie paused, nodded, and looked at Marc. "Do you think Sheila could be a link to the smuggling ring Blain was apparently part of?"

"I think we need more evidence. At this point, we're not even certain there is a smuggling ring."

"I know, but logically, just think about it." Addie rubbed her chin. "How could a department store merchant like Blain Fielding in little old Greyborne Harbor have gotten his hands on so many rare books and antiquities?"

Her eyes widened as Marc moved toward her. She held her breath as his thumb stroked just under her bottom lip.

"You have a little bit of chalk right here." His gaze seemed to penetrate her.

"Guys, I'm still here," Serena chirped from behind them.

He jerked his hand away as if he'd been burned. Clearing his throat, he backed away and sat back down on a box. "I . . . ah . . . think it's a possibility. No one knows what Andrew was up to in Europe all those years. Blain never talked about it."

Addie could still feel the pressure of his thumb. Ordering her heart to quit quivering, she continued as if nothing had happened. Because it hadn't. "So we have a lot of unknowns: the two women from my shop, Catherine Lewis, Sheila, Andrew, the black Honda, the antiquities smuggling." Addie tapped her foot, staring at the board.

"Oh, and we can't forget," she said as she started writing, "three break-ins; one verified murder, Blain; my father's suspicious death; my aunt's death; and Raymond's untimely death. Who" — she kept writing next to his name — "just happened to be executor of my estate. What are we missing so far?" She stood back and studied the names. "Oh, the fact that Raymond didn't feel it was important to have a security system installed in my aunt's house . . . which, looking at all this" — she stepped back, eyeing the board — "seems strange to me."

Serena wiggled excitedly on her crate. "What about the Alice in Wonderland book that was stolen from your shop — you never did find it, did you?"

Addie's eyes narrowed as she stared at the board. "No, I didn't." She shook her head. "But I don't think that's important. It wasn't worth much, a few dollars maybe; certainly not enough to justify breaking into my shop for. Besides, it might still be in one of those unpacked crates you guys are sitting on. No, there has to be something else we're missing."

Marc's phone rang. "Sorry, it's the station; I've got to take this." He stood and moved to the far side of the storage room.

"What are you thinking?" Addie glanced sideways at Serena.

"Besides the fact that you and my brother would make the cutest couple ever?" At Addie's withering look, she wiped the grin off her face. "Well, add the strange tea request made by the tall woman and your keys being found *mysteriously* outside your shop."

"And Catherine Lewis buying the same tea as Raymond was drinking when he died." Addie wrote excitedly. "And . . . her inviting me to come for tea today."

"What? When did she invite you?"

"This morning. She came in when I was out and left a note with Paige."

Serena's eyes widened. "Plus she knows the two women." She pointed to the chalk writing. "So it could be something."

"And . . . she knows Raymond and would have easy access to him." Addie examined the board. "Well, we don't have much so far, do we?"

"No, and Raymond's death hasn't been ruled a murder yet." Serena's eyes jumped from one name to the other. "But this is a start. At least we can keep everyone straight now."

"That's what I'm thinking, too. We can add more when we think of it or something new develops." She looked up when Marc rejoined them. His face looked strained. "What's wrong?"

He rubbed the back of his neck and stared at the blackboard. "I think we have a few more things to add."

Addie's eyes narrowed. "What's happened? Your voice sounds ominous."

Marc plucked the piece of chalk out of Addie's fingers.

"What are you doing?"

"Well, I guess" — he started writing, bits of chalk exploding with the pressure — "you can add . . ."

Addie stared at the board as he wrote. "Request . . ."

He paused and looked down at her, his face rigid, uncertainty in his eyes, then he let out a deep breath and started writing again.

Over his arm, she read aloud. "A . . . court . . . order . . . to . . . exhume . . . aunt's body?"

She grabbed his jacket sleeve. "What did you find out?"

"Another early report came back from the coroner's office. It seems the coroner who attended Raymond's crime scene also tested for organics and herbs, since the suspected poison, if there was one, might have been administered in the tea, and there was a hit."

"What was it?" Addie leaned closer.

"Foxglove." Marc and Serena replied in unison.

Marc's eyes bulged, and he looked at Serena.

"I knew it," she cried.

"How would you know that?" He eyed her warily.

"Because when the tall woman came into my shop, she was looking for something to help her husband sleep. She said he hated fruity-tasting teas and wanted something almost tasteless and odorless."

"Really." Marc looked at the tall woman's sparse profile on the blackboard.

"And she did mention that he had a heart condition and couldn't take regular sleeping pills." Serena took a breath. "I told her about the usual — you know, chamomile, hops, and valerian — but she didn't seem interested. The next thing, she was digging for information about belladonna and hemlock and stuff." Serena's gaze shifted from Addie to Marc. "I was shocked and told her those were poisonous and I'm not into that. I told her that I only blend teas and maybe she should talk to a witch."

Addie's mouth dropped. "You never told me exactly what she said she was looking for, just that it was weird."

Serena's shoulders rose. "I didn't know it would be important then. It was just creepy at the time. I know I never told her anything, because I don't know a lot about poisonous herbs and plants, only enough to stay away from them." She shivered.

"Well, someone gave her some information, apparently." Marc slammed his hand against the board. "There were high levels of foxglove in Raymond's system. The coroner just told me it's like digoxin, a heart medication, but in the wrong dose it can cause a heart attack that will easily be mistaken for natural causes unless you're specifically looking for it. It's virtually undetectable, especially if the victim already has heart issues and is on other medications, as Raymond was."

"Lucky thing you and the coroner clued in to the odd aroma in the tea, isn't it?" Addie stepped back and surveyed the crime board, glanced at Marc, and stopped herself from rubbing her chalk-covered fingers across her chin. "And you think perhaps my aunt was killed the same way?"

He nodded. "It's possible. Her death was ruled to be from natural causes, since she was sick and on other heart medications. There's only one way to tell."

Addie's eyes narrowed, her mind reeling with the information. "But why kill a sick old woman?" She bit her lip. "The killer was looking for something, obviously, and thought my aunt had it. I guess the easiest way to search for it would have been to get rid of her. That way he could slip in and out of the house and not worry about being caught." She sat down hard on one of the book crates and groaned.

"It could be a *she*," Serena whispered, looking at the list of names.

Marc rubbed the back of his neck, stretching it out.

Addie stared at the board. "You're right. What do you think?" She glanced at Marc.

His eyes creased around the edges. "Whoever it is thinks you now have what they are desperate to get their hands on, and they're quite willing to kill to get it." His gaze danced from Addie to Serena.

Addie looked up at him from her perch and cocked her head to the side. Her brow rose. "Come on, Marc, spit it out."

He frowned, his lips tightening.

Serena smirked. "Someone's about to deliver another lecture."

"Can't a guy just think? Jeez," he muttered. "But since —"

"Ah, here it comes." Serena leaned forward, her chin resting in her hand.

Marc shook his head and looked at the blackboard. "It's just that . . ."

"Yes. We're waiting." Addie tapped her foot. "What's on your mind?" She rolled her eyes.

He surveyed the blackboard, then turned and looked from one woman to the other, his face drawn.

"Come on, just say it, Marc. You're still worried this is too big for us amateurs to wrap our heads around." Addie stood up and walked over to him. "And you're afraid that with everything we have here, it might put us in danger from whoever the killer or killers are? Right?" She looked up at him and their eyes locked.

He placed his hands on her shoulders. "If we can connect all these dots together in the back room of a bookshop, and the killer or killers find out, you two could be in danger, do you understand?"

Her heart hammered in her chest. She wanted him to hold her close and make all this disappear. She opened her mouth to speak. He placed his finger over her lips.

"Addie, I think this is big, really big — FBI and Interpol big. You have to be very careful."

"We will be." Serena leapt to her feet.

"Here, I saw this before when I was helping Addie clean up after the first break-in." She pulled a painter's drop cloth off the top shelf of the broom closet. "We can keep the board covered with this." She held it up. "No one but us will ever see it."

Marc raked his hand through his hair. "I guess it'll be a start."

"It's perfect." Addie took it from her. "And just the right size to keep away prying eyes."

"I want you both to swear to me," Marc said, looking steadily from Serena to Addie, "that you won't tell anyone what you have here. No one, understand? Not even Paige. We aren't certain who else could be involved and can't take any chances."

Chapter Twenty-Six

"I'd better get back to the station and call the coroner and get the court order for the exhumation." He smiled and turned to leave. "I almost forgot." He looked back at her, his brow creased. "Why was it so important for you to take one of Raymond's sticky notes?"

She slapped her hand to her forehead. "I'll be right back." She dashed to the storefront and returned waving a postcard. "This!" she announced smugly, grinning and handing it to Marc.

Marc glanced at it and looked up at her. "What's this besides a nice picture of a key?"

"Look at the back."

He flipped it over. " 'Be careful'?" His eyes narrowed. "What does it mean?"

"Look at this." She retrieved the evidence bag from behind her back. "A perfect handwriting match."

Marc studied the sample against the note

on the postcard and looked at her. "I need to get this analyzed by our handwriting expert."

"I *am* a handwriting expert."

"Since when?"

"Since college. Part of the job as a researcher is to analyze the authenticity not only of old and rare books but also of ancient manuscripts, which are all handwritten. You have to be able to tell the clever copies from originals."

"Well, well, Miss Greyborne." His head bobbed as he studied her face. "You and your many talents never cease to surprise me."

"I told you I could be useful." She winked. "And" — she pointed to the sticky note and the postcard — "this is an exact match. Raymond knew something and was trying to warn me."

Serena peered over Marc's shoulder at the picture of a key in a red silk-lined box. "Wow, I wonder what the key means?"

"That's what we have to find out now." Addie wrote the word *key* on the blackboard and drew a line to Raymond's name. "There." She stood back, looked at the scribbles and lines, and crossed her arms.

"What are you thinking now?" Marc leaned closer for a better look.

"I'm now thinking that whatever the killer has been looking for . . . the key is the answer."

"Or it's the key itself," piped in Serena.

Addie nodded. "You know, you might be right. We just have to figure out what it opens."

Marc's phone rang again. "Damn, I've got to go. I'll be in touch as soon as I hear anything else." He flashed them both a look of warning and plucked the evidence bag from Addie's fingers. "I'll take that back now, thank you, and you two stay out of trouble." He turned around at the doorway and called back, "Do you hear me?"

Addie saluted. He shook his head and disappeared out the door.

"Now what?" Serena scanned the board. "I don't feel like we're any farther ahead, except that I have all the names straight now."

"We start by the process of elimination. That's what I do in my research, and it seems to work well."

"But how do we eliminate any of these people? We don't even know how they're connected."

"We have a couple of obvious links so far, and they might lead us to others. I'm going to start by calling Catherine Lewis and accepting her invitation."

"Be careful. Remember what Marc said." Serena frowned. "And you promised no investigating on your own."

"I'm not investigating." Addie winked. "I'm going for tea."

A few hours later, Addie made her way up the winding sidewalk of Catherine's nineteenth-century, two-story, saltbox house to meet her and the friends she had mentioned on the phone that she wanted Addie to meet. Flower beds that were probably beautiful in the summer wound around the span of the house and carried down the sides of the front walkway to the street. She peered up in time to see the curtains flutter in the window and knew she was being watched. She knocked and waited, and waited and knocked again. After several minutes of silence, she tiptoed through the flower bed, crunching dead stems as she walked, and peeked through the window where she'd seen the curtain moving. The panels were parted a few inches, and she pressed her face to the glass, cupping her hands around her eyes, and squinted into the darkened room.

She gasped. Catherine lay lifeless on the floor. She fumbled for her phone and dialed

911. In moments, she heard the sirens heading in her direction, and the next thing she knew Marc was at her side and officers were surrounding the house.

"She needs an ambulance, too." She turned to him, tears burning behind her eyes.

He held her shoulders and looked into her pinched face. "They're here. They've gone in with my men," he murmured.

She could feel the rapid pounding of her heart and took a deep breath, the aroma of his aftershave calming her. "I'm okay. It was just such a shock to see her lying there. I talked to her not two hours ago."

The door opened, and two paramedics wheeled the stretcher out. Addie stared at Catherine's ashen face. It was almost lost against the white sheet of the transport trolley, but the stark contrast of the blood-stained dressing around her head was too much. Addie bit the inside of her cheek to fight back her tears.

She straightened herself and looked at the paramedic. "Is she . . . is she dead?"

The paramedic shook his head. "Unconscious but alive."

"Thank God." Addie gripped Marc's jacket sleeve. "Do you know what happened? I mean, it was only minutes since I saw the curtains move, and she was looking forward to my visit."

"I don't know yet." Marc shook his head. "I'll have to go in and take a look around. Will you be okay waiting out here?"

She nodded, and he moved toward the house.

"I'll be back as soon as I can see anything that might give us a clue." He turned and looked at her from the door. "You stay put, do you hear me?"

She nodded and sat down on the step. Her head in her hands, she tried to think back to what Catherine had said to her on the phone that might give her some clue as to what happened. Then she jumped to her feet and dashed into the house.

"Marc." She stopped short at the living room door when his eyes flashed her a warning.

"I thought I told you to wait outside." He finished taking a swab of the coffee table corner.

"I just thought of something." Addie's gaze went to the three teacups on the coffee table. "But I see you already know it." Her eyes widened at the chaotic state of the room. She spun around and looked at the dining room behind her. The buffet drawers were tossed on the floor, their contents scattered about the room. She looked back at Marc.

"What is it?" He rose to his feet and strode toward her.

She fought to compose herself, realizing the crime team's eyes were focused on her. She bit her lip and looked at Marc. "Nothing. I came to tell you I know she wasn't alone." She cringed under his glare.

"I know."

"She told me that there were a few others here already and wanted me to stop by for tea, too, on my way home."

He looked back at the cups of half-finished tea. "Did she tell you who was here with her?"

Addie shook her head. "No, she was really vague, and I didn't press her. I just thought I'd wait to see who it was when I got here. Oh, she also mentioned she had something important to give me."

"Did she say what it was?"

Addie shook her head. "Only that she was really looking forward to seeing me again, that we had a lot of catching up to do."

Marc rubbed his hands over his face.

"I know. I never met her, as far as I know, before last week, so I don't get it." She bit her lip. "Is it possible she was mentally unbalanced or something?" She looked up at Marc.

"Pftt, not that I know of, but I guess unless you were close to her, you wouldn't know."

"Maybe she's confusing me with someone else?"

"Chief," an officer called from the living room doorway, "what do you make of this? I found it under the sofa."

Addie peered around Marc. The officer was holding two pieces of a heavy crystal vase. What looked like blood appeared to be smeared across the base portion.

Chapter Twenty-Seven

Addie tossed and turned. It seemed as though if it wasn't the hard hotel bed, it was too bright in the room from the parking lot lights shining through the window, or it was the ice machine rattling at the end of the hall, or the elevator bell, or one of a hundred other things — but Addie knew better. Names from the blackboard swam through her head. There were too many suspects, not enough links, and worst of all, no obvious motives. She watched the minutes pass on the bedside clock much like a countdown on a bomb. Her fear was it might come to exactly that if she couldn't figure out soon how all the pieces fit together. There'd be an explosion, and somebody else would end up dead.

When the morning light did stream through the curtains, Addie was perched on the side of the bed drinking a cup of coffee and staring at the clock. She shook her head and stumbled into the bathroom in hopes that a shower would revive her and help make this soon-to-be very long day somewhat bearable.

Two trucks — Brian's and one other — were already waiting outside her house when she got there. She hurried and let them in and put on a fresh pot of coffee for the crew. She told Brian to call her when they were finished and she'd be back, and then she dashed down the hall toward the front door. As she flew past the living room, she stopped. She had only been in the house once since the last break-in, to get fresh clothes, and Marc hadn't given her any time to tidy up the mess that had been left.

Addie stood in the doorway, scanning the ransacked room, and closed her eyes. Her mind went back to the day Raymond had conducted her house tour. When he had slid open the double-wide pocket doors, she'd almost burst into tears. The room was a breath of fresh air. As much as she loved the rest of the house, this room had no remnants of the relic wallpaper. There was a comfy, overstuffed sofa facing the large stained glass window, the furnishings were traditional, and she noted a few antiques dispersed throughout — her aunt's favorites, she'd assumed — but it wasn't formal and ornate. It looked lived-in. She had immediately felt as if she were home.

She wilted against the doorframe. Lived-in was one thing, but this wasn't what she'd had in mind. Her eye wandered to the writing desk, its antique drawers tossed on the carpet, their contents scattered across the floor. Her heart ached. She loved that desk and hoped it hadn't suffered any damage. She walked over to it, her fingers trailing across the desktop, which was ingrained with the fingertips of previous owners gone and forgotten. But not by this desk. It held on to them deep in its grainy wood.

After she moved in, she'd spent hours polishing it to bring it back to its original glory. It was then that she discovered its many hidden compartments and found carved inscriptions on the undersides of the drawers. It made her wonder what the history of it was. Who were those people? What secrets had they kept tucked inside? What love letters had they hidden in it? This desk had a heart, and she could feel it beating under her fingertips.

Secrets. Her chest constricted. "That's it." She began clicking the tiny wooden peg levers in the inside of the now-empty drawer recesses. Hidden trays popped open one by one. She had originally found three that had been filled with small trinkets and a few love notes, but she had a feeling there might be more still to be discovered. Now that she knew what to look for, cracking the puzzle desk might be easier.

She got on her hands and knees, swept the clutter away from beneath the desk, and crawled into the kneehole. She looked back over her shoulder at the sound of a throat clearing to see a bewildered Brian leaning against the doorframe.

"I guess you're wondering what I'm doing down here?'

He shook his head. "It's your house, carry on. But I was surprised to see you still here. Do you need help finding something?"

"Um, no, I was just inspecting the desk. It's an antique, and I wanted to make sure it hadn't been broken the other night when . . . well, when —"

"I get it. Marc told me you've been staying at the hotel since then. Well, I'll leave you to it. Unless you do need anything?"

"No, I'm fine." She smiled. "You carry on. I'll be going soon anyway."

He nodded, and she turned back to the desk and ducked her head underneath the kneehole, her backside waving high into the air. She shivered, and her skin prickled. Was he still watching her? She quickly flipped over and looked at the door just as he disappeared around the frame.

"Men," she mumbled and resumed pushing and prodding at the underside of the desk. Her cell phone vibrated in her pocket.

"Hi, Paige . . . it's what time? Really? . . . I'm sorry. I'll be right there." She bolted straight up and banged the top of her head on a low-hanging drawer rail.

The panel beside it clicked, and a concealed tray popped out. "I knew there must be more." She pulled the tray out of its recess and peered inside. It was empty. Disappointed, she returned it to its slot and crawled from under the desk. She headed toward the door but looked back at the desk one more time. Was the key in the picture the key to open another compartment hidden somewhere in its depths? Or was it to open something else that might be hidden inside it? Not having the time to mull over her questions now, she grabbed her handbag from the side table and dashed to the car.

She screeched to a stop in her parking space behind the store, disarmed the alarm, and darted to the front door to let in Paige.

"I'm so sorry, Paige," she panted. "I had to meet Brian at my house and I got delayed."

"Don't worry about me." Paige smiled,

taking off her coat. "I was worried about you. You know, with all the weird things that've been going on around here lately."

"Yes, 'weird' is a good word for it. Want a cup of coffee?" Addie dropped a pod into the machine and leaned against the counter, trying to catch her breath. "No wait, you told me already that you're a tea drinker." Addie dug into her purse on the counter and pulled out her wallet, retrieved a five-dollar bill and handed it to Paige. "Go next door and get one. It's on me, and buy a treat for yourself, too."

"You don't have to do that."

"I know, but it's the least I can do for keeping you standing outside waiting half an hour. And don't let Serena frighten you. Remember, she's all bark and no bite."

Addie went behind the counter, put her bag away, and scratched her head. She was certain she had a plan for Paige today, but couldn't think what it was. She pulled a notepad out of the drawer to see if she'd jotted anything down yesterday, but it was no use; her mind was as blank as the pad. "I guess no sleep tends to do that," she muttered, fixing her cup of coffee and taking a big gulp as Paige returned, tea in hand.

"Cheers." Paige toasted her cup and took a seat on the other side of the coffee bar. "I was thinking . . ."

"Yes?" Addie studied her.

Paige flashed a smile, then shifted in her seat. "Well, I was thinking it would be a good idea if you trained me to open the store. You know, just in case something comes up again and you're running late."

Addie palmed her forehead. "That's what I was trying to remember. Yes, you were late yesterday, and we never did go over the opening procedures."

Paige appeared to relax and sipped her tea.

"Let's get started." Addie smiled at her and pulled an instruction manual out of the drawer beneath the cash register.

They went through the security system manual, and once again, Paige proved she was a quick study. The only dilemma Addie was left with in the end was the problem she had with giving Paige the keys to the store so soon after she'd started to work for her. She needed another plan.

"I'll be right back," she said to a startled-looking Paige and darted out the door, heading to SerenaTEA.

Addie dashed back from Serena's shop just in time to see a red-faced Martha exiting Beyond the Page. She glared at Addie and slammed the door. The chimes jingled in protest. She stomped toward her door, huffing and wheezing as she went.

Addie flew through her door to find a very calm Paige placing new stock on a bookshelf, a satisfied smile on her lips.

"Are you okay?" Addie approached her, afraid the girl would erupt into tears as per usual.

Paige looked at her, confusion in her eyes. "Yes, why?"

"Umm, well . . . I saw . . ."

"Mom was in here, trying to bully me into quitting."

"And?"

"I stood up to her and asked her to leave and told her she wasn't welcome in here until she apologized to you."

"Really? Wow. That's kind of you, but I don't want to come between you and your mother."

"You're not, don't worry. There's a lot more wrong between us than me working here." Paige picked up another stack of books from the cart. "There's no room for these. Do you want me to display them on the trolley? If customers see them, they might sell faster than if they're sitting in the back room waiting for shelf space."

"Great idea." Addie looked at her as a smile tugged at the corners of her mouth.

"You're a very smart young lady."

Paige beamed and began organizing the top of the trolley as a display unit for the extra books.

"Just in case I'm not here to unlock the door, Serena will have a spare key to let you in when you need it."

Paige nodded and smiled.

Addie went back to the counter, downed the last of her now-cold coffee, and placed another pod in the machine for a fresh cup when the phone rang. Paige raced past Addie and picked it up before the second ring. Addie shook her head and laughed. The girl's energy today was impressive. She appeared to be handling the phone inquiry as well as though she had worked there for months.

A pile of books on the floor between the two window chairs caught Addie's attention. She started to pick them up so she could re-shelve them, but then she noticed Marc's patrol car parked outside and a somber-faced Marc heading for her door. Addie tapped on the window. His eyes lit up, and her heart surged. She cursed the warm blush sweeping across her cheeks as he stepped inside. She glanced at Paige, who was leaning on the counter, chin in hand. She grinned as her eyes flitted from Marc to Addie.

Addie squared her shoulders and walked toward him. Her knees trembled. Why did this man have such a profound effect on her?

"Would you be free to join me in an excursion, Addie?" He glanced over her head to Paige, who clapped. "There, Paige said it was okay. Get your handbag."

"Do you mind telling me where we're going?" She ignored Paige's thumbs-up as she retrieved her purse and handed it to Addie over the counter.

"Catherine is awake, and she asked to see you."

"Me? Why?"

"I don't know. 'Danger' was all she mumbled."

Chapter Twenty-Eight

A burly police officer nodded at Marc when he and Addie came around the corner from the nursing station. Addie swallowed hard at the sight of an armed guard outside the room. Maybe the danger Catherine had spoken of was real and was coming after her, too. She couldn't help but remember this woman had bought the same variety of tea Raymond had been drinking when he was poisoned, and a shiver ran through her. She looked at Marc. He nodded. She took a deep breath and pushed the door open.

The curtains were drawn, making it difficult for her to see Catherine in the dim light, but then Catherine's face turned toward her, her eyes brightening. Addie walked to her bedside, took Catherine's cold, frail hand in hers, and smiled down at her.

"It's good to see you awake." She pulled a chair closer to the bedside. "You're looking much better."

Catherine patted her uncombed hair. "I must look a fright."

"Nonsense. For having gone through what you just have, you look wonderful." Addie gently squeezed her hand.

"You're such a dear to say that." Catherine weakly laughed. "But you always were such a kind child. I wouldn't expect anything less of you as a grown woman." A slight smile curved at the corners of her lips.

Addie gulped. "Catherine, that's not the first time you've mentioned knowing me when I was a child."

"No . . . I knew you well." She squeezed Addie's hand.

Addie slowly pulled away and shifted on her chair. "How did you know me? Where? Here or in Boston?"

A faint smile crossed her lips. "Both, my dear. There was a time when I saw you most every week, here and in Boston."

"Then why don't I remember any of it?"

"You were so young, just a child. It was too much for me to expect you'd remember me when I went into your store that day, but you and your father were such an important part of my life for so long, I did hope."

"My father? You knew him, too?"

"We were very close for a few years."

"Close how?" Addie's eyes bored into her.

Catherine took a deep breath and gazed into Addie's eyes. "This isn't the way I planned on telling you," she sighed. "I wanted to do it over tea or dinner, but you need to know, since you're living in Greyborne Manor and the Harbor now." She bit her lip, looked at Addie, and swallowed hard. "I was your father's lover."

Addie felt the color drain from her face. She sat back, her breath caught in her throat, and she choked. "His lover? But how? What about my mother?"

"It wasn't like that. Honest. When we first met, you weren't more than a baby. He was visiting your aunt. Your mother had become very ill by then, and he needed to get away for a few days. It was hard on him to go to the hospital day after day and watch her slowly getting sicker, and him knowing there was nothing he could do."

Addie's eyes narrowed as she looked at this woman who was telling her about a side of her father she had never known and that her mother had died a slow, agonizing death. She leaned closer to Catherine, dreading but needing to hear what she might say next.

"I was at your aunt's house with my

mother. They were very close friends, and we met. He was so afraid and so lonely. We just came together as friends. I swear." She paused and looked at Addie, her eyes searching for reassurance to continue.

Addie's trembling hand reached over and patted hers.

Catherine swallowed hard again. "We visited back and forth, taking you on weekend getaways. I was newly divorced, and it was the perfect companionship for both of us. We were happy, all three of us. You were too young to miss your actual mother — not much older than a toddler — so it was natural you clung to me so much."

Addie shook her head. "No, I wouldn't have. I don't believe you."

Catherine's pale eyes fogged with tears, and she nodded and whispered, "Okay."

"So you were friends." Addie cleared her tight throat and coughed. "My father never mentioned it though. I never knew I had visited here before. I didn't even know I had a great-aunt, let alone a town named after my family. So forgive me for not understanding any of this, or why a friendship of my father's so many years ago plays an important role in my life now." She sat back and crossed her arms, staring at the pale woman lying in the bed in front of her.

"Because you need to know what happened and why you were never told about Greyborne Harbor or your aunt."

Addie leaned closer again and folded her hands on her lap to keep them from shaking. "Go on. What happened?"

"As I said, we were friends for a long time, but . . . the sicker your mother got, and the more time we spent together, the closer we became, and . . . it developed into something more."

Addie clenched her jaw.

"We became lovers." She let out a deep breath.

Addie's head began to spin. She couldn't focus and grabbed the side of the bed. "If you were lovers, why did he never tell me about you?"

"Because it almost killed your grandmother, and it destroyed her relationship with her sister-in-law, your aunt."

Addie sat back. "Why? What happened between them?"

"Your grandmother found out about us and the fact that we'd been involved for some time. She was furious with your father, and then when she found out Anita had known for a few years and encouraged it, they had a horrible fight."

Addie bit her lip, thinking back to her

grandmother and how strict she had been when she was growing up. Addie hadn't been allowed to start dating or even attend a party where boys might be present, so this didn't surprise her.

"Your grandmother was a very dear, sweet woman, but she had strong morals, and when she discovered Michael and I had been seeing each other when your mother was still alive, despite the fact she was so sick and there was no hope, and then when she found out I was a divorced woman, she . . . well, she threatened to take you away from him if we didn't put an end to it immediately. Your aunt was furious and tried to reason with her for your sake, but she wouldn't listen, and they never spoke again, as far as I know." She rubbed her face with her hands and sobbed.

Addie took a tissue from the box on the bedside table and handed it to her. Numbness crept through her body, and her chest tightened. She tried to imagine how horrible that time must have been for her father, being threatened with losing his only child.

"I'm sorry." Catherine sniffled. "It still hurts. You see, he broke it off right then. I didn't see him again until the day, the day he died."

"Wait a minute. You saw him the day he died?"

"Yes." She nodded. "I always lived in hope that after your grandmother passed away he would come back, but he didn't. Then I lived in hope that when you grew up and went out on your own, he would want to see me again." She shook her head and wiped her eyes. "Then one day, out of the blue, he called and said he was in town and needed to see me." She half smiled. "I was so happy. I thought we'd finally be together." Her shoulders slumped. "He wanted to meet for coffee at a small restaurant near the harbor. As soon as he walked through the door, I knew something was wrong, and that he wasn't there to reconnect with me. He looked horrible, his face drawn and pale. His eyes looked, looked —"

"Like what? He looked like what?" Addie grasped her thin arm.

"Afraid. He looked afraid and nervous. He kept watching the door and checking out the window. I didn't know what to think. I had waited so long for this moment, but it wasn't to be."

Addie frowned. "Well, why did he call you, then? Didn't it seem odd after all those years?"

"I was hopeful at first," she sighed. "But it

didn't take long to find out why he called."

Addie leaned forward. "Why?"

"He said I was the only person he could trust and wanted me to know he had dropped off a package for you with Raymond James. That if anything ever happened to him, he wanted to make sure someone else knew Raymond had the package, and I was to make sure it got to you somehow and no one else."

Addie shivered. "What package? Raymond never gave me one."

"I know. I just found that out the day Raymond . . . died." She sobbed and blew her nose. "I always thought that he had given it to you when you first came to Greyborne Harbor, but the morning he . . . died, he called me and asked me to come to his office. It was a Sunday, but I knew Ray often worked weekends, so I thought nothing of it."

Addie's skin prickled. "Was he alive when you got there?"

"Yes, very much so. He was a bit pale, but seemed fine. He gave me an envelope with what felt like a small box inside and told me not to open it. He said it was something he should have given you months ago but didn't. He then said for me to give it to you, and that I was to tell no one I had it. He said you were to tell no one as well."

"Where is it now?"

"I was so confused when I left his office. He seemed afraid of something, almost like your father did that last time I saw him. I went directly home and put it in my secret hiding place."

Addie let out a deep breath. "You do know your house was ransacked the day of your accident, don't you?"

Catherine's eyes filled with horror.

"Which means it's more than likely —"

"No." She shook her head. "Impossible. My hiding place is virtually undetectable. I'm sure of that."

Addie chewed on her bottom lip. "Well, I guess we'd better hurry up and get you well so you can go home and we can see what's in this mysterious envelope." She rose to her feet.

Catherine grasped Addie's hand. "I'm so glad I had the opportunity to tell you about your father." Tears filled her eyes. "I want you to know what a loving and kind man he really was and how important you were to him. Your mother, too. Even after he and I became involved, he still visited her most every day. He truly loved her."

Addie smiled down at her. "I know." She patted her hand. "I know." Tears burned her eyes and she quickly turned and headed to the door, but then stopped. "Catherine, who are the two women you were having dinner with the other night at the hotel?"

"Nobody, really — why do you ask? Were you there?"

"Yes, I saw you with them. I was just heading out, and they looked familiar. I was just curious, that's all."

"They're friends . . . actually, *were* friends" — her voice dropped to a hush — "of Raymond's. They're collectors from Boston and came to town looking for antiques. He said I was the perfect person to show them around and introduce them to some of our local residents who had been known to sell to dealers. Surely you must have met them in Boston?"

"Yes, that's probably why they looked familiar."

"Well, when I first met them, they mentioned you by name and said they were interested in getting together with you sometime during their stay. So I decided to have all of you come for tea so you could chat, thinking you knew them."

Addie winced and sucked in a sharp breath. "Perhaps, but I met so many collectors through my work." Addie bit her lip. "So they were at your house just before I arrived?"

"Yes, we'd had a cup of tea already, and I got up to refill the pot because you were expected shortly, and — well, I must have stood up too fast and . . . then my head felt like it was going to explode and that's the last thing I remember until I ended up here."

Addie flinched, then forced a wooden smile and patted Catherine's hand. "Chief Chandler mentioned to the officer who was here earlier that you thought I might be in danger. What was that all about?"

"The envelope. I mean, your father and Raymond seemed to be so nervous about it, and they both ended up dead. I'm afraid if I give it to you . . ."

"I'm sure it's not cursed, if that's what you're thinking." She smiled reassuringly at her. "Well, I'll leave you to get some rest. We have to get you well soon."

"Thank you, Addie." She turned her head and stared toward the window.

Addie watched her close her eyes. Maybe Catherine was thinking of Addie's father. Well, whatever it was that she was thinking about, Addie's head was spinning, and she needed air.

Chapter Twenty-Nine

Addie teetered into the hallway. Pressing her back to the wall, she took deep breaths.

"Are you all right?" Marc leapt to his feet from the chair by the door.

All she could do was nod.

"Whatever she said, it looks like it's shaken you up pretty badly." He clasped her shaking shoulders.

She stared blankly at him, trying to understand his words. When she opened her mouth to speak, words wouldn't come out.

"You were in there a long time. She must have said something about what happened?"

"She, she said lots, but I'm still trying to get my head aroun—"

"Thanks, Chief, I needed that break." The young officer swept around the corner, a steaming paper cup in his hand.

"No problem," Marc said. "I'm going to take Miss Greyborne back now." He placed his arm protectively around her and ushered her down the hall. "Jerry will be along in a few hours to relieve you," he called over his shoulder.

"Thanks, Chief."

"Oh, and remember" — Marc turned around and stared at the young man — "no one except hospital staff goes in that room. Call me immediately if anyone else tries to."

"Yes, sir, will do." He sat down and pulled a newspaper from under his arm.

Addie looked at Marc. "No visitors? Did you find something out?"

"I'll tell you outside."

Addie took a deep breath. The fresh air relieved the burning in her lungs and the pounding in her head. The information Catherine had thrown at her was way too much, but the one thing that she could focus on now was the gnawing she had in her gut. It told her the envelope was the key to it all, but what exactly was in it, and why were people trying to kill for it? That is what she had to work out. The rest was just too raw and painful to absorb right now, and she breathed deeply, trying to push it all from her mind.

Marc, his brow furrowed, looked steadily at her as he opened the car door. His face was pinched, and his eyes were filled with concern. He reached across her, secured the seat belt, and gave her a faint, reassuring smile. She laid her head back and closed her eyes, thinking he really was a tender man under the staunch police chief exterior.

"It's obvious that whatever she said has shaken you up pretty badly." He fastened his seat belt and turned on the car.

"Yes, yes it has." She gazed unseeing out the window as they pulled onto the road.

Marc made a sudden turn down a side street, pulled the patrol car over to the curb, and shifted into park. "We can sit here for a few minutes if you want before you go back to the shop."

"That's probably a good idea," she whispered and took a deep breath. She could feel his eyes on her as she rested her head against the cool glass of the side window. Despite her best efforts to push Catherine's revelations from her thoughts, her mind kept replaying the news she had shared with her. Everything Addie had known her whole life now seemed like a lie, no matter if it was meant to protect her.

"Serena said once she felt like she already knew me before the day we met in front of my store." She shifted upright and looked at Marc. "Do you know anything about that?"

Marc's eyes narrowed. "I don't know. Why?"

She shook her head and peered out the window again. "It's nothing. Just wondering."

"I think you'd better start from the beginning and tell me what Catherine said to you."

Addie counted to ten, took a deep breath, and then relayed Catherine's story to him. When she had finished, Marc was staring straight ahead, rubbing the back of his neck. He looked over at her, his eyes wide. "And you knew nothing of all this before?"

"No, I'm in complete shock. I understand my father not wanting to share a lost love affair with his daughter, but to find out I had spent a great deal of time here in the Harbor and never knew it is, well, it's . . ."

He grasped her hand and gave it a gentle squeeze. "I'm sure if he had told you, you would have had questions, and the answers would have been too painful for him, so because it was over and she wasn't part of your lives anymore, he just thought it better not to mention it at all."

"You're probably right, and it does answer the question of Serena saying she felt like we had met before, doesn't it? We probably did."

"Come to think of it" — he put his head back on the headrest — "I remember our mother taking us to the playground at the top of the hill by your aunt's house one day. She was reading, and Serena was playing in the sandbox with another little girl. Mom had told me to keep an eye on her, and I was mad because a few of my school friends were there, and I wanted to go off and play with them but had to watch her."

Addie chuckled. "I bet you were a great big brother."

"Well, not really." He scratched his head. "I did eventually run off into the trees to play hide-and-seek, and then I heard Serena crying and my mom calling me."

Addie winced. "What happened?"

"Serena was fine. She toddled over to me and wrapped her chubby little arms around my neck, crying because her new best friend had to leave with her daddy. Mom was furious at me for leaving her alone, and I was grounded for a week." He shrugged. "Guess that's why I remember it so well."

"Well, who knows. Maybe I was the friend she made that day." Addie smiled and put her head back. "But I guess we'll never find out. Just like I'll never know the real reasons my father didn't tell me about Greyborne Harbor."

A slight smile crept across Marc's face. "Attagirl. Let's move forward."

"Right." She sat up straight and looked at him. "We have to focus on what we do know, or at least what we can find the answers to."

"I think a good place to start is with that envelope Catherine told you about. I have a feeling it's more important than we think it is."

"Yes, I've got to get my hands on it, and soon. What did the doctor say about her collapse?"

"That's the thing. He said there was a large external hematoma. A bruise and swelling at the back of her head. She'd been knocked out."

"The vase. I knew it. That means they were still in the house when I knocked. Someone had to have been keeping watch, because I saw the curtains move."

He sat straight up in his seat. "Did she say who *they* were?"

"Yes." She slapped her forehead. "Sorry, I meant to tell you right away, but she said so many other things that my mind's —"

"That's all right." He tucked a wayward strand of hair behind her ear. "I understand."

"I asked her very casually who the two

women were that she had dinner with the other night at the hotel and told her I thought I recognized them from somewhere — because I did. They were the same two women who had been in my shop. When Serena came, she pointed out the tall one as being the woman who wanted to buy the knockout tea from her."

"And they are friends of hers?"

"Only recently; apparently Raymond introduced them to her." She looked at Marc, her mind raging. "He told her they were collectors from Boston, and since she knew everyone in town, she might be able to set them up with some local antique sellers or dealers, and they told her they wanted to meet with me. They even knew my name."

"Interesting." Marc rubbed his chin. "Raymond seems more involved with all this than I first thought."

"Yes, and he called Catherine the same day he died. She said he was really nervous about something and appeared to be afraid. That's when he gave her the envelope for me and said he should have given it to me a long time ago but wanted to protect me."

Marc looked out the window, appearing to be lost in thought. "Whatever is in that package is the key to what's going on. First, your father was afraid and told Catherine about it, then —"

"That's exactly what I've been thinking. Dad's killed, then Raymond gives it to Catherine, and he dies, and then she gets attacked — maybe these two mysterious women are behind everything."

Marc started the ignition and pulled onto the street. "I'm taking you home. You've had a rough day with lots of surprises."

"No, I need to get back to the store. There's something I have to do."

"That's why I'm not taking you there. I know exactly what you have in mind, and it's too dangerous. Stay out of it. Let the police take it from here. Please?" He glanced at her.

"No. Take me to my shop. I just have to check a few things out before I can go home. You know, Paige is there on her own, and —"

He heaved a loud breath. "That'd better be all you're checking out."

"I promise." She crossed her heart and smiled, glancing down at her other hand, where her fingers were crossed.

Chapter Thirty

Addie stood back from the blackboard, studying the names and links she and Marc had identified earlier. Deep in thought, she stroked her hand over her throat and squinted at the white squiggles, trying to get a mental picture of the story they were telling her.

She threw her hands up in the air and spun around on her heel, coming face-to-face with a red-faced Marc. "I knew you were up to something when I dropped you off. I'm so glad I decided to park and come in."

"Well, you can stop worrying. I give up. I can't see how these people are connected except by suspicion."

"Good." He glared. "Now maybe you'll leave it alone and get back to running your bookshop and let me get on with *my* job."

"But, but —"

"No buts. You broke a promise, and you

even crossed your heart on it." His eyes bored into hers.

"Yes, but . . . that's not all that I crossed." She winced and held up two crossed fingers.

His eyes widened.

"So . . . you see . . . it really doesn't count as a broken promise, right?" A slight smile graced her lips.

Marc thudded down onto a box, raking his hair with his hands. "Darn it. You're the most stubborn person I've ever met." He shook his head, stared at the board, and let out a deep sigh. "Well, at first glance, it looks like these people are all connected by the envelope, but we have no idea what the motive is or how they all know each other."

"Did your investigation into Andrew or Blain turn up anything — any connections to the two women?"

"Nothing so far, I'm afraid." He blew out a loud breath and stood up. "I just don't know right now," he rubbed his eyes. "I think we'd better call it a day though and think on it."

"I guess you're right." Addie frowned and looked back at the board. "Besides, I have to go meet Brian soon and then was planning on having dinner with Serena. Have you heard from her today?"

"No." Marc shook his head. "It's strange.

Usually, I get at least one call from her in a day."

"Maybe before I leave I'll pop in and check on her."

"I've got to get back to the station anyway, so I'll look in on her now." He picked up his hat. His brow rose. "Maybe we can talk about all this later. You know, after we give ourselves a break."

"After dinner I was planning on a massive cleanup at my poor house, but you're welcome to drop by and help." She coyly smiled. "We can brainstorm while we work."

"Sounds good. I'll see you there about eight." He nodded and left.

Addie checked her cell for missed messages and sighed when there still wasn't one from Brian to say the work was complete. She walked to the front of the store, surprised to see how busy it was and how adeptly Paige seemed to be handling the customers. Mentally she practiced her see-I-told-you-so dance for Serena before taking over the cash register duties while Paige worked her customer service magic on the floor. Addie's gaze wandered to the window and the street beyond.

"Sheila?" She stared at the tall woman standing at the curbside across the road. "What the . . ." She raced out the door and waved, calling her former colleague's name. A red SUV pulled up. Sheila looked coolly across the road at Addie, slipped on a pair of sunglasses, and got into the passenger side. Addie couldn't make out the plate number, but she knew she'd seen that same car around town before.

"Are you okay?" Serena's voice echoed through her muddled thoughts.

Addie spun around. "Did you see that?"

Serena scanned the street. "See what?"

"That woman. It was Sheila. She was standing right across the street. I waved and called to her, and she just took off." Addie frowned, staring at the corner the SUV had disappeared around. "I can't believe it."

"Why wouldn't she have come over and said hello?"

"Exactly," cried Addie. "Unless she doesn't want me to know she's in town, which makes me think —"

Serena's eyes lit up. "She has something to do with everything that's been going on."

"Bingo." Addie rushed back into her shop.

"Where are you going?"

"To call Marc. I have to tell him about her and the red SUV."

"Let me lock up, and I'll be right over." Serena headed to her store. "Wow, this is getting weirder."

"You said it." Addie swung her door open and raced inside toward the back room.

She fumbled to pull her cell phone and noticed a text from Brian. She pressed reply and said she'd be there shortly. Then she called Marc. To her amazement, he answered on the first ring. Still breathless, she managed to tell him what had just happened. He said he knew a couple of people in town who drove red SUVs, but that he would check the vehicle registration database to make sure and call her back.

Paige popped her head around the corner.

"Hi, what can I do for you?" Addie tucked unmanageable strands of her hair behind her ears and glanced at the clock. "Oh my, it's closing time."

"Yes, and everyone's gone. Is it all right if I leave, too?"

"Yes, yes of course. I'll come upfront and lock the door behind you, then I'll be off soon, too."

"Are you sure? You look a little shaken. Do you need me to stay?"

"No. I'm fine." Addie said walking her to the door. "Serena's coming over, and I have to meet Brian. All's good, don't worry." Addie flashed her a reassuring smile and locked the front door behind her young shop assistant.

She returned to the blackboard, wrote *Sheila, red SUV,* then stood back and studied the other names. "I know the answer is here. But where?" Her fingers traced the white lines and then stopped at Catherine. "God, I've got to get my hands on that envelope. It has to be what's behind all this." She flipped the drop cloth over the blackboard, grabbed her coat and purse, punched in the alarm code, and dashed into the alley to her car.

Serena's head appeared out her back door, and she looked frantic. Addie turned off the ignition and rolled down her window. "What's wrong?"

"A customer just came in, so I can't leave yet. I'll meet you at the Grey Gull at six."

"No problem. I have to meet Brian first anyway. See you then." Addie waved.

Brian wasn't his usual flirty self when she arrived at her house, which was a relief. Dark circles stood out under his eyes, and he kept muttering about slow contractors. She welcomed the reprieve from his constant gaming with her and actually enjoyed his company while he showed her what they had done and explained the features of the new alarm system.

As his car pulled away, she stood at the open door and took a deep breath of the crisp evening air, remembering why she loved fall in New England so much. She leaned her head against the edge of the door and smiled. At the top of her driveway, headlights flashed on. She shivered as the car made a quick U-turn and sped off down the hill. She closed and bolted the door. Someone had been watching her. Even having the new alarm system didn't take the dread away. Her first instinct was to run. She pressed her back against the heavy mahogany door and breathed in and out, slowly focusing on the fact that she was safe. When the initial fight-or-flight instinct had passed, she looked at the alarm box on the wall and reassured herself that this was now a fortress. She noted the time. As per usual, she was running late. She activated the alarm and dashed off to meet Serena.

When she arrived at the Grey Gull, Serena was waiting at a table downstairs by the window. "I'm so sorry I'm late." Addie collapsed into the chair across from her.

"No worries." Serena took a sip of her water. "I was running a few minutes late, too, and was going to call you when I got here, but realized I must have left my cell phone at the store."

"Let's eat. I'm starving." Addie picked up her menu. "God, what a day I've had."

"Tell me about it. I don't think I've ever been so busy since I opened." Serena glanced over her menu and closed it.

"You've decided already? I haven't even had time to focus." Addie laughed and glanced back at the menu. "But it's good that you were busy and the whole murder suspect thing hasn't kept customers away."

"Oh, I'm sure that's exactly why I was so swamped." Serena waved the server over. "People are curious and nosy. Say, you said you saw that woman Sheila on the street?"

"Yes." Addie peered over the top of her menu. "What are you thinking?"

"Is she tall? Auburn hair, swept up kind of?"

"Yes." Addie laid down her menu. "She does wear it like that sometimes. Why?"

"English accent?"

Addie nodded.

"She was in my store today." She cracked her knuckles and smiled.

"No way? Really?"

Serena grinned.

"You are the Watson to my Sherlock. What did she want?" Addie leaned across the table.

"She was very friendly, asked about my tea blends and how I came up with them. But when she was leaving —"

The server approached their table and cleared his throat. "Are we ready to order, ladies?"

"Yes, we are." Serena ogled him and only slightly flinched when Addie kicked her under the table.

Serena eyed him as he walked away. "Hate to say good-bye, but love to watch him leave."

Addie slapped her playfully with her napkin. "You're too much."

Serena laughed. "Well, he's cute. Don't you think?"

"Come on, focus, don't leave me hanging. What did Sheila say?"

Serena leaned forward, and her voice fell to a hushed whisper. "She asked me about the bookstore next to mine and wanted to know if it was a new shop and if it carried rare books or just used books?"

"And? What did you say?" Addie sat back and gripped the edge of the table.

"Of course, I didn't know who she was and told her, you know, thinking hey, a new customer for you? I said that you didn't keep any of the rarer books in the store but had a personal supply."

Without taking her eyes off Serena's, Addie took a drink of her water.

Serena looked down. "I told her" — she

took a deep breath — "I told her, if that's what she was interested in buying, she should go in and talk to you, that you might have something she wanted in your private collection."

Addie sat back in her chair and stared unseeing at Serena.

"I'm so sorry. I didn't know." Her face became pinched and drawn. "I thought I was doing you a favor."

"I know you thought you were helping out my business." Addie's mind whirled with thoughts of Sheila and what she really knew about her, which wasn't much, it seemed. She shook her head. "You didn't know. How could you?"

"I just feel so bad."

"No, don't." Addie sat forward. "I don't think Sheila being here is a coincidence. She didn't want me to know she's here, and knew she'd been found out when I saw her."

"But why keep it a secret?" Serena's eyes widened. "Are you thinking what I am? That she has something to do with the break-ins?"

"Yes. The question is, what is she looking for? And why was she in your store asking questions when she probably already knew the answers?" Addie shook her head and chewed on the inside of her cheek.

Serena sat forward, glancing over her shoulder at the table behind them. Her voice dropped to a whisper. "I think it was that she hoped I'd slip up and tell her something. She did spend a lot of time at the counter with me."

"Maybe. . . . If she's the one who has ransacked my house twice, plus the store, she obviously didn't find what she was looking for, so . . . so she was hoping you'd tell her about another place I might have whatever it is she's after." Addie pounded the table in victory and then looked apoplectically at the couple sitting behind Serena.

"That must be it."

"If it is her, then she hasn't been working alone either." Addie leaned forward and whispered, "I've seen her in the black Honda, and today, a red SUV." She sat back and drummed her fingers on the table. "She has a partner or two."

"Wait, she left in a red SUV? I assumed it was the black car."

"Nope." Addie shook her head. "It was definitely a red SUV; something fancy and expensive looking."

Serena's eyes widened. "What make?"

"I don't know. It sped away so fast I couldn't tell. Why?"

"The only person in town who drives a

fancy, expensive red SUV" — Serena blew out a deep breath — "is Andrew Fielding. He drives a Porsche Cayenne."

Chapter Thirty-One

Addie pulled up behind Marc's Jeep in her driveway. He waved from the porch as she got out and raced up the front steps. "Sorry," she panted, "dinner with Serena ran a bit late."

"No problem." He stood aside while she opened the door. "I just got here myself."

"Not working tonight?" Her eyes skimmed over him, admiring how nicely his jeans hugged his muscular thighs.

"No, finally took an evening off." He chuckled and walked into the foyer. "Did Brian show you the features of the new security system? And you understand how it works?" He took off his jacket and hung it on the coatrack behind the door.

"Yes, sir." She saluted and headed toward the kitchen. "I don't know about you, but I need coffee. Want any?"

"Yes. I'd love some."

"Did you eat? I can make you a sandwich,

if you want."

"No, I'm good, just coffee's fine." He sat on a stool at the kitchen island. He looked over at her. His eyes glimmered with a hint of self-satisfaction. "I have some news for you."

She leaned across the counter. "Me, too."

"Okay." His jaw tensed. "You first, but you better not be going to tell me that you and Serena ran late because you were out conducting some amateur investigation."

"No. As you keep reminding me, you're the cop and I'm not. So you tell me your news first." She dropped a pod in the coffee maker.

"Well, on my way home to change, I drove by Andrew's."

"Don't tell me." She smirked. "He drives a red Cayenne."

"What? You knew?" His eyes narrowed as he studied her. "How?"

"Serena told me he drove one." She handed him a cup of coffee.

"Serena — of course, should have known." He added a teaspoon of sugar and stirred his coffee. "I have more." He took a sip and looked at her over the rim of his cup.

She leaned her elbows on the counter and rested her chin in her hand. "Go on, I'm listening."

"I drove by because I thought I saw him driving one the other day, and sure enough, in the driveway was a red SUV. I needed an excuse to stop, so I decided to drop in to inquire about Blain's funeral arrangements, telling him lots of people at the station were asking and no one had seen anything about it in the papers."

"Did he buy it?"

"Yes, but the interesting thing was that when I walked past his SUV, I put my hand on the hood. It was warm. But when I told him I thought I'd just seen him downtown, he denied having driven it at all, saying he'd been home all afternoon making the funeral preparations."

"Really?"

"The best part is, either he has a new potpourri thingy in his foyer or a woman who drenches herself in expensive perfume was there for a visit. His foyer was filled with the scent of a woman's perfume."

"Well, Sheila wears some pricey perfume she picked up in Paris just before I left London, and I saw her get into that car, so there's no question she knows him somehow."

"I thought that, too. So when I left there, I went to have a chat with Elaine, Blain's assistant."

"Good thinking."

"Yes, well, the police are known to have one or two good ideas once in a while." He choked on his sip of coffee.

She handed him a napkin. "A blind squirrel is bound to find a nut at some point." She slapped his back when he started choking again. "Is it something I said?"

"If you don't behave, I won't tell you the next tidbit of information."

She put on her best angelic face. "I promise to be a good girl, until I'm asked not to be." She grinned at the blush creeping up under his collar. "Go on. I'm listening."

"Elaine's house is empty and has a sign out front. It's been sold."

Addie's eyes widened. "No way, she's skipped town?"

"Looks like it. Strange timing. But she wasn't put on the witness list after she gave her initial statement, so in reality, she has every right to come and go as she pleases."

"I get that, but don't you find it suspicious that I saw Andrew hand her an envelope, and then she suddenly leaves town?"

"I do, but the DA reviewed the reports and decided she had nothing to add to the case, so she was dropped from the investigation."

"Maybe they need to take a harder look at

her now that's she vanished."

"I don't know about 'vanished,' but tomorrow I'll look into it and see if anyone knows where she went."

"Are you going to search her house for any clues?"

"Like I said, it was empty. Any clues would be long gone." He looked at her over the rim of his cup, draining it.

"My guess is that she knows something, and Andrew wanted to make sure she wasn't here to answer any questions."

"Based on what we know now," he said, setting his cup on the counter, "you might be right."

She scrubbed her hands across her face. "This is getting to be too much."

"Come on, then, let's take your mind off it. You said you needed help cleaning up. Let's get started." He pulled her behind him out of the kitchen.

She laughed. "I don't *need* help. I said you could help if you wanted to."

"I want to. Where do we start?"

"Right here." She pointed at the dining room. "I think every room was hit, by the looks of it. But let's leave the living room for now, because I want to show you the puzzle compartments that I discovered in the desk when we're done."

He raised his brow, looked at the living room doorway and then back at her, and shrugged.

They worked their way through the downstairs and then the second floor. Through their inspection of the rooms, they found every one of them had been searched, some more than others. Her aunt's old bedroom had been hit the hardest.

"Any word on her autopsy report?" She put the last of her aunt's belongings in the drawer of the bedside table.

Marc was standing at the closet door. Without a word, he closed it.

"I asked if there was any word on my aunt's autopsy yet." Addie stopped what she'd been doing and looked at his broad back; his shoulder muscles flinched. "What is it? What did they find?"

He turned to her slowly, his face contorted. "I knew there was something I forgot to tell you." He winced.

"Okay." She sat on the edge of the bed. "Tell me now, is it bad news?"

"Well . . . yes and no." He sat down beside her.

She sucked in a sharp breath. He took her hand, stroking his thumb over the back of it.

She quivered at his touch. Could he feel

her pulse race? She slowly let out her breath, hypnotized as his thumb stroked small circles across her skin.

"It seems," he started, then blew out a deep sigh, "that when old Doc Smith, her doctor, discovered the exhumation order, well, he flew into a rage. He came to see me first, then went directly to the DA and had it rescinded."

Her eyes widened. "Why?" She bit her lip. "Do you think he's trying to hide something?"

"No, no. He said that she suffered from a heart condition for years and had begun failing rapidly in the couple of months preceding her death. He'd wanted to hospitalize her, but she wouldn't go."

"I hear she was stubborn."

Marc looked at her. "I'd say it runs in the family." He chuckled.

She pulled her hand away. The electrical charge that had bound them broken, she playfully slapped his hand.

"Anyway, he went on to say — and none too calmly, I might add — that I was a fool to think anything other than natural causes were to blame. When she refused admission, he did insist she have round-the-clock nursing homecare."

"No one told me that." Addie pursed her

lips. "So with a nurse always with her in the house, no one could have come in and poisoned her?"

"Doc said her visitors were limited in the last months, since she wasn't up for company, so only a few close friends came to see her."

Addie nodded. "Understandable."

"But he did mention something strange." Marc's eyes twinkled. "He said the night nurse, who slept in her bedroom on a cot, did mention that she was woken a few times by strange noises in the house."

"Did she report it?"

"No," he sighed. "He said she just put it down to the house being so old and guessed it was normal. So that's that. No autopsy needed."

Addie stood up and went to the window, crossing her arms. "Then we'll never know if someone did give her some tainted tea to try to rush things along."

"It's very unlikely, but you're right. We'll never know, but to be honest, I think Doc Smith is right and it was natural causes."

Addie shook her head, gnawing on her bottom lip. "I guess so." She glanced over the bedroom. "Well, I think we're done up here. It didn't take long with the two us working on it. Thank you."

"What about that old desk you mentioned? I've been itching to explore it all evening."

"Come on then." She motioned toward the door. "Let's grab more coffee and go have a look, and you can tell me what you think."

"You're the expert on it, not me, but anything with hidden compartments to be explored sounds like my kind of thing."

She stopped at the top of the landing and looked at him. "You really do love your job, don't you?"

"Well, yes." He scratched his head. "I can't imagine doing anything else. What makes you say that?"

She laughed and bounded down the stairs. " 'Cause you love a good mystery and sorting out the clues as much as I do."

"Then maybe you should join the police force."

"Nah, I'm a rule breaker. Don't think I could follow orders." She winked at him and walked toward the desk.

"Gee, I hadn't noticed." He chuckled and glanced around the living room. "That's a great-looking desk, it appears to be really old. I hope the intruder didn't damage it?"

"I don't see any damage, but as you can tell by everything tossed on the floor, they did search it," she said, wiggling into the kneehole.

He bent down as she flipped onto her back and shifted over to one side. "Here, I think there's enough room for the two of us." He slithered in beside her. "It dates back a few hundred years. I think. I haven't really had time to appraise it though. I love the old pedestal design. Too bad it's so bulky and heavy. Take a look at what I found this morning." She pressed on a panel above his head. The drawer popped open easily, and she pulled it out of its recess. "See, it's full of these. I think I've only discovered about half."

They continued to poke and probe every inch of the underside and side pedestal panels but nothing else popped open. Addie wiggled out from under the desk. "There's one more option we haven't tried."

"What's that?" Marc slipped out and stood up.

"This desk wasn't made to be placed against a wall. It's only here, I'm assuming, because the room's too small. On the front side is a modesty panel."

"So it's finished?"

"Yes, it's the front of the desk, not the back, at least if it's like the others I've seen, and it probably has fairly ornate carvings. I just haven't pulled it out because it's too heavy for me on my own."

"Looks like someone has." Marc bent down and traced his fingers over scratches on the hardwood flooring by the foot of the desk.

"Really?" Addie leaned over his shoulder. "They aren't too bad, pretty faint, but it looks like the desk was pulled out at one time at least."

"They're barely noticeable, and that's a good thing. Probably why whoever broke in here didn't pull it out. They didn't know this wasn't the front of it." He stood up and grabbed the side of the desk, inching it away from the wall.

"Wait." Addie ran around the other side. "You'll strain your back if you do it yourself. I'll walk this side, and you do yours. We should be able to get it far enough from the wall to take a look."

When the massive mahogany desk was far enough out, they began to explore the carved wood front. Addie pointed out the intricate features on the trim and details in the modesty panels that might mean it concealed a drawer. They ran their fingers over the ornate design, pressing and pushing on anything that could be a button.

"This doesn't make sense," Addie fumed

when they had been over every inch of the design. "There has to be something here. I can feel it."

"That gut feeling of yours again?" Marc stood up, offering her his hand. "Well, I'm done. Kneeling this long reminds me that I'm not a kid anymore."

Addie clenched her fists and studied the desk, then walked around to the other side and dipped down into the kneehole. "I see it." She popped her head back out. "Of course that's where it would be." She jumped up and ran around to the modesty panel again.

Marc grunted as he kneeled beside her. "What did you find under there?"

"Here under the top lip. Run your fingers under here, pressing along the length of the desk. See if you feel any crevices or a peg or piece of rough wood — anything out of the ordinary."

"Why?" Marc ran his fingers under the desktop overhang.

"The depth under the knee hole is shallower than it should be, given the top width of the desk. It must mean there is a hidden drawer or two somewhere."

They each started at one end and worked their way to the center, but nothing happened. "Darn it. I was certain I was right."

She slapped her palm against the modesty panel. There was a click. She turned to Marc and swallowed hard.

"Well, well, well, let's see what we have here." He reached over her arm and opened the small door that swung outward.

Addie reached inside and pulled out an elaborate jeweled box. "Look at this. Wow. It must be worth a fortune." She glanced at him and then back down at the box in disbelief.

"Maybe this is what the thieves are looking for." He rubbed his fingers over the inlaid diamonds on the lid. "Does it open?"

She turned it over in her hands. "Yes. Here's a keyhole. I wonder where the key is." She shook the box, the contents thudding against the sides of it. "Sounds solid. I wonder what it is?" She shook it again.

"It's large enough to hold a lot of things: a book or papers, wills, a smaller jewelry box. Who knows?" He shrugged.

"We have to find the key. It must be hidden in another compartment." She began pressing the sides of the niche that the box had been in.

Marc groaned, rubbing his knees, and stood. "Well, there's a lot of gold and diamonds on there. The box has a fairly high value by the looks of it."

"Do you think they're real?" She looked up at him

"They must be. Why else would someone be willing to kill so many people to get their hands on it?"

"Yeah, you're right." She stared at the exquisite gold filigree design with diamond insets.

"I don't like the fact that it's here in the house with you."

She stood up and placed the box on the desktop. "What are you saying?" But he was walking toward the window.

He pulled back the curtain enough to peer out a small crack, then closed it. "Just as I thought . . ." His voice trailed off.

"What?" Her veins ran cold, and she shivered.

"Earlier I thought I saw a flash of headlights across the curtains. Then you started searching the trim lip, and I shook it off. Because I know some traffic doesn't realize the street's a dead end and turn around up there at the top of the driveway, but . . ." He shook his head, his jaw tense.

"But what?"

"Look," he said, stepping toward her, "it's pretty dark out there, and I can't see it clear enough, but the streetlight is reflecting off —"

"That black sedan's out there again, isn't it?"

He nodded. "I know you have a new security system and all, but I don't think you should stay here tonight." He pulled his phone out of his jeans pocket. "But don't worry, I'm going to call it in and have a patrol car come by and check it out."

She crossed her arms and planted her feet. "No, I'm not going anywhere. I've done enough running. The house is secured now, and I'm not putting myself or anyone else out tonight. Not anymore."

"If you insist" — he took a deep breath — "then I insist . . . I'm staying here for the night, *and* I'm still going to call the station to send someone to check out the car." He locked eyes with her, mirroring her stance.

Chapter Thirty-Two

Addie awoke to a text alert on her cell phone. She fumbled to grasp it from her bedside table. Who would be messaging her at six-fifteen a.m.? She pulled her phone close to her eyes and bolted straight up, her hand against her chest. "Thank God, Jeremy."

She continued to read the message. Initially, she was disappointed to see he was still away, but then he went on to say that he hoped to be back in Boston this week and would come and visit her for a few days before he had to return to work. He would explain it all when they got together and wanted her to know that he hadn't forgotten about her book appraisals. They were almost finished. "What a relief." She bounded out of bed, wrapped her robe tightly around her, and headed down the hall to the bathroom.

She basked in the calming effects of the

steamy shower and vanilla body wash cascading over her skin and hugged herself. *Jeremy's coming back soon!* She hadn't realized until she read those words this morning just how worried she'd been about him. Her heart feeling lighter than it had in weeks, she stepped out onto the bath mat and dried off, snuggling her face into the soft cotton towel and inhaling the heavenly aroma of fabric softener mingled with the fragrance of her body wash and peppermint shampoo. She smiled, humming to herself, and wrapped the towel around her wet hair.

A scuffling sound came from the corridor, and her chest constricted. She stood motionless and held her breath, gritting her teeth as her lungs burned for oxygen. Then there was a rap at the door, and she gasped.

"Addie, it's me. Sorry to disturb your shower."

"Marc." She heaved a sigh of relief.

"I don't mean to rush you, but . . ."

"Sorry, I'm on my way out." She pulled her robe around her and opened the door.

His eyes scanned her robed figure. "Good morning." He thumbed a piece of towel lint from her cheek. "Sorry to interrupt you, but —"

"I should have told you there's a bathroom off my aunt's room and a half bath —"

"No, no, I don't need to use the facilities. I'm heading out and need to talk to you before I leave."

If he could be nonchalant about her being in nothing but a flimsy robe, so could she. "I had forgotten you were here."

He leaned against the doorframe, crossing one leg over the other, and lazily reached out to finger the ties of her robe. "Really?" His brow rose. "You forgot there was a man in the house?"

"Yes." She stepped back and slapped his hand away. She unwrapped the towel from her head and hung it over the rack. "What's up?" She began combing out her hair.

"I told you I'd call the station and have them check out the car at the top of your drive last night, and it paid off."

"Fantastic, whose is it?"

"Well, we don't know yet, but they ran the plates, and it's registered to a car rental company in Boston. I'm heading in to request a warrant for their client records."

"So your officers didn't catch the driver or talk to him, or her, whatever?"

"Afraid not." He shook his head. "Andy came up the hill just as the car was heading down. He did get the plate number, but by the time he turned around and headed after it, they were gone."

She blew out a sigh. "I guess that's the best clue we've had so far. How long will it take to get the client records?"

"Probably a few days, but I'm going to put it in as vital to a murder case and see if that will hurry the process along."

"Good. Are you hungry? Did you get anything to eat, any coffee?" She stepped toward him to pass.

He didn't step back. For a full second, time stopped. The old grandfather clock even quit ticking. All she could smell was her vanilla body wash and his day-old cologne. The scents, merged together, took her breath away. His eyes held fast with hers. She wanted nothing more than to dive into their depths and lose herself. He broke the spell when he stepped back, and she sucked air into her burning lungs, only aware then that she had forgotten to breathe.

"No, I'll grab something later, thanks. I have to be in court for another case by nine. Busy morning." He turned to go. "I also forgot to tell you — the nursing station called, and it looks like Catherine will be discharged this morning after doctor's rounds. I had said I'd pick her up, because I need to ask her a few questions but —"

"I will, and I'll tell her you'll drop by later.

I planned on being there anyway. I need to get my hands on that envelope, and soon."

"I don't like the idea of you and her being alone in her house."

"Why not?" Addie spun around from her bedroom doorway, the fine hairs on the back of her neck bristling. "Don't you trust her?"

"No, it's not that. It's just that her house was ransacked, and she was knocked out. The culprits still haven't found what they're looking for, and I'm afraid they may be back. Especially if they know the two of you are there alone."

Her hand clung to her doorframe. "I thought you were worried about her attacking me."

He stepped toward her and began twirling her robe ties around his index finger. "I am worried about you, but not about you coming to harm at the hands of Catherine."

"How worried?" Again, her lungs rebelled and refused to breathe.

He tugged slightly at the ties. "Don't ask." His voice turned husky, and she swallowed hard. "But be careful and watchful, promise?"

"I will, and I'll call the station at the first sign of trouble."

"No, I'd rather you call 911." He tapped

her nose with the end of her robe tie. "Don't forget to lock the door behind me."

She heard the door click shut and went down to secure the dead bolt. Then she headed for the kitchen to make coffee.

By eight-thirty, she was already exhausted. One more hour of sleep would have made all the difference, but this way she arrived on time to open for Paige and get her set up for the day, then race to be at the hospital by nine.

Catherine's face lit up when Addie walked through the door. She was up and dressed and sitting in a chair by the window, waiting for the discharge order from the doctor.

"This is a wonderful surprise, Addie. The nurse said I had a ride home, but I never expected it to be you."

"Marc was supposed to come, and I was only going to tag along to make sure you got settled just fine, but he got called to court, so here I am. I hope that's all right with you?" She smiled and moved closer to Catherine. "He asked me to tell you that he'd drop in on you later to talk about what happened, if that's okay?"

"Yes, of course it is and this is wonderful. It gives us more time to get reacquainted, and I can give you that envelope that seems to have caused so many problems lately."

"Yes, the envelope." Addie breathed a sigh of relief at having dodged her burning question. She sat back and studied Catherine. Maybe she should give this woman a chance. At the very least, she could glean more information about her father. "Has the doctor come by yet?"

"Yes, and he explained that I also received a bump on the back of my head? Honestly, I have no idea how that happened." Addie glanced down at the floor. That was something she'd better leave for Marc to explain later. "Now, I just have to wait for the doctor to write the discharge order and the nurse to give me the go-ahead. Then we can leave." Catherine placed her hand over Addie's and smiled.

Addie squeezed her fingers and smiled back. The nurse came in and gave Catherine papers to sign and information about what to watch for after she went home and told her that if she had any of the symptoms, she should go directly to the emergency room. Other than that, she was to follow up with her own doctor in a few days.

The drive to Catherine's was quiet, for the most part. Addie glanced sideways at her passenger, thinking how tired she looked. Visiting could wait. Catherine needed rest. She checked her rearview mirror and sucked in a breath. A black sedan was stalking them. She made a quick left turn.

"This isn't my street." Catherine pointed out her window.

"Isn't it? I must have gotten confused, sorry. I'll turn right up here and go around."

Addie kept checking her mirrors and was relieved. The black Honda didn't reappear. She pulled up in front of Catherine's house and got out. Her heart started thudding against her chest wall. Parked at the far end of the street was a black sedan. She fished her cell phone out of her purse and put it in her front pocket and went around to help Catherine into the house.

Catherine collapsed on the sofa, her forehead covered in beads of perspiration. "I had no idea I was this weak." She closed her eyes. "I'll just catch my breath and then get the envelope for you."

"I can get it if you like."

"No, you'd never find it. It's well hidden." Catherine heaved herself up. "I'll be right back, and then I think I'm going to have to lie down. Sorry to cut our visit short today." She disappeared down the hallway.

"I understand," called Addie after her.

She went to the window and peeked through the curtains. She couldn't see the end of the road from her vantage point, so she had no idea if the sedan was still there. She listened for any unusual sounds outside or at the doors. A scraping noise came from the direction Catherine had disappeared in. The hairs on the back of her neck tingled. Then Catherine came around the corner, holding a small brown envelope in her hand, a wide grin across her face.

"See, I told you no one would find it." She held it out to Addie.

With trembling fingers, Addie took it from her and turned it over in her hands. "I can't believe such a small parcel could cause so much trouble. Thank you for keeping it safe for me." She looked at Catherine, tears burning behind her eyes.

"It's all in the floorboards, my dear." She tapped her foot on the hardwood floor under them. "An old trick my mother taught me that she learned from your aunt. It seems your aunt had a number of very valuable items over the years and didn't trust their safekeeping to anyone else, so she developed her own safe security system."

Addie laughed. "It sounds like my aunt was a real character. I only wish I could remember her."

Catherine squeezed her hand gently, her eyes filling with tears. "She was. After my own mother passed, she took me on as her daughter. I'll always be ever so grateful to her."

"Well, she sounds like an amazing woman."

"Yes, and she would be so proud of you. It was her dying wish that you would continue her legacy."

"Her dying wish? You were with her when she passed?"

"Yes — myself, old Doc Smith, and Raymond. I held her hand as she took her last breath."

"So there was no reason to believe any foul play was involved?"

"Heavens, no. Your aunt was very old and had been suffering from a heart condition for years. Doc Smith was surprised that she lasted as long as she did, considering the extent of her heart damage." Catherine smiled, sucking in a deep breath. "But she was a fighter and wouldn't give up." She tucked a wayward strand of Addie's hair behind her ear. "You've very much like her, you know."

Addie bit her bottom lip, studying the wistful look in Catherine's eyes, and wished she could remember meeting her aunt, just once, as she seemed to be a dynamic person who had a great impact on the lives of all who knew her. Addie squeezed Catherine's hand, thanked her again, and quickened her pace to her car.

She started her engine and pulled out onto the road. At the same time, the black car pulled out from the far end of the street and made a quick right turn at the corner. Addie stepped on the gas, hoping to be able to catch a glimpse of the plate number, but when she got to the intersection and checked the road to the right, the car had vanished. She made her way home, keeping a close eye on her rearview mirror, reassuring herself that the envelope was tucked safely in her handbag.

The closer she got to home, the more anxious she became to open the package and discover its secret. She was certain it must be the key for the jeweled box, but was it the box that had created such murder and mayhem? If so, then why was the key so important — or was it? The box itself was worth a fortune. She shook her head. None of it made sense.

Chapter Thirty-Three

Addie raced up her front steps and took a quick look over her shoulder to be sure she was alone. She disarmed the alarm and pressed her back against the door, pausing to take a deep breath, and then dashed into the living room. She tossed her bag on the sofa and tore into the envelope. A small, white box fell into the palm of her hand. With trembling fingers, she pulled the top off and gasped.

It was exactly like the picture in the postcard: a red silk-lined box with a small gold ornate key tucked into the center. "My God, Raymond," she murmured. "That card was an actual photo of this, not a postcard. How much did you know?" She frowned, tucked the box into her jacket pocket, and then turned toward the desk.

Marc and she had returned the desk to its original position against the wall last night. Addie had insisted on storing the jeweled box in one of the other secret compartments underneath the desktop for easier access when they had to retrieve it later. After all, she had told him, the intruders hadn't discovered it in the past. Therefore, it should be safe in there again.

On wobbling legs, she navigated herself across the room and crawled under the desk. She wiped her clammy hands on the knees of her trousers and slowly pulled the box out of its hiding place. Her heart raced. This was the moment she had been waiting for. She took a deep breath and wiggled out from under the desk, fished the key from her pocket, and fit it into the small lock. Nothing happened. She jiggled the key; still nothing. Her breath came short and fast, and her heart crashed to the pit of her stomach. She took the key out and refit it into the lock. Still nothing. It turned, but the top wouldn't open. "Darn it. What's your secret?"

She placed it on the desk and glared at it. "Secret . . . that's it." She grabbed the box and turned it over. Her fingers traced the contours of its underside, but she felt nothing out of the ordinary. She tried inserting the key again and began pressing and prodding the gem and gold filigree design, but to no avail. She moved her hand to the box's side and discovered an irregularity in the pattern where the base and sidewall met, and pressed the center diamond of that pattern. The lid popped open in her hand.

Her face dropped. There was nothing but a roll of newspaper clippings bound by an elastic band, which she easily removed. The elastic didn't break, so it told her it wasn't that old and hadn't dried out with age. She unrolled the pages across the desk and checked for the date of publication. She wavered and grabbed the side of the desk. The date was the day after her father had died. She scanned through the pages, looking for a clue as to why this would be in the box, but only found advertisements and comic strips. It made no sense. Why would her aunt have gone through the trouble of stashing these in the jeweled case?

Her cell phone in her pocket chimed a text alert. She pulled it out, relieved to see it was from Serena.

Where are you? I need to talk to you right away.

Addie's fingers flew across her screen. I'm home. Come over. Leaving the door unlocked. If I don't answer, follow nose to the kitchen.

She rolled the newspapers back up, secured them with the elastic and placed them into the box, then tucked it under her arm and unlocked the front door. After she got the kettle on for Serena's tea, she flew off a text to Marc.

> Found the key! Contents a little disappointing. Serena's going to meet me here at the house. Should be back at my store within the hour if you have any juicy tidbits to share.

"I'm back here, Serena," she called out when she heard the front door open. "That didn't take you long. I'm just making a late lunch. I hope you're hungry?" she yelled, placing meat and cheese on buttered bread.

"Not really," a cold voice said behind her.

She spun around and looked directly down the barrel of a black gun. She stared across the barrel to the hand and then to the face of the person holding it. Her jaw clenched as she looked into the steely eyes of the tall woman from her store, the same one she had seen with Catherine.

"We're not very hungry, my dear," chirped another voice. The elderly lady from her shop appeared from behind the tall woman. "But I do think you have something that we are looking for." She smiled sweetly. Her gaze traveled to the jeweled case sitting on the counter. "If you would be so kind as to give me the key," she said, holding out her frail hand, "we'll be on our way and let you have your lunch."

"What makes you think I have the key?" Addie wished she had kept the carving knife she'd used earlier in her hand.

"Please give us some credit, my dear." *Tsk tsk,* she clucked. "We know much more than you're aware of." Her eyes bored into Addie's, and the corner of her lip curled up. "Now I'm losing patience. Hand it over."

The woman with the gun took a step forward.

Addie flinched and reached into her pocket.

The old woman took the key from her trembling fingers. "There, that wasn't so hard, was it?" She turned to the box and inserted the key in the lock. It didn't open. She wiggled it and then slammed her palm on the counter. "Open it. Now."

Addie took a breath and shook her head.

"I said now." The old woman glared.

Addie heard the sound of a trigger being cocked. Her heart pounded against her chest so hard she could hear the thudding in her ears. She clenched her fists at her sides and grabbed the box. She almost dropped it. The woman reached out and grasped Addie's arm, steadying it. "There, there, that's it, just give us what we want, and we'll be off." Her silky voice grated inside Addie's head.

Addie turned the key in the lock and pressed the gemstone to release the lid. It popped open. The old woman snatched it from her hands and pulled it toward her. "What's this?" She pulled the roll of newspapers out. "Where's the book?" She glared at Addie. "Where is it?"

Addie glanced at the two women, their faces red with rage. She stepped backward. "I, I don't know anything about a book. I swear. I thought you were just after the box. It has to be worth a lot of money." She inched away until her back pressed into the counter.

The old woman tucked the case into her large handbag. Her eyes remained fixed on Addie's. "Not half as much as the book, and you know that. Where is it?"

"Honest, I don't know anything about a book. I just found the box yesterday. Until then, I didn't even know it existed." Addie placed her hands behind her and searched the counter until she felt the handle of the carving knife. She drew it close to her back.

"We're not done yet," snapped the old

woman, turning on her heel and heading out of the kitchen.

The tall woman inched backward. Her gun never wavered from Addie. When she was close enough to the front door, she turned and bolted. Addie slithered down the side of the cupboards and sat, shaking on the floor. She turned the carving knife over in her hands and wondered, if given the opportunity, she would have actually been able to use it on a person. She dropped it on the floor beside her.

She pulled her phone from her pocket, knowing she had to call Marc. Not only to report this but so he could tell her how she should feel after staring down the barrel of a gun. Tears burned at her eyes as she entered his phone number. The front door banged open, and she jumped. Her phone flew from her fingers and skidded across the floor. She gritted her teeth and tried to stop the whirling motion in her head. She strained to listen and heard the scuffle of footsteps, but nothing more.

Addie swiveled onto her knees and peered over the island counter. "Marc," she cried.

"Addie, are you okay?" He lowered his gun to his side.

She nodded.

"You're shaking." Marc walked over to

her. "Are you sure you're all right?"

She looked up at him and nodded. "How did you know to come?"

"Because I was standing in front of your shop with Serena when you sent me the text telling me she was on her way to your place."

Addie frowned and stared blankly at him.

His fingers grasped her shoulders. "She's lost her phone. You couldn't have gotten a text from her."

"I didn't know." She bit her lip and looked at him. "Why were you at my shop?"

"Long story. First, I need to know what happened here and why you're so shaken up."

"All clear, Chief. There's no one else in the house."

"Thanks, Kurt. You guys can wait outside. I'll just get Miss Greyborne's statement."

Kurt looked from Addie to Marc, a slight smile crossing his lips as he turned and left.

Marc wrote down her statement and offered a few hums and nods while she made it. However, she noticed his brow did rise when she told him about the mysterious book the old woman had said was supposed to be in the box — but that was it. His staunch, detached chief-of-police demeanor through it all was infuriating. What she really needed from him right now was some hint of personal warmth. After all, she had stared straight down the barrel of a gun. When she finished giving her statement, she shot him a glaring glance.

"What's wrong with you?" He stared at her. "What did I do besides come to your rescue?"

"My rescue? Really, that's what you think?" She crossed her arms. "I think the threat was over by the time you arrived — and by the way, staring down a loaded gun barrel isn't as bad as everyone thinks it is." She tossed her head back.

"Addie, come here."

"I'm fine, really I am." She tapped her toe.

He tilted her chin up with his fingertip, his soft eyes searching hers. "It's okay if you're upset. It isn't easy. It never is when something like this happens and you walk away thinking how lucky you are to survive."

She nodded, tightening her lips.

"Well, I will say," he said, gripping her shoulders gently, "that you handled things pretty well. You made sure you could get your hands on that knife. It shows that you can think on your feet and not lose your head in a crisis."

"Yup, I sure did that."

Marc focused on her taut face. "Look,

Addie, I know you're in shock now and holding it together, but sometime out of the blue it's going to hit you, and hard. It does even the most seasoned soldier or police officer. But please know, I'm here when you need to talk." He tucked a wayward strand of her hair behind her ear. "The anger and confusion you're feeling right now is a natural reaction. Talking about it comes later."

She sniffed. "Why were you at my store?"

He shook his head. "You are something else."

"What happened?"

He puffed out a deep breath and scratched the back of his head. "Well, I was there to break up a protest that got out of hand."

"A protest in front of my place?"

"Yup. Haven't had one of those in years."

"Who and what was the protest?"

"Well," he said, and leaned back and stroked his chin, "your neighbor, Martha, has it in her head that you are the leader of a major crime ring and is demanding the town shut you down."

Addie stared disbelievingly at him. "You're kidding."

He rubbed the back of his neck. "Nope. She got a few of her cronies together, and they staged a protest, complete with signs and chants telling the townsfolk to force you out."

Addie dropped onto a counter stool. "So her petition wasn't enough. Now she has to publicly humiliate me."

"Yup." He rocked back on his heels.

"That's not all though, is it?"

"I knew you were smart." He winked and brought his hand out as if he wanted to touch her flushed cheek. Instead, he dropped it back to his side. "Paige went out to tell them to leave and got into an altercation with Martha, and then Serena went out to break that up, and . . . well, long story short, it ended in a full-out sidewalk brawl."

Addie scrubbed her hands over her face. The next time she saw Martha, she'd . . . she'd . . .

"That's why I didn't get here sooner. I couldn't hear my text alert over the noise." Marc's voice broke into her thoughts of revenge.

"I can't believe this." She shook her head. "If Martha ever knew the truth about what's been going on, she'd have a lot more fuel for her fire, wouldn't she?" She sighed and leaned on the counter, her chin cupped in her hand.

Marc patted her on the back. "Keep your chin up." He slid onto the stool beside her.

"We now have a few other pieces of the puzzle, which takes us one step closer to ending this whole mess once and for all."

"Yes, and the big one now seems to be a mysterious book." She twirled the carving knife in circles on the counter.

"Yes, the book." He placed his hand over hers, stopping the knife from swirling. "Remind me to never really get on your bad side."

"I'm not sure I could use it, even if I had to." Her eyes dropped to the blade in front of her.

"You'd be surprised what people can do when they have to."

"Yes, I guess, but we now have to figure out what this book is and why it's so valuable that even a gold- and gem-covered box wasn't enough to make the two women happy."

"Were you aware of any of the books your father had been tracking down for clients?"

"None that would have been worth that much." She shook her head. "It's strange though."

"What are you thinking?"

"Well, obviously the book had been in there, because the newspaper clippings were only six months old and were dated the day after my father was killed. Which means my aunt must have taken the book out and replaced it with them to throw off whoever she thought might come looking for it."

"She was a smart lady." He patted her hand.

"And smart enough not to keep the key anywhere it would be found, which is why she gave it to my father."

"Who then gave it to Raymond, but he also told Catherine about the package just so someone else would know Raymond had it."

"Yes . . . and probably because he knew he was being followed by someone who was onto the book."

"Then he's killed because somehow the thieves knew your aunt gave him the key when he left her place, right before his accident." He rubbed the back of his neck.

"Right, but because of the fiery crash, which maybe they didn't count on, they assumed it had been lost and they'd have to go directly after the box. They were probably planning to smash it if they had to so they could get to the book." She chewed her lip and drummed her fingers on the counter.

"But that would have destroyed the box, and it's worth a lot of money itself, and you said the older woman knew that you had the key. But how?" His brow furrowed.

"And how did my aunt open the box the day after she'd given my father the key? You know, when she replaced the book with the newspaper clippings. There must be a second key hidden somewhere. Arg, I don't know anymore." Addie groaned and put her head on the counter. "It's so confusing." Marc lightly caressed her hair. If she were a cat, she would have started purring. Instead, she glanced sideways at him. "I wonder who my aunt would have told about the key and the book? She seems too smart to have shared something so important with just anyone." Her head shot up.

"Raymond," they cried in unison.

"That must be it. He was her lawyer for years. Why wouldn't she trust him?" Addie clasped Marc's hand in hers. His warm gaze fell on her. She let her hand fall from his.

He stroked his chin. "I wonder if your father suspected Raymond might not be so trustworthy, and that's why he told Catherine about the package in the first place."

"And why Raymond never got the security system installed. He wanted to make sure they, whoever *they* are, would have had plenty of opportunity to search her house." She stared at the countertop.

"Yes, after all, she was an elderly woman

living on her own, and if they were such good friends, besides him being her lawyer—"

"He might have had another key to her house?" She looked at him. "But then if he did have a key, why was my back door smashed open?" She bit her lip.

Marc sucked in air between his teeth. "Maybe Raymond did double-cross them somehow."

"Which is why he was murdered."

Chapter Thirty-Four

Addie arrived back at her shop to find Serena and Paige hunched over the counter, deep in conversation. Her eyes widened when Paige turned to greet her.

"You have a bruise coming up on your jaw, Paige."

"Don't worry about me. My mother's needed a good hair-pulling for a long time. Although, I never realized she had such a solid right hook." Paige rubbed her chin.

"Look, I really don't want to come between you and your mother. If you're having second thoughts about working for me, I'd understand."

"No, of course not." She grinned. "It's the best job I've ever had." She gathered up her belongings. "See you tomorrow," she called over her shoulder from the door.

Addie shook her head and studied Serena. "And what about you? Any battle scars?"

"No, I fared pretty well, although it was

fun to pin Ingrid Smith from the Dollar Store down on the sidewalk."

"What? Oh, it sounds like such a mess."

"You'll be able to watch it on the news tonight. Television crews were here and everything."

"No." Addie slumped into a counter stool. "I want publicity for the store, but not this kind."

"Well, you know what they say." Serena tossed her paper cup into the trash and stood up. " 'All publicity is good publicity.' "

Addie groaned. "They may as well have been selling cotton candy and caramel corn to bystanders."

"Now, why didn't I think of that?" Serena plopped back onto her stool. "I forgot to ask. How come Marc grabbed a couple of the guys and tore out of here so fast? He mumbled your name and left."

Addie sighed and told Serena about her lunch guests and her afternoon adventures. Serena's face paled and her mouth gaped open, but she didn't say a word until Addie scrubbed her hands over her face and growled.

"Wow, that's incredible. How are you feeling? A gun, jeez." She shook her head and clasped Addie's hand. "I'm here if you need to talk."

"Thank you." Addie smiled. "I think I'm okay though."

Serena eyed her warily.

"But it's too bad the whole thing isn't over."

"Why, isn't it? You know who the women are now, so I'm sure Marc will catch them soon."

"Yes, but the older woman said she was more interested in a book that was supposed to be inside the box. I've been wracking my brain to think what books would be worth more than a box covered in diamonds."

Serena's eyes widened. "Are they large ones?"

"No, tiny, but there are quite a few of them, and they're inlaid in gold, so the box must be worth a fortune, but she said the book she was after was worth more than it." Addie tapped her finger to her forehead. "Hmmm. The only one I can think of would be a 1455 first print run of the Gutenberg Bible. A single leaf is worth thousands, and a complete version — well, tens of millions. Or maybe the original journals of the Codex by Leonardo da Vinci?" She raked her hands through her hair. "I don't know, there are a few worth more than the gems probably are, but who knows what we're dealing with."

"Well, the women can't have gotten too

far. I'm sure Marc will track them down in no time, and then maybe we can find out exactly what it is they're looking for."

"I hope you're right. I need all this to end so badly, and then I can focus on saving my reputation in town."

Addie's cell phone rang as Serena stood up to leave.

"I hope that's Marc with some good news." Addie pulled it out of her pocket.

Serena sat back down.

She checked the call display. "No, it's Roger Moore, from London. Sorry, but I have to get this." Serena stood up again, but Addie motioned for her to stay, and she sat back down.

"Hello. . . . Yes, Roger, this is me. You're in town now? But I thought it wasn't till — Oh, yes. I understand. . . . Sure, I can meet you at seven. . . . Yes, I'm looking forward to seeing you again too. . . . Right. . . . Yes, bye for now."

Serena dug around in her purse. "Roger? I thought he wasn't coming until next week sometime? Voilà." She jingled her keys from her fingers. "What's wrong? I thought you were looking forward to seeing him?"

"I am." Addie rubbed her temples. "I just wasn't expecting him to come tonight, and it's already been a long day." She sighed.

"Well, I'll go and hear him out and then decide if I want the job. Are you off?"

"Yes, we're supposed to meet my parents for dinner at Mario's. I hope Marc makes it. He had to cancel last week 'cause of work. Oh well, guess it goes with the job." She kissed Addie on the cheek and gave her a hug. "I'll give him your best." She winked and zigzagged toward the door, dodging Addie's half-hearted slap. "Remember, I'm here if you need anything." She closed the door behind her.

Addie checked the time and shook her head. What was she going to do for two hours? She decided that if she went home she'd probably fall asleep, and she couldn't go to Mario's and grab a quick dinner, because she didn't want Marc to think she was following him. In the end, she decided she really didn't feel like eating now and would grab something on her way home from the meeting.

She perched on a box in the back room and stared at the blackboard, trying to make sense of the names and links they had come up with, but she couldn't see how all the pieces fit together. The two women were only linked with Catherine . . . and Raymond, but he was linked with everyone in town, so that was no help. It was the same with her aunt. She bit her lip and looked harder, fighting to concentrate.

Sheila was only linked to the black Honda from Boston and the Porsche Cayenne, which Andrew owned, so there was a connection there. She focused on the white line to Andrew's name. He was linked to Blain, who was dead, and Sheila, who was seen getting in Andrew's car, but he couldn't be linked to anyone else, except Elaine, who had mysteriously left town. "Arg." She rubbed her tired eyes.

Her appointment alert rang. She checked the time, dragged herself off the box, and stretched. "Okay, Roger, let's hear what you have to offer." She grabbed her purse and coat and headed off to the Grey Gull Inn.

Addie made her way toward the main entrance and followed the arrows directing her to the open staircase that led up to the guest rooms on the second and third floors. When she got to the second-floor landing, she pulled a slip of paper out of her pocket with Roger's room number on it and wandered down the corridor, searching for room 201.

She came to the last door, took a deep breath, and knocked. The door slowly swung partially open, but no one greeted her. "Roger. Are you here?" She peered in and saw a small living room, and beyond that a closed door, which she assumed led into the bedroom. "It's me, Addie. If you're busy, I can come back." She doubled-checked the number on the door.

A shadow fell across the doorway, and she jumped. "Jeremy?" Her face lit up. "I had no idea you were coming." She stepped back and looked at him. "I can't believe you're really here. Why didn't you tell me you were coming, too?"

He smiled down at her. "I wanted to surprise you. I ran into Roger at the airport in New York. We landed about the same time. He mentioned that he was coming to meet you — something about a contract. Since I'd gotten back a bit earlier than I thought I would, we decided it would be fun to come together so we could celebrate your accepting his offer." He raised his shoulders and grinned. "Surprise!"

"Best surprise ever." She squeezed his arm. "To tell the truth, I haven't decided about accepting it yet." She winked. "But never mind that, look at you. I've never seen you sporting facial hair before."

He rubbed his chin and laughed. "Oh, this? My miserable attempt at growing a beard."

"Well, I like it. It makes you look rugged

and handsome." She reached up and brushed strands of dark hair from his brow. "I even like the longer hair; it suits you." She beamed up at him. "I still can't believe you're here."

"Come in. Have a seat. Do you want a drink?" He walked to the kitchenette counter and retrieved two glasses from a cupboard.

"After this, I need one. I'm still stunned to see you." She took a seat at the small table. "I'm shaking — look at my hands."

He dropped a handful of ice cubes into the glasses, turned around, and laughed. "I figured since you left Boston that it would also be a good chance to catch up with each other. What's your poison? I have vodka and whiskey."

"Whatever you're having, thanks." She looked around the small living room. "Where's Roger? I can't wait to see him, too."

Jeremy handed her a glass and sat in the chair on the other side of the small table. "Cheers." She lifted her glass in a toast.

"Bottoms up." He clinked her glass with his and then set his down. "Now, who starts with the latest news, you or me?"

"You start. I'm sure you've been up to much more exciting adventures lately than I have. This is a pretty sleepy small town." She chuckled and set her drink down, too.

He smiled, curling his fingers around his glass and swirling his drink.

"Where did you say Roger was?" She leaned forward. "I expected him to be here. He did say seven, didn't he?"

Jeremy's steel-gray eyes bored into hers.

A shudder rippled through her. Addie shifted on her chair and reached for her drink, but stopped. His was clear amber liquid over ice. Hers was fizzy. "So, Suzanne told me it was something to do with your sister?" She shifted back in her chair.

"I'm more interested in hearing about you." He reached over and clasped her hand. "It appears by the books you've sent me that you found some fairly good treasures in that old house." His fingers tightened their grip.

Her skin prickled where he touched her, and she flinched. She pulled her hand away. He grabbed her wrist.

"Jeremy, what are you doing?" She struggled to pull free. Her eyes skimmed the room, and Jeremy's grip on her tightened.

She realized there weren't any signs of Roger. She'd heard from her coworkers at the British Museum that he was an avid reader who never left home without a stack of books. In fact, it had been a joke among the staff who had traveled with him to other museums to attend their latest artifact reveals, but she saw only one book on the end table beside the sofa. She craned her neck to get a better look and gasped. It was a copy of *Alice's Adventures in Wonderland* with her store price sticker clearly visible on the cover. "I asked you what you're doing — and where is Roger?" She jerked her arm away from him.

Jeremy stood up and leaned across the table. The bedroom door flung open.

"Sheila? What are — what's going on here?" Addie leapt to her feet. "You two know each other?" She shook her head and stared at Jeremy. "I don't understand."

"Come on, Jeremy, obviously doing it your way's going to take all night. It's time I step in." She pulled a gun out of her jacket pocket.

Addie sucked in a deep breath. "Jeremy? What's this all about?"

"Sit down." Sheila motioned toward the chair with the gun.

Addie sank back into the seat.

Chapter Thirty-Five

Jeremy sat in his chair, too, and folded his hands on the table in front of him. "I'm afraid my sister's right."

"Your sister?" Addie's mouth dropped open. "You're British, Jeremy?"

"No," Sheila snapped. "We're both as American as they come. But it really didn't hurt that I easily picked up the accent when I lived there. I fit in better and it opened a lot of professional doors for me."

Addie glanced from one to the other. "I don't understand what this is all about. The two of you here? I just don't get it."

"There's nothing to get, my friend," Sheila sneered at her. "Remember that book you found last year in a crate, the one that made you the shining star at the British Museum? You all thought at first it was the original handwritten copy of *Alice's Adventures in Wonderland.*"

Addie nodded. "I remember." Her eyes

fixed on the gun in her face. "We thought it was the one that had been stolen from the British Library warehouse a year before, when it was being prepared for shipping to be on loan to Oxford."

"But you see, we knew better — it couldn't have been that one." Jeremy looked at Sheila and winked. "Because that book was safely tucked away in our possession when you made your discovery. What you may not know," he said, leaning toward Addie, his sour breath wafting across her face, "is that my talented sister also does consulting work for the British Library and is well acquainted with their security features. She just worked her magic, and poof, it was ours." His eyes mocked her.

"So as you can see," Sheila said, shifting her weight onto one hip, "I became rather curious about just what it was you did discover. To everyone's surprise, including mine, it turned out to be the second copy, also handwritten. Not the initial fifteen-thousand-word version that the library had been displaying, which of course I knew, but the twenty-seven-thousand-word copy where Carroll had added the scenes about the Cheshire Cat and the Mad Tea-Party."

"Do you see now?" Jeremy's brow cocked. He looked at Sheila and grunted a gasp of exasperation.

Sheila rolled her eyes at him and sighed. "What my brother is trying to say is, we know you're not stupid."

Addie shifted in her chair, slipped her hand into her pocket, wrapped her fingers firmly around her cell phone, and pressed what she hoped was record.

Jeremy stood up and slammed his hand on the table. Addie flinched. "There were two originals, and they make a very rare set worth tens of millions."

Sheila urged Jeremy back with her gun hand. Addie's eyes held fast on it as the woman thrust it in her face. "The first book is Carroll's first edition, and then you discovered the second one. The one he'd expanded in preparation for publication — the one he had given to the real Alice, Alice Liddell, which I knew had sold at auction some ten years ago for millions to a private collector who later reported it stolen. We were in the process of tracking it down when, voilà, it fell in my lap."

"Do you think I was the one who stole it from the collector? Is that what this is all about?"

Jeremy laughed. "No, my dearest Addie, we thought you stole it from the museum. You see, right after your discovery became big news, you went back to Boston and that second book disappeared from the museum. We thought that, like us, you had your own little side business going, and we'd be damned if you were going to take away our chance at the millions that the two-book set would bring us."

"I must say I did wonder at the time how Miss Lilywhite could have fooled me all those months. Then Jeremy reminded me what line of work your fiancé was in, and we figured the two of you were our competition."

"But I didn't bring anything back. It was sent to the British Library for further analysis."

Sheila tossed her head back, laughed, and then glanced at Jeremy.

He walked to the kitchenette counter, leaned on it, and shook his head. "We know that now, but unfortunately for poor David, Sheila discovered where the book had really gone after I had already paid a little visit to your apartment."

"What do you mean?" Addie felt the color drain from her face. She looked at Jeremy's back, then at Sheila. "*You* killed him."

"Yes, but it wasn't in vain. You see, as David pleaded for his life — and yours, by the way — he did share a tidbit of information with me before he gasped his last breath. He told me about a rather shady broker who might know about a third book that, if added to our collection, would make us even richer. I of course at the time still thought he was keeping the second book from me for your own purposes and eventually lost patience, but his information about this third book's existence was rather enlightening."

"But David didn't know anything about the book you thought I took."

"Yes, and his death was truly tragic, but, as you see, it served a purpose."

Tears burned at Addie's eyes. "Why did you have to kill him?"

"Well, he could have been competition, you know." Jeremy studied his cuticles. "Especially since he'd discovered what we were after, and then had the lead on the third book for our little priceless set of three, instead of just the two. I couldn't take the chance he might go out on his own and find it, causing us to lose a fortune."

Addie heaved a heavy breath, fighting back her tears. "You mentioned a broker." She squared her shoulders and held her head high. "Did this broker tell you I had the third book you're looking for?"

"No, but he was well connected and had

discovered someone who did have a lead on it." He flashed a grin.

"Who?"

"Raymond James, of course."

Addie shook her head. "That's how he got involved in all this."

Jeremy cracked his knuckles and brought his hands to the back of his head. "It seems a number of years ago your aunt found something during her travels and had it appraised by an old antiquities dealer who has long since passed, but the copy of the evaluation was in her files in Raymond's office. Once Raymond shared that information with us . . . we *convinced* him to work with us, and everything else came into play."

Sheila lifted her chin and stared down her nose at Addie.

Addie stretched out her tight shoulders and glanced down at her jacket pocket. "So your plan is to find this third book that you think I have and then go back to the British Library and steal the second one, just like you did the first?"

"Sheila is a wizard with security systems." Jeremy smirked.

Addie balled her fists. "And what happens now?"

Sheila took a step closer. "Unless you tell us where you have hidden that book . . . I'll shoot you."

"I have no idea what book you're talking about. You already have the two that are worth millions. I only know about a diamond-covered box."

Sheila's lip curled and she glared at Jeremy. "I told you I'm tired of all this. We should have had that book months ago, and here we still are." Her eyes narrowed, she straightened her arm, supporting her elbow with her other hand, and took steady aim at Addie.

"Wait a moment, Sheila." Jeremy grasped her arm, securing his sister's hand and lowering it to her side. "Let's try one other option first. Be patient just a few minutes longer." He headed for the bedroom. "I think I might have someone here who may convince her to talk before it comes to that."

"Let's hope so, or this one won't be any use to us anymore, and . . ." Sheila raised her hand, wielding the gun in Addie's face.

Addie rolled her wet palms on her knees and scoured the tabletop with them, her eyes fixed on Sheila.

"What's taking so long?" Sheila glanced over her shoulder. "This is getting tiresome. Hurry up."

Seeing that Sheila's attention was momentarily diverted, Addie grabbed her drink and tossed it in Sheila's face, knocking the gun out of her hand. She grabbed the lamp off the table, brandishing it over her head, and brought it down across Jeremy's head when he bolted back into the living room.

A hot, sharp pain slammed into Addie's right temple. She spun around. Sheila took another lunge at her, wielding the whiskey bottle from the counter. Addie ducked and rolled onto her side. Sheila grabbed her hair and jerked her violently backward, seizing Addie around the throat. She reached behind her and managed to grab hold of Sheila's hair with both hands. With a hard yank, she pulled Sheila's head forward and smashed her forehead into the back of hers. Sheila lost her grip. Addie lurched toward the door. It flung open and Marc, gun drawn, burst in.

"Thank God," she panted and looked up as officers swarmed the room. One placed his knees on Sheila's back and slapped handcuffs on her.

Marc bent over Jeremy, who attempted a weak swing in Marc's direction. Marc dropped the weight of his body across him. "Cuff this one, too, and read him his rights."

"Chief, I think you'd better come in here."

An officer secured Jeremy, and Marc made his way into the bedroom. "Another one?"

"Another what?" Addie jumped to her feet and dashed for the bedroom door.

Marc grabbed her before she could get by him. "You'd better stay out here." He gripped her shoulders. "Give my men room to work."

"What? Why?" She swerved to the side to peer behind him.

He moved to block her view.

"Marc, who's in there? Who is it?" She pushed him away. "Jeremy said he had someone who could make me talk."

"Well, this guy's not going to be doing any talking for a while. It looks like a bad blow to the head. An ambulance is on its way."

"Roger?"

"Yeah, that's my guess. He probably refused to cooperate with Jeremy's next plan to convince you to talk, and Jeremy had enough playing around, tried to force him to — The paramedics are here now. Step back, we need to let them do their job. You can ID him later." Marc shuffled her to the side.

Tears pooled in Addie's eyes. Moments later, two paramedics wheeled a stretcher out of the door. Addie stared at Roger's colorless face as they passed her, dark red oozing through the contrasting white gauze binding his forehead. She shuddered, thinking of Catherine.

She looked up at Marc. "Yes, it's him. Thank God you came in when you did. Poor Roger. He could have died, too."

"Yes, Jeremy doesn't seem to have an issue with disposing of people to get what he wants."

Addie shivered. "I know. And I thought he was someone I could trust." She puffed out her cheeks, exhaling hard. "He's probably already sold the books I sent him." She frowned and looked up at Marc. "But . . . how did you know I was here?"

"Serena, of course."

"Of course, but how did you know to come in?"

"When she told me this fellow Roger had come a week early and was insisting you meet him tonight, I had a gut feeling." He shrugged and scratched the day-old stubble on his cheek.

"A gut feeling?"

"Yes, you're not the only one who gets those. So I took a drive through the parking lot on my way home just to see if you were still here."

"How did that tell you there was something wrong?"

"I spotted the Cayenne and the black

Honda and knew something was up."

"Thank heavens for gut instincts."

"You can say that again." He put his arm around her shoulder and pulled her close to his side.

She laughed and gave him a quick hip-check. "Now what, partner?"

"Partner nothing. I go back to the police station and hope I can wrap all this up by morning. You — you go home."

"Not a chance."

Chapter Thirty-Six

Addie paced back and forth across the police station waiting room. Every time the door behind the desk opened, she spun around in hopes of seeing Marc walk out. The night desk sergeant glanced up at her each time, shook her head, and then returned to her work. Addie sat down, leaned forward on her elbows, and rubbed her palms together. She checked the time. Two-fifteen a.m. Five minutes after the last time she'd checked. The sergeant walked around the desk and poured a cup of coffee.

"Here." She handed Addie the cup. "You look like you need this."

"Thanks." Addie looked up at her. "Any idea what's taking so long?"

The sergeant shrugged. "Who knows. Interrogations can take all night."

"Great." Addie took a sip. "I guess I'll need this, then."

"We could call you when it's done if you'd rather."

"No, no, I'll wait. Thanks though."

"If you change your mind, let me know." The sergeant walked back to the desk.

Addie looked over the rim of her cup. "I don't think we've met before. I'm Addie Greyborne."

"I know who you are." She chuckled. "You're the only person everyone around here talks about lately."

"Nothing too bad, I hope."

"No, nothing bad. You've just kept us pretty busy lately, that's all. I'm Carolyn, by the way. It's nice to finally put a face to your name."

Marc appeared in the back doorway, stretching out his neck and shoulders. Addie jumped to her feet. His head jerked. "Addie." He stared at her. "You're still here?"

"Of course I am. Do you really think I could go home and sleep after all this?" She set her coffee on the end of the desk.

He rubbed his hands over his face. "No, I guess not. I wasn't thinking." He gestured to his office. "Come on, let's go in here."

She sat in one of the chairs in front of his desk, and he slid into the one beside her. "Are you off duty now?"

He shook his head. "I wish, but no. I'm

just too tired to even walk around the desk, I guess. You must be, too. It's been a long day for both of us." He yawned and slouched back in his seat. "Where do I start?" He scratched his head and leaned forward on his knees.

"Start by telling me it's over." She looked at him. "Please, let it be over."

He tossed his head back and laughed. "Yes, it's over. They were both very co-operative, especially since we had the recording. There wasn't much they could deny, either of them. By the way, making that recording was fast thinking on your part. I'm not sure how you managed to press the right button given the circumstances, but I'm glad you did." He took her hand, rubbing his thumb over the back of it.

She felt a wave of heat rush up her collar to her cheeks and looked away. "They said they . . ." She gulped. "They said they killed David, too."

His thumb kept stroking her hand. "Yes, that was on the recording, and Jeremy confessed to being the one that did it."

Her face crumbled, and she fought back tears. "They'll be charged with his murder, too, then?"

"Yes — his, and Blain's, as well as Roger's

assault."

"What about Raymond's?"

"That one was apparently Elizabeth and Gwen's work. Jeremy was only too happy to squeal on everyone else involved." Marc smirked. "He said Raymond went soft in the end. He had second thoughts about the whole thing and made free access to the house impossible. They wanted it back and were afraid as time went on that his next move was going to be turn them all in."

"Wait a minute. Who are Elizabeth and Gwen?"

"The two women."

"Go back." She slid to the edge of her chair. "I got lost there. You said they wanted free access back. They had it before?"

Marc nodded. "It sounds like Raymond had given them a key to the house when this whole thing first started. Your aunt was old and sick. It was easy for them to slip in and out at night to search for the book. But just before she died, he went soft on them. He threatened to change the locks if they didn't stop the whole thing. He felt too many people had gotten hurt already. Jeremy informed him that wouldn't be a smart move, but then just before you moved in, he did."

"So the two women were working with

Jeremy and Sheila. It's starting to make sense now."

"Ah, but there's more to it than knowing their names." He sat back. "Elizabeth, the younger one, is married to Jeremy."

"What? He was married this whole time?"

He nodded. "And Gwen is her mother."

"I don't believe it." She slapped her knee. "It's a family business."

"It gets better. Sheila is married to Andrew, and Andrew is the one who apparently ran your father off the road — not meaning for him to go through the guardrail and end in a fiery crash. But nonetheless, he caused the accident by trying to stop your father on the roadside. Andrew has been picked up now and charged with manslaughter."

"No way." Addie's eyes widened.

"Yup, and wait for this: Sheila killed Blain, her own father-in-law, because he started to ask too many questions."

"So Blain didn't know what they were up to? But the books and antiques were in his office and the hidden room, so how could he not have?"

"Apparently, at first he wasn't aware that it was an illegal operation. He was just happy to help his son make a success of his life finally, but after a few years, he got suspicious. He started digging around and asking questions and found out the business wasn't as squeaky clean as he'd been led to believe. He threatened Andrew, told him he was going to turn all of them into the authorities. So he became a liability."

"And that's when they decided to kill him, Andrew's own father?" She shook her head.

"They must have decided to get rid of two roadblocks at the same time. With him dead, one issue was solved, and with you in jail for his murder they would have free access once again to search your house. They just needed to get a copy of your key, a job given to Elizabeth and Gwen."

"Really? Then I was right about them taking my keys." She shook her head. "Serena was the one who ended up in jail, though." Addie brushed her face with her hands. "Oh no, I was the one who was supposed to find Blain's body and be charged."

"Exactly."

"That's why Elaine called me to meet with Blain that day, and Serena showing up was an accident." She sat back, shaking her head.

"A very unfortunate one, but it also forced them out into the open. They were desperate to get their hands on that box and some book they thought was inside it. Otherwise, we never would have known about all this or caught them."

"So Elaine was part of this."

"No, it doesn't sound like it. Sheila told her all the squabbling around town wasn't good for the store and asked her to call you to come for a meeting to smooth things over. Apparently, Blain knew nothing about that meeting."

"Which is why Andrew paid her off to leave town, I'm guessing."

Marc leaned forward. "Plus the fact she knew Sheila was Andrew's wife, and they couldn't take the chance of word of that getting out, because you knew her as someone else."

"She must have been wearing disguises though. I know I saw her in the crowd after the break-in happened at my shop, and then again in the hotel parking lot. But every time I saw her, she never looked the same. I guess that's what threw me off and made it so I couldn't place her."

Addie couldn't believe what she was hearing. It was all making make sense though. She leaned her elbows on her knees and cupped her head between her hands. "Did they say which one of them broke into my shop the first time? I'm guessing it was Andrew. He's about six five and the only one tall enough to reach the chimes."

"Probably it was him and Jeremy, although who did what is something we still have to figure out. But I can tell you that they certainly aren't afraid to turn on each other. I guess with the recording and so much evidence, they want each of them to take a share in the blame and not go down alone."

"Just one big happy crime family." Addie chuckled, staring down at the floor lost in thought, coiling a lock of hair around her finger.

"And we found Serena's phone in Sheila's purse. She must have been the one who sent you the text, and then sent Elizabeth and Gwen over to get the box and key."

Her head snapped up. "That's why she was hanging around the front counter chatting Serena up for so long — waiting for a chance to grab her cell phone." Addie frowned and rubbed her temples. "But how did they all meet and get together?"

"That is a mystery. Probably Andrew met Sheila when he was in Europe. He had already been on a crime path here, so I guess it all followed from there. Once Sheila married Andrew, she was related to Blain and they were both rare book experts — and, well, everything else, the thefts and smuggling, just fell into place after that."

"And the murders." Addie glanced sideways at him. "Was Roger involved in all this, too?"

"No, it seems they just used him tonight, because everything else they'd tried had failed to get to you and the box with the book. They thought that's why he was meeting you here, to make a deal for it with the British Museum."

"Did they say what the book is, or why the set of three books is more valuable than a diamond- and gold-covered box?" She rubbed her hands over her knees.

"No, Jeremy hasn't said yet, and Roger still isn't awake."

"I guess the big question is, what's the book and where is it?" Addie threw her head back on the chair and moaned.

"I don't know. It all sounds pretty farfetched to me, this mystery book and why it's worth so many people's lives, and maybe we'll never know."

"What?" She leaned forward. "We can't stop searching for it now, not after all these people died because of it."

"My thought is it burned up in your father's crash and it's gone."

"But then why did they keep looking for it?"

Chapter Thirty-Seven

Addie pursed her lips, looked at the clock on the wall behind Marc's desk, and stood up. "It's late, and I'm exhausted and need time to think. This is just so much to take in." She rubbed her tired eyes, grabbed her purse, and headed for the door. "Besides, I'm sure you still have paperwork to do. Serena told me you had a family dinner tonight. Sorry you had to miss it."

"The paperwork can wait, but you missed dinner, too. We can still grab a late-night bite and talk this through. Maybe we can figure this whole book thing out."

She paused. "But there's nothing open."

"I know a great little place."

"Not that awful greasy spoon up by the highway." She shuddered at the thought.

"No, but the kitchen's open all night, and it serves the best food in town, or so I'm told. Want to join me?"

"Um, no." Her face grew warm. "I'd better not. It's so late, and . . . thanks anyway though." She opened the door and blew out a deep breath.

"It serves wine, coffee, tea, anything you like."

She paused and rested her hand on the doorframe. "And does this chef make a good burger by chance?" she asked without turning around.

"The best homemade ones in town."

"You're pretty cocky about your cooking skills, aren't you? I mean, I'm only guessing but assume you mean your kitchen?"

"Hey, when you're good you're good."

"Well, I suppose I could be persuaded then." She looked at him over her shoulder. "Just dinner though, right? I'm still not ready."

"I promise, just dinner." He leapt to his feet and grabbed his jacket from the coatrack. "I'll drive. You've had a tough day. Two guns waved in your face and a down-and-out struggle for your life." He turned toward the back staircase.

"Do you mind if I drive?"

"I guess not. I just thought —"

"Actually, would you mind if we went to my house instead?"

He frowned. "Sure, if you'd rather."

"It's just that I don't feel like it's over yet,

and there's something I want to check out."

"Are you parked out front?"

"Yes, by the door." She turned and walked across the waiting room, her mind and heart fluttering with anticipation and unanswered questions.

Addie walked into the living room and dropped her purse on the side table. "I'll start some food in a minute. There's been something gnawing at me since we talked about it in your office."

"What's that?" Marc tossed his jacket on the sofa.

"The book. I can't leave this hanging. I don't believe it was lost in the crash, and they all knew it somehow, too, which is why they kept looking for it. So, obviously, it was inside the box at one time — or why would my aunt have gone to the trouble of disguising the weight of it with some useless newspaper clippings from the day after my father was killed? She was trying to throw someone off. So it has to still be here." She gazed around the room, trying to find the slightest nook or cranny where a secret lever or button could be hidden.

Marc stood behind her, his eyes following her gaze. "I don't even know where to begin tonight. The suspects have searched several times that we know of, and they never found it."

"I know, but I just have a feeling."

He laughed. "You and your feelings."

"They've been pretty right on so far." She glanced sideways at him.

"You're right. So, what are you thinking?"

She looked at the desk. "That's it. Here — help me move it." Marc went to one side, and she grabbed the other. "Try to keep it right on the scratches that are already on the floor. Line them up exactly."

"Mind if I ask why?"

"I have a hunch."

When it was out far enough and the scratch marks lined up, she dropped to her knees behind it. "Do you have a pen knife on you?"

"Yes." He pulled a small one out of his pocket and handed it to her. He leaned over her shoulder. "Mind telling me what you're doing?"

"It's something Catherine said."

"What was that?"

She looked up and smiled. "It's all in the floorboards."

He scratched his head. "Okay."

"Yes," she cried. "Look at this." She pulled a brown paper package out from its hiding place and stood up. "This has to be it."

He slipped off the paper wrapping. She flipped the cover open to the title page and gasped. "Look at that."

"What is it? Is it valuable?"

"Well, it's a first print run edition of *Alice's Adventures in Wonderland* by Lewis Carroll."

"Then being a first run makes it worth more?"

"Yes, especially since only two thousand of them were ever printed. That run got held back to make print quality changes to the illustrations. As far as anyone knows, only six are still surviving."

"And you're certain this is one of them and not a later printed copy?"

"No, it's a first run. The next edition was printed after the illustrator, John Tenniel, raised issues with the first one and had an 1866 print date. This one says 1865."

"So it is one of the six original copies still around."

"Yes, but this isn't just any one of them. Look, it's signed by Charles Dodgson, Lewis Carroll's real name."

"And that's what makes it worth so much?"

"Not only is it a signed copy." She flipped through the pages. "Look at the handwritten notations in the margins. This was

Dodgson's personal copy."

A loose page fluttered to the floor. "Oh dear, I think it's falling apart." Marc bent down and picked it up. He started to hand it to Addie, glanced at it, stopped, and sucked in a sharp breath. "You'd better look at this."

"Why? Is it a letter or note he wrote and tucked into the book?" She reached for it.

"Not him." He handed it to her.

"It's from my aunt." She frowned, staring at it. "Oh my God." She wavered as her knees turned to jelly. "Look at this. It was written the day after my father was killed." Marc took the letter from her quivering hand and began reading aloud.

April 4

If you are reading this, you have discovered my secret — one I have been in possession of for over fifty years. I came across this book enclosed in its beautiful case at a small market in England. The family was clearing out their grandmother's house after her passing and only too happy to get rid of everything they could to save them from having to pack it all up again and dispose of at a charity shop. I assumed the set had little value considering the meager price I paid for it. When I returned to the States, thinking the box was a mere trinket, I displayed it prominently in my home for many years. It was lovely to look at, and family and friends had such fun trying to solve the puzzle of opening it. I knew the book was old by the publication date, and it made a nice addition to my collection in the study.

Eventually, at the urging on my dear friend and lawyer, Raymond James, I had it appraised. Much to my delight, Raymond informed me that the box was actually covered in genuine diamonds and the book wasn't just old, but rare. He convinced me to lock up the book and box for safekeeping. Feeling only the jeweled case was the possession of value, and that it would be a tidy inheritance one day for my nephew, Michael, and his beautiful baby daughter, Addison, I agreed.

I forgot about it completely until a week or so ago, when Raymond came to me inquiring as to whether I still had the book. He said a collector had come across two books that were related to the one I had. He went on to say that if mine were added to those, and then sold as a three-book set, with the box as a nice bonus, it would be priceless. I told him to tell the collector I didn't intend to sell anything.

When he relayed that story to me, he grew increasingly nervous and afraid. He said the book I had made this one-of-a-kind collection extremely valuable, and some very bad people had been trying to find it. I needed to get rid of it immediately, as I was in danger now.

I offered to give it to him for safekeeping, but he said that would place him in grave danger, too. He advised me to get it out of town. Then he suggested that perhaps my nephew could take it for the time being to keep it and me safe. I called Michael and asked him to come, and when he arrived, I told him the story. He was well versed in these areas because of his work, and he said he had heard about the book possibly being somewhere in the States and knew that people had been hunting for it. He was shocked to discover that I had the book.

Michael became very nervous, not even wanting to use the telephone to call and report it to authorities in Boston. He said he would have to go to them, as it would be safer to speak to them in person. He warned me not to talk to anyone about this. I begged him to take the book with him, as Raymond had made me very anxious about keeping it, but he said no. He didn't want to take the risk of anyone else getting their hands on it, just in case he was followed when he left. He reminded me that it had been safe here for all these years, and another day wouldn't hurt. However, if I was nervous, then I should separate the box from the book and hide them in different places, so that if someone searched for them before he managed to return, at least the book or the box would remain hidden and not as valuable. The thief would then be forced to return for the missing part, but the authorities would be aware by then and be able to catch them in the act. I must say that if I were forty years younger, I would find this adventure rather exciting, but at this time, it only places a greater stress on my heart.

I was disappointed that he left without the book. I called Raymond immediately to let him know but it reassured him somewhat to know that Michael had taken the key. His thinking had been that if the thief did search the house in the meantime he wouldn't be able to open the box without it. So before he left we opened the jeweled box and left it open, in case I decided to do what he had suggested. Raymond was frantic, but I reminded him that my nurses were here with me. I told him not to worry, as Michael would be back the next day.

Hours later, Michael was killed in a horrible accident. I don't know if that was connected with the book, but as a precaution, I am taking his advice and separating the book from the jeweled case. As my health is failing me rapidly now, I felt obligated to write this so whoever finds this book will make certain that my beloved Addison receives what belongs to her.

      Anita Greyborne

Addie faltered and leaned against the desk for support. "I could hear her reading that." She sniffled. "It brought back a memory flash. She used to read me stories when I was little. I do remember her now, and how she made me feel loved."

"I don't know what to say." Marc's voice cracked.

"I know. I'm numb." She took a deep breath and squared her shoulders. "But it does sound like Raymond did know that my dad didn't have the book. He must have told Jeremy, or at least let it slip."

"Yeah, that's how they knew to keep looking for it." Marc cleared his throat. "You were right not to give up."

She chuckled. "What have I told you about gut instinct? It's not always about the facts and the evidence."

"You proved that again." He scratched his head. "And it helped you find the last piece to this crazy puzzle."

"I think there's one or two things left for me to teach you, Chief." She glanced sideways at him, a coquettish grin on her face.

"Now, now, don't get carried away. But I guess working in a small town like Greyborne Harbor hasn't taught me much about the world of antique book theft."

"See?" She smirked. "There's something else you can learn from me."

"Okay, teach. Then explain this." He playfully tapped his finger on the tip of her upturned nose. "If this book is considered to be part of a priceless collection, then who besides a museum could buy it? Especially since the first two books are known to have been stolen from the British Library? Wouldn't Jeremy, or Raymond, or anyone trying to sell it, show up somewhere on a list, alerting authorities that it was being traded on the black market?"

"Yes." She rubbed her neck. "There's an Art Retrieval Registry that looks out for things like this hitting the market. My dad and David worked with them a lot. Probably how David knew about the broker who had the lead on Auntie's book in the first place."

"Which," Marc said, snapping his fingers, "originally must have come from Raymond making inquiries about it — he did have the appraisal."

"Yes. Jeremy did say it was in her file. But" — she chewed her lip — "it sounds like Raymond may have first agreed to work with them but then got more than he bargained for with Jeremy and his crew."

"Well, Jeremy is ruthless, and he's proven that a few times."

"He is, and I think Raymond may have been getting cold feet by the end and was trying to make things right again, by the sound of this letter, but it was too late; it had gone too far."

"Yeah, Jeremy and his bunch were in too deep to give up, and Raymond knew too much." Marc scratched his chin. "I wonder if that's why he never gave you the key your dad got to him? He wanted to keep it as insurance."

"Hmmm, maybe. But it didn't work, did it?"

"No, it certainly didn't." He rubbed his neck. "How much actual money could someone get for selling this? Enough to kill that many people for?"

"Well, not in my book, but yes, there are some who would think it was worth it. It could fetch millions. Sure, the British Library would pay a hefty finder's fee, but on the black market, there are some collectors who would pay anything, because just possessing something this rare is their payoff. Plus, there are lots of disreputable collectors who use antiquities as currency for drugs, arms, or whatever else."

"I guess I'd better brush up on my art history skills and get in touch with some bigger law enforcement agencies to find out how to look out for these kinds of things."

"That's a whole specialized field, I think. They also track down brokers who find buyers, like the ones who would give anything to get their hands on something like this. Are you thinking of making a career change?"

He threw his head back and laughed. "Not right now, but if the short time that you've been in town is any indication of what it's going to be like in the future, I might have to."

"Don't worry about that." She smiled up at him. "My crime-fighting days are officially over." She closed the book.

"So, after we turn this over to the authorities, you're *not* going to join the Harbor police force?" His brow rose. "You'd be a perfect fit."

She laughed. "Thanks anyway." She tucked the book into a compartment in the desk. "I think from now on I'll stick to solving the murder mysteries in my books."

"I'm going to hold you to that."

"But you have to admit," she said, turning to him and clasping his collar with both hands, her voice dropping to a husky whisper, "we did make a pretty good crime-solving team."

His thumb traced the outline of her jaw, and his breath wafted across her cheek, stirring the remembrance of his velvety lips caressing hers. She arched upward, tugging at his collar, urging his face closer. She stopped when their eyes locked. He kissed the tip of her nose. His silky lips swept across her cheek, to her mouth. A shrill alarm sounded. "What was that?" She jerked away, glancing around the room.

"Damn it." He pressed his damp forehead

against hers and pulled his phone from his pocket. "It's from the desk sergeant — an all points alert."

"But I thought you were off duty now?" Her hands dropped to her sides.

"As chief, I'm always on duty."

"But it's late; couldn't someone else investigate?"

He shook his head. "I think I'd better handle this one."

"What happened?" Addie gripped his arm.

"Apparently, our local cat lady, Mrs. Crawly, who has a tendency to roam the back alleys and the municipal park at night looking for stray cats to rescue, reported a strange buzzing noise and flashing lights coming from the utility shed behind the library."

"A power surge?"

"I don't think so; it's been investigated before. This isn't the first time we've had this same report." He looked at her from under a creased brow. "Though the others were mostly made by townsfolk who frequent the park after bar closing time."

"Can't it wait until morning, then?"

"No, I happen to be very familiar with her because she regularly calls in reports of her cats being stolen. She's learned to trust me. So I have to go and talk to her now, because she's in the park screaming alien invasion or something else just as crazy and riling up a growing group of people pretty badly." He tucked his phone away and shrugged. "Sorry."

Addie grabbed her purse and headed toward the door.

"Where do you think you're going?"

She flipped her hair and glanced back over her shoulder. "Why, with you, of course. There's a mystery to solve." She winked.

ABOUT THE AUTHOR

Lauren Elliot grew up devouring Nancy Drew before graduating to Agatha Christie. Eventually, she tried her hand at penning a novel herself. *Murder by the Book* is her first mystery.

The employees of Thorndike Press hope you have enjoyed this Large Print book. All our Thorndike, Wheeler, and Kennebec Large Print titles are designed for easy reading, and all our books are made to last. Other Thorndike Press Large Print books are available at your library, through selected bookstores, or directly from us.

For information about titles, please call:
(800) 223-1244

or visit our website at:
gale.com/thorndike

To share your comments, please write:
Publisher
Thorndike Press
10 Water St., Suite 310
Waterville, ME 04901

CPSIA information can be obtained
at www.ICGtesting.com
Printed in the USA
BVHW072136030122
625417BV00001B/11